HIGH AND OUT

HIGH AND OUT

JUSTIN WEBER

BLACKTIP BOOKS

First Edition

For information about bulk purchase discount, please email us at contact@blacktipbooks.com

Interior design by Ray Coughlin

Printed in the United States of America

10 9 8 7 6 5 4 3 2 1

Library of Congress Control Number: 2024909088

ISBN (hardcover): 979-8-9901460-0-6
ISBN (paperback): 979-8-9901460-1-3
ISBN (ebook): 979-8-9901460-2-0

For my Mom,
Stacey,

My Wife,
Shayley,

and

My Son,
Gregory

"All hockey players are bilingual.
They know English and profanity."

— GORDIE HOWE

PROLOGUE

Jason Wagner opens his front door to greet Paul Bissonnette and Mike Grinnell. They're there to get set up for their interview, which will be recorded for the next week's episode of *Spittin' Chiclets*. The other two hosts will be joining via video conference as they live out on the east coast. *Spittin' Chiclets* is among the top hockey shows on the internet, if not the top. The show is presented by *Barstool Sports* and hosted by former NHL players, Ryan Whitney and Paul Bissonnette, as well as sports writer Rear Admiral, and the show's main producer Mike Grinnell. They typically have a segment where they interview current or former NHL players and coaches. Despite it being Jason's first podcast appearance, he isn't nervous.

Wags and Biz have gotten to know each other somewhat over the years, having run into each other at the rinks or seen each other around town in Scottsdale. There has always been a question that Jason has been dying to ask Biz, but never felt it the right time nor place. There are always too many people around and too much going on. Here, he figures it will either be good for their show, or they'll cut it out.

After the welcome and introduction, each host has a quick player history question. RA kicks it off in his thick Bostonian accent, "So Wags, before we dive into the current, we always like to uh, you know, get a little idea for where ya come from. I guess firstly, when, uh, did you realize this was what you wanted to do wit ya life?"

"Well, I had tried the other sports when I was young and wasn't too good at any of them and didn't really like them either, but something about hockey was different. I wasn't good at all, but I loved it, you know? Loved watching it, playing it, talking about it, just obsessed, right? But the moment I knew I wanted to be in the NHL was during my first real season. I was six. My team got to go to a Coyotes game and do a little scrimmage for the intermission show between the first and second period.

"Just being there under the stands and getting dressed down where the players were was incredible. There was a little TV in the corner of the room that had the game on. We were watching while our dads helped us get dressed and tie our skates, then just before the end of the period, Brad May and Derian Hatcher dropped their gloves and went at it behind the Stars' net."

"No way," says Biz.

"You kids are just lovin' it I bet, huh," says Whit.

"Oh yeah got the boys going for sure and there was only like ten seconds left in the period, right before we were about to go out. So he went off the ice to the room, you know? Instead of going to the box."

"Right, yeah, cause if you fight with less than five minutes in a period they just send ya off," says Biz.

"Yeah so, he goes into his dressing room, takes his jersey and shoulder pads off, grabs a bunch of pucks and signs them for each of us kids and takes the time to meet all of us before we head out."

"No shit... fuckin' May Day... what a guy," says Biz.

"That's a pretty tough customer there," says RA.

"I always forget he played for the Yotes," says Whit.

"I just remember when he scored that fuckin' goal in overtime against the B's in ninety three. The announcer was just shoutin', 'May Day, May Day,'" says RA.

"That was a little before my time, but I heard that was huge. Then, yeah, my next season I changed my number to thirty-two and decided I wanted to be like Brad May when I grew up."

"That's unreal. Who were your other favorite players from that era?" Asks Biz.

"Back then, I liked everyone. Once I got to... I wanna say peewee or bantam, I jumped on the Wings bandwagon and became obsessed with Pavel Datsyuk. He was unreal."

"Oh yeah he was, made me look like an asshole out there at least a couple of times," says Whit.

"I was never even allowed on the ice at the same time as him," says Biz which gets a good laugh from the boys.

"But also being from Arizona, there was Doan, Peter Mueller,"

"Muellsie," says Biz.

"Yeah. You, obviously."

"*Obviously,*" RA and Whit say together in a sarcastic tone.

"Yeah. Carcillo always got me fired up."

"Car-Bomb!" Says Biz, in reference to Dan Carcillo's nickname from his time playing.

"You've always liked the grinders, hey Wags? What about Sid or Geno, huh?" asks Whit.

"I was more of an Ovi kid, so Ovechkin and Datsyuk were my skilled guys then yeah grinders, fighters, guys with good style. Mueller always had such sick style out there."

"He did man, and an absolute magnet out at the bars too," says Biz emphatically.

"Also, how underrated was Shane Doan? I mean I know I feel like we talk about it but he's just such an unreal dude, and such a horse to play against. Makes sense 'cause I hear he loves horses," says Whit.

"Oh yeah, you should see him up on those things, when I played with him, he was always trying to get me to go for trail rides with him and his kids and shit."

"You ever go?"

"Yeah, I went a few times."

"Oh yeah, sure ya did."

Jason laughs, "He means so much to the state for hockey and he's such a great guy. You guys know."

"Best human being in the world, hands down," says Biz.

"Hey so, Wags, what happened with Vegas?" asks Whit.

"Oh man that's a crazy story. But first, I've got a question for Biz, if it's okay. We can cut this part or whatever if we need to."

"For me? Uh-oh," says Biz.

"Uh-oh," Whit echoes. "What'd that animal do now?" asks Whit.

"No, no, it's not bad, I've just been wanting to ask a long time and have never been able to. It's old enough to where I can't imagine any trouble comes from it."

"Alright, shoot, whaddya got? asks Biz.

"Did you ever know a chick named..." Jason leans over to Biz whispering the name.

"Uh-oh. Oh no. This can't be the first time Biz's had this conversation," says Whit.

Paul looks up and says seriously, "No. Why? She your old lady?"

Jason starts laughing and says, "Get the fuck out of here, are you serious?"

"I'm so fuckin' confused right now boys," says RA.

"Swear to God. On my life. Who is she?" asks Biz.

"I'm with RA, what the fuck is going on here?" asks Whit.

Jason is cracking up and Biz is trying to figure out whether or not he's being made fun of. He continues to repeat the name in his head to make sure he didn't miss an innuendo like good old *Eileen Ulick*.

Jason calms down and says, "Man that's so funny. Alright so I was catfished. Plain and simple."

"Wait, what?" Biz asks.

"No way," says Whit.

"You gotta give us the story now, Wags," demands RA.

"Alright, alright, alright. This is a long time ago."

"Before the NHL?"

"Way before the NHL, before juniors even. I was in Colorado playing AAA U16, and Twitter had just launched."

"Oh, I know where this is goin'," says Whit.

"Our whole team was on there, wheeling broads, racking up followers, you know, trying to be like Biz."

"Yeah, there's a scary role-model for yahs," says RA.

"Oh fuck off, RA, that Twitter account got me an extra five years in the league and you know it."

"Take it easy there Biz, I'm just bustin' yah balls."

Jason laughs at the banter and continues, "So anyways, I stumble across this absolute rocket and we start following each other, and then we're in the DMs."

"Yeah ya are," says Biz.

"This is where it starts getting crazy though. At some point early on she goes, 'Oh yeah, I've got an off and on thing with Paul Bissonnette on the Coyotes,'"

Paul's eyebrows raise.

"No shit," says Whit.

"Just wait. She goes on to tell me she's had a very well-known goalie, can't say his name on air, tongue punch her from behind, and I'm going, 'Holy shit, this is above my pay grade, I'm only sixteen, what's this chick talking to me for? But being that I was young and dumb, I just kept it going, you can understand why."

By now Whit and RA are howling and Biz is just eager for more of the story.

"Young, dumb, and fulla cum," says Whit.

"Where'd it lead to?" Biz says.

"Yo and you gotta tell us who the goalie was after," says Whit.

"We made plans for her to come out, but they all fell through. Then all of the sudden she told me her dad was a mob boss or something and she got all weird."

"Oh yeah, those are all the red flags of a textbook catfish right there," says RA.

"Real pro at being catfished, hey RA?" says Whit.

"I had my fair share of bouts with the catfish back in the day. We didn't have all the tech the kids have. But you know, these days, fuck. It's a-a-a whaddya call it? An occupational hazard," says RA.

"I guess so, but yeah she'd send pictures and stuff so I just went with it, you know, seemed real."

"This is unbelievable," says Biz.

"Wanna know the even crazier part?"

"It gets worse?"

"In the summer before I went to Kamloops, I texted her one morning. The response came back like, 'Hey I hear you're talking to Boobs, nice. This is Paul by the way,' It was early so I guessed that you and her had spent the night and you were kinda marking your territory or whatever. It was before you and I had ever met so I responded and was just like, 'Oh yeah, nice to meet you, how's it going?' Or whatever. Then you were like, 'Boobs tells me you're thinking of going to college instead of the Dub,' and then you went into this whole long text about how going to Saginaw and Owen Sound were the best things you ever did and told me why I should go to Kamloops and how great it was for your career to go major juniors."

Biz is listening to all of it with his hand covering his mouth in utter shock and disbelief.

"Get the fuck out of here! And Biz, you said you never met this chick?" Whit asks.

Biz raises his right hand, "Boys, I've never been so creeped out in my life, I promise you, that was not me."

"So let me get this straight, one of the deciding moments that led you to the Dub instead of going to college was a text message conversation with Biz that wasn't actually Biz?" says Whit.

Jason smiles an embarrassed smile and nods his head, "I guess so." Causing them all to bust out laughing at the story then continuing to talk about how weird the whole ordeal was.

"Yo, and I love how Biz's callsign for this broad is just, 'Boobs,'" says Whit.

The rest of the interview is pretty much par for the course with the show's hosts asking Wags about the upcoming year. They ask about any other juicy stories, and all-in-all they have a good conversation.

The interview wraps, and as quick as Biz and Grinnell were in, they're out. They thanked Wags again for his openness and hilarity. Jason and Biz made loose plans to get together for a night out at some clubs in Old Town or maybe the lounge at The Global Ambassador.

PART I

1

Four Months Earlier.

"The Lightning are down against the Hurricanes in the series, they're down in the game and oh, look at that, Lemieux just absolutely clobbered one of the Lightning forwards, I wasn't able to see exactly who it was. But Wagner immediately skates over to Lemieux and gives him a customary shove. Are they gonna go?"

"Hun, game's on. Jason's about to drop the gloves."

"I'll be right there," she says as she slowly gets up out of bed.

"I'll pause it 'til you get here."

Jason's mom is recovering from a surgery. They had to remove a few parts of her organs that were covered in cancer, along with a fairly large mass. She'd had no idea about it, and it wasn't even discovered until the surgery. The doctor was luckily qualified to be able to remove the cancer down to a microscopic level.

"How are you feeling?"

"I'm okay, I think all the drugs from the surgery are finally starting to flush out and so I feel a little more sore today than I have."

"Yeah, that's probably normal, but you're not in pain like before?"

"No, not at all."

"Well, that's good."

He resumes the TV coverage of their son's game.

Wagner and Lemieux continue to shove one another and are saying things back and forth that wouldn't possibly be audible through the TV.

"Oh no, I hate when he does that," she says as she makes her way through to the couch in the living room.

"Why? Honey, he's been fighting with Brendan Lemieux since they were what, twelve or thirteen?"

Wagner and Lemieux's gloves come off at the same time and they grab a hold of one another, jostling for the better position.

"They're gonna go. Wagner and Lemieux's gloves are off and they're wrestling to see who's going to get the upper hand. Lemieux is the first to throw, doesn't quite land. Wagner with a body shot, Lemieux returns and connects, Wagner comes back with a couple of his own, the linesman tried to step in, and they said no. This is old school hockey ladies and gentlemen. They're still going. Wagner switches to south paw and now they are just throwing punches. As they go to clinch up here, the linesmen are going to intervene and break this up."

"Yeah and that's a scary job right there, being one of the linesmen that has to go in there and get in between two gladiators as they're duking it out. Certainly not a job I envy."

"You're right about that, and every now and then, you know, you see 'em get clipped by a stray punch and I just think how grateful I am to be up here in the broadcast booth and not down there doin' that."

"It looks like Wagner is going to be heading down to the dressing room, hopefully he'll be okay."

"Yeah, he looked like he was holding onto his hand as he was coming off the ice and going down the tunnel."

"That's a tough one to lose for the Tampa Bay Lightning, although, I'm not sure anything can be done this late in the series."

"Well it was a hard hit that maybe could've justified a fight in the regular season but when you're this far into the playoffs, it's usually smarter to just let that kind of stuff go."

"Yeah, hopefully it's nothing too serious. Jason Wagner was a deadline acquisition in his last contract year for the Tampa Bay Lightning and was brought in to bring a solid physical presence that can put the puck in the back of the net."

* * *

"FUCK!" Jason screams as he storms into the dressing room. The team trainer is following closely behind. Jason puts his left hand on his hip while the right dangles. He tries to make a fist but can't. He inclines his head to the ceiling as he paces around like a caged lion.

"Come in here, let me see it." The trainer was making his way into the trainer's room.

"Moth-er FUCKER!" Jason walks in his skates to the trainer and despite his rage, is careful to avoid stepping on the team's logo in the center of the dressing room.

"Pop up here," he says, pointing to a massage table.

Jason uses his good hand to brace as he lifts his butt up onto the table. He raises his hand for the head athletic trainer. "Gah!"

After taking a quick look at his player's hand, the trainer says, "Sorry Wags, it's broken."

"Can I still play?"

"That's between you and Coach. It's not a concussion, so it's out of my hands. Can you hold a stick?"

"I can play with one hand, maybe you could give me a brace or wrap it or something though."

"Let me see what I got."

Jason sits on the table and watches the game on the small TV in the corner of the room. There is no volume on the TV, only the video feed. It's halfway through the second period and his team's down by two goals. Jason brings his hand up to eye level and examines it for himself. It's already swollen up like a balloon. He winces as he tries to close it into a fist but is still unable. He looks back up at the screen and watches his long-time friend and current teammate Mikey Eyssimont get the puck in the offensive zone and fire a shot that finds the back of the net.

"Fuckin rights, Mike!"

The trainer walks back over to where Jason is sitting, "Hey, hey alright, one to go. Let's see if we can get you back out there to be the one to put it in."

"Let's do it, whaddya got?"

"I've got this splint here, then I've got this set of gloves that we made for McDonagh when he played with his broken hand, and lastly, I've got a shot of Toradol."

"Fuckin' rights, that'll work."

The trainer goes about fastening the splint while Jason

watches the game and keeps his mind off the excruciating pain that's lighting up his hand.

"Good to go, how does it feel?"

"'Bout as good as it's gonna. Thanks for your help."

"Just don't break it any worse than it already is."

"I'll try." He puts his helmet back on, only using his left hand to strap it, and gingerly puts on the modified gloves before stomping back toward the sound of the game. Jason comes back through the tunnel and joins his team on the bench.

"You good?" Coach asks.

Jason nods affirmatively, "Just a broken hand."

"Alright, get back with your line, you guys go next."

Jason nods again and continues to watch the play. When it's his turn to get out there he fumbles a pass for a good scoring opportunity and hardly gets a shot on goal. He skates back to the bench utterly embarrassed and is worried that his night is done. "FUCK!" he yells for what feels like the hundredth time that night.

He ended up getting two more shifts in the third period, but no one passed him the puck. Both of them were penalty-kills where he was either going after the guy with the puck or getting in the way of someone's shot. The buzzer sounded and the game ended. Carolina wins the game and the series. Jason is forced to endure the ceremonial post-series handshake with his broken hand.

2

THE FRONT DOOR to the boutique doctor's office swings open. A man in his late twenties with dark, wavy hair, a scruffy beard, and a missing tooth rushes toward the receptionist's desk. The woman on the phone is an attractive and friendly looking woman who seems to be around the same age. The man politely waits at the desk, doing his best not to interrupt despite his obvious impatience.

"Alright, we'll see you tomorrow at nine... uh-huh... You too, bye," the receptionist says. She hangs up the phone before turning to size up the visibly rattled but fit and rugged looking man that had just burst into her waiting room. "Hi, are you here to see Dr. Sutton?" she asks him with a smile and a hint of flirtation in her eyes.

"Yeah, hi, sorry I'm running a little late, my appointment's at ten. My name is Jason Wagner."

The receptionist looks at the clock and says, "It's only ten-fifteen, you're fine, some people come in like an hour late and expect to still be seen. You can have a seat and I'll let him know you're here," she says with a smile that reveals her perfectly white teeth, a kind attempt to ease his worry about being late.

"An hour late? That's brutal, I felt terrible for not calling. I thought I could make it. Thanks," he adds, taking a few steps over to the fish tank where he becomes mesmerized by the varieties of salt water fish inside. "This a saltwater tank?"

After her intercom message to Dr. Sutton about Jason's arrival she says, "Sure is, I was the one who recommended we make it saltwater, the fish are so much more beautiful and vibrant."

"Yeah, cool spots and spines too," he says in an attempt to keep the conversation going. She smiles again and the phone rings.

Dr. Sutton walks down the hall toward the waiting area decked out in Lululemon. "Jason? Great to meet you." Dr. Sutton says as he puts out his arm to shake Jason's hand.

"Likewise, really sorry about being late, I thought I'd get here a little quicker but traffic was unreal," says Jason.

"No, no, don't worry about it. Come on back."

Dr. Sutton leads Jason back to his office which is set up like a nice therapist's office, though it was clear that this therapist was a high-level athlete in a past life and had the memorabilia to back it up.

"These are pretty sweet, you wrestled at Michigan?" Says Jason while admiring some of the trophies and accolades on his walk to what he assumed would be his chair for the session. It wasn't exactly one of those therapy chair-bed things like from *What About Bob?* Still, it was more comfortable looking than the chair he assumed belonged to Dr. Sutton, which was like a gamer chair. Next to his seat was an end table with an iPad sitting atop. *Pretty casual,* Jason thinks.

"Sure did, all four years. Then tried getting into mixed martial arts in the nineties after college."

"No way!"

"Yeah, I strung together a couple wins. But when I saw that guy get punched in the nuts *twenty times* at UFC Four, I was out," he says. "Obviously they've reigned it in to be a very legitimate sport and the UFC is a legit league now, but man, it was wild in those early days."

Engaged and entertained by the conversation, Jason has made the determination that this guy is the real deal. He takes his seat in the chair, "No way that actually happened. Did he get kicked out?"

"No, he won. It was totally legal. To this day, it's the craziest thing I've ever seen," he says with a plop onto his chair.

"That is *insane*," says Jason.

"Yep, after that, I went to Arizona State for my masters and doctorate degrees in psychology, and have specialized in athletes ever since," says Dr. Sutton.

"You deal with a lot of hockey guys?" Jason asks.

"Oh yeah, all the time. I don't work for a specific team but lots of guys'll work with people like me during the off season. Lot of hockey guys, lot of combat sports guys, all the savages it seems."

Jason chuckles at the quip, knowing full well the man himself was at one point if not still, quite a savage. "Takes one to know one I guess."

"I guess so," Dr. Sutton says with a chuckle. "I still get to the gym and train every once in a while."

"Oh yeah? Where do you train?"

"I go to Fight Ready off the 101 and Shea."

"No way, my younger brother trained there for a long time.

One of his buddies from there started his own gym, but he always loved Fight Ready."

"What a small world."

"Definitely."

Under normal circumstances with non-athlete clients, Dr. Sutton probably wouldn't spend so much time talking about himself or his history in sports. However, if he didn't do it with his athlete patients, the chances of them trusting him enough to open up would be less in his favor. It behooved him as well as his clients to spend a little bit of time reliving his glory days before the first session. After that, it was all about the athlete he's working with.

His job is about making them a better version of themselves as athletes, sure. That is important and that's why most of his clients come to see him. But more importantly for him, his job is to help them become better versions of themselves as human beings.

"So, Jason, have you ever meet with a sports psychologist before?"

"Yeah, there was one in New York when I played for the Rangers, and we had one for my last two seasons I was with LA before that. I think all the teams have them now. But pretty much I'd just do the annual beginning-of-the-year check-in session, and I had never actually sought them out for anything on my end. It was all just what was required."

Dr. Sutton reaches over to his iPad on the end table beside him and places it in his lap, detaching the Apple Pencil from the side of the device, ready to write.

"Got it, and those sessions that you did, they were just like, 'Hey welcome back, how was the summer? Just checking to make sure you're not bringing any emotional baggage into the new season' type thing?"

"More or less, yeah, making sure we had a healthy summer mentally. They'd always ask about family, outlook on the upcoming season, if we had any injuries, stuff like that, you know. Real basic where, unless a guy was really going through something, the sessions would last maybe fifteen to twenty minutes, tops. Main thing was like, you said, to make sure there was no baggage going into a new year."

"Sure," the doctor says while jotting a quick note. "And since those are the only sessions under your belt, I assume things have always been good throughout your career until now?"

What the fuck does that mean? He plays it cool, knowing things weren't currently what he would consider ideal. "I'd say for the most part. I mean it's been a tough road to get here. I spent my first four seasons as a pro in the American Hockey League, which they call *the jungle* for a reason. Those guys are animals.

"The first three were with Grand Rapids after being drafted to the Red Wings. Then I got traded to Los Angeles and played for the Reign, which is the Kings' AHL affiliate team. The next season, I spent about half my time with the Kings and half with the Reign. Then the year after that, I finally became a regular in the NHL.

"Ever since, I've just been doing whatever I can to stay in the league long enough to win a Stanley Cup."

"How does your body feel?" Dr. Sutton asks. He's starting to put the pieces together as to why his client is there.

"My body feels good. I've had a few nicks here and there

but nothing so bad that I've had to miss many games," says Jason maybe more for himself than Dr. Sutton.

"Well, you've certainly had a great career and are a fierce competitor. As well as protector from what I see on that *Hockeyfights* Instagram page. It's good to hear the body's holding up alright."

"Yeah, all in all it's been pretty special," Jason says. He sniffles and looks down, starting to get emotional.

"Are you here now because you're worried that it's over?" Dr. Sutton asks with utmost care. That was the moment when he noticed a silent stream of tears flushing down the face of what he knew to be a very tough guy. Knowing the momentum would be lost if the next words spoken were his, Dr. Sutton sits in silence while the question echoes through his client's skull.

Finally, Jason composes himself enough to realize he's broken down, wipes away the tears, and rips out a couple of tissues. After giving a good, hard honks he says, "Yeah," *sniffle*, "I guess I just figured that once I finally made it, I'd get to stick around for a while. It felt like I was just getting going with the Kings then bam, traded to the Rangers. Had a couple good years there and felt like we had a good team to make a run for the Cup, but then I got dealt to Tampa at the deadline this last year and I didn't play great while I was there. Now I'm back to being a free agent."

"Why do you feel like you didn't play well?"

"I didn't score as many goals as I should have. Took dumb penalties. It just didn't click."

"Well sometimes that happens. The teams know that and they don't just write guys off, right?"

"Yeah, I guess."

"What makes you think it's over now?"

Jason's sadness turns to frustration, "I don't know, it's just a feeling. When I was a free agent before, there was more communication with my agent about what might be in the works, but I haven't heard from the guy in like three weeks. Instead, I have my parents calling everyday wondering whether I've got any news or not."

"Have you tried reaching out to him?"

"Yeah, a few times a week. Fuckin' guy is always at lunch, in a meeting, or out of town and never gets back to me."

"Have you looked around for another agent?" Dr. Sutton asks, wondering just how fragile the relationship with his agent is. He knows agent problems can be a point of great strain on an athlete that can hinder their ability to worry exclusively about their play and health.

"I mean, I don't really have time for that right now and for the most part, he's had my back, so I feel bad for even doubting him... I just can't help but feel like nothing's getting done."

Dr. Sutton takes a couple of notes, attaches the pencil to the side of his iPad and sets it back on the end table. To many psychologists, it could seem that whatever Jason is suffering from is something to just *get over*, but to the former athlete, this despair makes perfect sense. Athletes dedicate their entire lives to a sport starting at such a young age and when they're faced with the prospect of it going away all these years later, it's terrifying. It's extremely common for athletes to feel this way, regardless of their age or time played.

It doesn't take long for Dr. Sutton to figure out that Jason is there because he's scared shitless of the fact that he's facing a potential identity crisis, which in and of itself can feel like its own little identity crisis. This was a part of the job Dr. Sutton had known would be pivotal to his practice. It was also the crucible in his own life which led him down his vocational path.

The day Dr. Sutton realized professional sports were not going to be in his future, it sent him spiraling. To him, it felt as though the person he'd spent his whole life becoming, was no longer a person. Devoid of direction and filled with anger, he began heavily drinking, started using drugs (more than the occasional pot he smoked while he was in his college years) and was quick to snap, with a fuse shorter than the last kid picked in gym class for basketball.

On more than one occasion he was kicked out and banned from bars after inciting full on fights. He usually instigated them by sinking a double leg takedown on which ever guy had the hottest chick there. He never once got the girl with this strategy, and just ended up starting brawls. Luckily, it was before cops got involved in every single altercation on the streets.

Not for nothing though, he ended up meeting the woman that would go on to be his wife after being escorted out of the last such situation. She had just got there and wondered what the commotion was about. Derek, as he was called before he was Dr. Sutton, told her that he was sticking up for some girl who was being poorly treated by the guy she was with. She bought it and became the catalyst for his road to recovery. First, she inspired him to help himself. Then she inspired him to help others as they transition from athlete to civilian. It was her ignorance towards sports in general that helped him to see that there was so much more to life than college wrestling, prize fighting, or the world of competition. Since then, he's grown his practice to be just the right size for him to manage by himself with one receptionist and his wife to do the decorating.

3

———

Jason pulls his blacked-out Chevy Tahoe into an industrial office complex and finds an open spot to back into. Dressed to work out, he exits his vehicle with his shaker cup in hand. It's filled with his pre-workout from Jocko Fuel, a brand his strength and conditioning coach has a hook up with through his time in service as a Navy SEAL.

He walks up to suite 103, but before opening the door, he sets his shaker on the ground and hops up with extended arms. He grabs the lip of the building's pop out above the door to execute ten perfect pull-ups before retrieving his pre-workout and entering the *fortress of pain* as his coach likes to call it.

Ryan Banning's NFL career hadn't panned out like he'd expected. False promises led to him playing one season in the Canadian Football League before he decided he wanted to come home and serve his country. Like many from Banning's generation, he loved the eighties action movies in which Navy SEALS would wipe their enemies off the face of the planet in pure decimation and figured maybe he could do that.

After successfully completing the selection process known

as BUD/S, he would spend the next eight years doing all kinds of crazy missions. One of his favorites to talk about was when he jumped out of an airplane while mounted to a specially and tactically modified dirt bike, armed with enough ass-whooping gear to inflict hell-on-earth for the terrorist forces he and his boys were up against.

When he got home, it was evident that he wasn't cut out for writing about his experiences or training civilians in the ways of war, so he made the next obvious choice; he went and got a job as a personal trainer at a local gym. He got all his certifications and six months later, applied for the job with the Fighting Artichokes at Scottsdale Community. That's when Jason, only thirteen at the time, and a few other kids started training with Ryan before he left to open his own shop. Now Ryan's got a place of his own that he's had for the last fourteen years. He's instilled strength and a warrior's mindset for all who enter his facility. A facility that is purposefully built and exactly how he likes it. He primarily works with football and hockey players, keeping track of it all by scheduling the football guys and hockey guys (some hockey girls too) on their own separate days.

The lobby doubles as a casual warm up area with three treadmills, two rowing machines, two stationary bikes, and one stair climber. There's also some room to stretch or use the foam rollers, which Banning makes himself by wrapping a thin piece of yoga mat around a thick PVC pipe. They really get in there and roll out the knots.

Jason is finishing up his ten-minute warm up on the bike and he hears the session before his start winding down. Four high school age boys come into the lobby area just as Jason is wiping down the bike. The boys notice the NHL player and quietly decide amongst themselves which one is going to be the one to say something to him.

Jason makes his way to the water dispenser to fill his now empty shaker cup with water and electrolytes for his work out. "How'd it go in there boys?" Jason asks them.

They look like they've been through the hardest work out of their lives and had spent a good bit of time spewing chunks. They seem somewhat reinvigorated after being acknowledged by a guy they watch on TV whenever they can.

"Brutal, RB seemed like he was in a mood," one of the boys says coolly.

"Yeah, definitely," another one adds, feigning nonchalance.

"Can't wait to see what he's got in store for me," Jason says with a hint of sarcasm as he finishes filling his cup then gives each of the kids a fist bump.

"Hey Wags, do you know where you're gonna play next year?" asks the third kid.

"Not yet buddy, sorry," Jason says, "still got some time though. Gotta stay ready for when we get the good news, you know? How's your guys' summer going? Staying on the ice?"

Each of the boys nods his head in the affirmative as Banning comes barreling into the lobby with his iPad mini in one hand and a big Honey Crisp apple in the other.

"Wags. What's up? How's the hand? You ready to go?" Banning says as he takes a violent bite of his apple.

"Yep. All good. Just catching up with these boys here, looks like you worked 'em over pretty good, hopefully that's not fore-shadowing for me."

Banning gives Jason a menacing grin as he sadistically bites into his apple again. He jets to the front desk area where he clicks around on the computer, "Thursday, same time. Right fellas?"

They each say, "Same time," in unison.

"See ya," he says without looking at them, already jetting back toward the door that leads to where the magic happens.

Jason watches the group of boys as they walk out the door, drop their stuff, and do their exit pull-ups as he follows his coach into the weight room with a smirk, eager to find out what lays ahead for him.

The actual weight room is warehouse space, converted into a perfect training facility that caters to elite athletes. To the right are mats laid out with a climbing rope secured to the rafter twenty feet up. The front center of the wall is covered with chalk board paint and is where the workout of the day is written out.

The right side of the facility are the various plate loaded machines, like the seated rows, chest press, shoulder press, a pec-deck, leg extension, curl, press, hack squat, and finally on the far end are the dumbbell racks with weights that go from ten pounds up to the big boy one-twenties.

All along the top of the wall on the right are the flags for each branch of the military, including POW-MIA, Coast Guard, and last but not least, the American flag. Signed and framed jerseys of players he's coached that have gone on to play professionally line the top of the wall on the left side.

Also, on the left side, running from the back of the room to front, are four Rogue power racks lined up, side-by-side. Next to those are stacks of Rogue bumper plates and an area to store the Rogue power sleds. Then there's a restroom that also serves as storage closet for cleaning supplies. The center of the room is divided by a strip of artificial turf that runs the length, all the way to the roll-up garage door at the far end of the gym that is hardly ever open this time of year, being that the lows are in the low-nineties.

Jason plays it cool, but on the inside, he freaks when he sees the workout posted on the board. He knew it was coming since it had been a while since his last Fallen Hero workout and Banning usually has him do at least three of them every summer.

Fallen Hero workouts have become somewhat popular over the years, with the most known being the *Murph Challenge*. It honors Lt. Michael P. Murphy and is a one mile run, followed by one hundred pull-ups, then two hundred push-ups, three hundred body weight squats, and another one mile run to wash it down, all for a time.

Today's workout would be to honor the thirty Americans that lost their lives in the shooting down of Extortion Seventeen and represents the greatest single loss of American lives during Operation Enduring Freedom. The workout is ten rounds of thirty push-ups, thirty pull-ups, thirty push-press with ninety-five pounds, thirty hang cleans with ninety-five pounds, and thirty double stack tire jumps, for time. *Fuck. Me.* Jason thinks.

Banning pulls out his phone and cues up the tunes via Bluetooth, his first jam being AC/DC's "Highway to Hell". Jason takes a second to get himself into the zone. He feels Angus Young's opening riff course through his veins, and when the drums enter, he walks over to the open area near the plates and stands to attention.

The stopwatch function of Banning's iPhone is already open and the menacing grin is back. "Ready?" Banning asks.

Jason nods his head and drops. He knew that his coach, a master of mind games, probably had started the clock as he said,

"Ready" but even if he hadn't, Jason knew it would definitely be started before the first push-up was completed. Now or never.

He pumps out his first thirty push-ups then makes his way to the pull up bar on the squat rack and cranks out eleven before dropping for a few seconds to catch his breath and give his arms a rest. The first time he did this workout he didn't afford himself any rest time, only taking what his body required. In doing so, his arms were reduced to cooked spaghetti by the fourth round. He jumps back up and cranks out another nine before another mini rest. After three to five seconds, he's back up to knock out the remaining ten.

In later rounds, it'll take him a few more sets to knock out the thirty, but for now he tries to keep the pace of three to five sets per round on the pull-ups. Next are the push press and the hang cleans, for each of these he is able to steadily knock out all thirty for the first few rounds, but eventually tapers to three sets of ten, a similar tactic used for the push-ups.

Banning wasn't a loud *rah-rah* type of trainer. Very seldom did he let his voice get above the intense and motivational tone that was his norm. He was direct and concise with his communications, as if every word he said was to save your life now or sometime in the future. He could tell when Wags needed a little extra push but didn't get in his face as it wasn't his way. He knew which buttons to press, and he wouldn't stop pressing them until he saw his client do what he felt he was capable of.

In the center of the room, on the artificial turf, was the double stack of giant tractor tires. Jason always much prefers the days when they use sledgehammers to beat the shit out of the tires to the days where he has to jump up and down on them, but such is life for an athlete of his caliber.

His final time was clocked at *one hour, forty-six minutes and thirty-two seconds*. After laying on the artificial turf like a human starfish for a few breaths, Jason feels himself come back to life. He stands and walks over to his shaker cup then hunches over in contemplation. Wondering whether or not the intake of any liquids will make him hurl.

While he ponders his dreams and life choices, Banning walks to the chalk wall where he writes the times for those who complete the challenge. Jason finally straightens up and stumbles over to his coach who loves to watch and observe the athletes in the moments after their torment has ended. It reminds him that humility can always be taught and achieved through working people past what they thought was possible for themselves.

"How do you feel?" Banning asks, no shit eating grin now.

"Pretty good... got a little rough at the end. Legs were howling on the tire jumps. How'd I do?"

"Compared to what? The U16 kids in here before? Your last time? Or your first time?" He asks, seeming genuine which coming from him, usually means he's asking sarcastically.

"Whichever is gonna make me feel the best about myself."

"Fuck off," Banning says, his smirk returning. "One-forty-one-thirty-two."

"That's not bad, right?"

Banning responds with raised eyebrows and a look that says, 'It's not good.'

"It's pretty much same as last time." Jason says. "You remember the first time you had me do this one?"

Banning cocks his head back amused at the thought and lets out a hearty laugh. "Do I remember?" He says, "You were so burnt out before halfway, it ended up taking you over three hours."

"You know, you could've said something before about taking little rests."

"Nah, you wouldn't have listened. None of you kids do. You needed to find out for yourself, and you did. You always have. Path of most resistance, right? That's what makes you stronger and that's what makes you better. Right? No matter what happens this summer, I'm proud of you, and more importantly, you should be proud of yourself," Banning says without breaking eye contact.

Jason can't tell if sweat is getting into his eyes or if he's starting to get a little emotional at the rare vulnerable moment between him and his coach. The two men usually show their love for one another by ribbing or playing practical jokes. "Thanks coach, I am," says Jason. He pats Banning on the shoulder before they head back out into the lobby.

Jason is Banning's last client for the day, so when they enter the lobby there is no one there to ask him what his plans were for the next season. He was relieved; knowing he didn't have fuck all to tell them. It was a conversation he'd come to dread over the years. It was one thing when he was young and had the whole world in front of him. Even then he didn't love it, but now? The future is absolutely his least favorite topic of conversation.

4

THE SUN IS SETTING as Jason climbs out of his pool and shakes his limbs like a big cat getting out of its bath at the zoo. He walks over to the lounge chair and grabs a towel to wrap around his waist and slips on his Crocs before starting into the house. Before he enters the sliding glass door which leads into the main living room, he sidesteps over to the outdoor kitchen and fires up the gas built-in grill so it can warm up.

Their pool is one that doesn't use chlorine or saltwater. Instead, they use what's known as an AOP system. It works by producing molecules that oxidize and eliminate the contaminants found in a pool's water. It was what his parents had at his house growing up. When he originally bought this place, the pool had a chlorine system and that was the first and only major thing they'd changed about the house since moving in.

Behind the sliding glass door stands a patiently waiting Ari, Jason's French Bulldog, named after the character from the TV show *Entourage*.

Jason's younger brother Nick and Jason's buddy from middle school, G, are sitting on the couch playing the latest version of EA Sports UFC. Nick is a six-foot-five, 245-pound monster, currently ranked number four in the UFC's Heavyweight division. He and Jason bought the house together a few years back. Jason uses it as a summer/vacation home while Nick and G live there year-round.

"Who's winning in the series?" Jason asks as he enters the living room, bending over to pet his excited dog, "Hi buddy, how are you? It's good to see you too."

"Your brother is but not... for... long."

"OHHH!" Says Jason, witnessing a vicious knockout combination.

"Got caught," says Nick as he tosses his controller up with a spin. "We got a couple more weight classes."

"I'll say. You better hope G isn't finding his stride there. I'm gonna get the chicken going on the grill. Slick, you playing tomorrow?"

"What time?"

"Early."

"I wish, I gotta train at nine."

The house rules for EA Sports UFC typically favored a tournament style. Multiple weight classes, with each guy having to choose between three randomly selected fighters. It was a way to keep the game both fun and honest. They have the same method for picking teams in any sport video game. There was nothing worse than playing video games with a friend who kept choosing the same, best in the league team every single time. The boys' method prevents that, and in some cases new bonds are formed with new teams or fighters. They have all the games for all the sports loaded on, then G's got his GTA, Warzone, and whatever else he plays.

Jason walks over to the large island in the middle of the

kitchen. On a stainless-steel baking sheet, he places three chicken breasts after patting them dry with a paper towel. Then he grabs his bottle of olive oil and his seasoning jar (a blend of salt, pepper, black garlic powder, and black truffle). Holding his thumb over the top of the bottle, he drizzles a fine amount of oil over each breast. Then from his jar, he pinches a liberal amount of seasoning and sprinkles it evenly. After that, he rubs the breasts so as to get the mixture firmly embedded into the chicken, then flips them to repeat for the other side.

After prepping the chicken, he pulls out a bunch of asparagus from the fridge and cuts off the base. Then places onto another stainless-steel baking sheet where he seasons them and sets them aside.

Before heading back out, Jason pours himself a few fingers of Cazadores Añejo Tequila on the rocks. He retrieves his grilling tongs and grabs the tray while holding his glass. He heads toward the sliding door, through the adjacent living room, where Nick and G are tied up in their best of five fight series. He clicks the tongs a few times to let them know he's coming.

G pauses the game to let Jason pass through without interrupting their fight.

"Thanks, G," says Jason.

G was an awkward and shy kid from Jason's middle school who got picked on a lot. He's never been into the popular Arizona team sports like baseball, football, soccer, or basketball. That made it difficult to maintain friendships at school, seeing as all the cool kids played those sports. Jason could relate, because he hadn't been very much interested in those typical sports either. Back then, hockey was extremely unpopular among the kids in Arizona, so much so that Jason never even went to the same school as someone he played with until seventh grade. Kids treated him as though he didn't play a sport, or he was bullied with remarks like, "hockey's stupid" or some other mean-spirited comment from some jealous little shit-head kid, too afraid to learn to play.

Jason's treatment in his younger years resulted in him acquiring a unique perspective when it came to people like G. Jason realized that, save for the fact that he was a very skilled hockey player and had some genetic advantages in the looks department, he was no different from the ones labelled geeks. In fact, he gets along great with those kids. Jason and G hit it off in seventh grade and have been close ever since.

The greeting of heat from opening the grill's lid coupled with the heat of the hot summer day coming to an end would be unbearable for some. But Jason is from the desert and so is used to its harsh conditions. He also knows there is a nice pool just a few feet away that he could run and jump into.

Cooking has become a favorite hobby for his time away from hockey. He first started after being hooked on reruns of that show *Kitchen Nightmares* with Gordon Ramsay. He now cooks the majority of his own food unless it's a game day, in which case the team provides him with meals. Every once in a while, he does still enjoy the occasional, guilty trip to a drive-thru.

The chicken breasts are placed onto the grill and immediately begin to sizzle. The smells of the black garlic and truffle are released into the air. Jason closes the lid and stands near the grill, taking small sips from his glass while he enjoys the desert sunset.

After a few minutes, Jason opens the lid and checks the chicken. Satisfied with the color and grill markings, he flips each breast over and closes the lid again. Jason pulls out his phone and turns on his music which begins playing through the Bluetooth surround sound speakers situated all around the patio.

He walks over to a chair at the fire pit table and sits down, throwing his head back. After what feels like five or six minutes, Jason opens his eyes, takes a sip of his tequila, stands up, and starts back to check each breast's internal temp. *One six five, that's what we want. No more, no less.*

The thermometer reads around one-twenty-five for each piece. Instead of leaving the chicken there, where it would end up sharing the same fate as the witches in Salem, he moves them to the other side of the grill where the heat would come indirectly. This continues heating the internal temp with ambient temperature like in an oven and helps prevent the exterior from being scorched, turning tough and dry.

Back in his chair at the fire pit, having put on the asparagus, too, he looks up at the now dark sky. He is able to make out only a couple of constellations due to the bright city lights. It was better out here than where he grew up, but he's been places where the sky doesn't even look real, like he's sitting on Space Mountain. Since he was a young boy, he's been fascinated with the vastness of space. He loved to study the constellations and try to pick them out at night in the sky. He was also fascinated with aliens and so he felt that the more he looked toward the sky at night, the better chance there was at seeing something weird.

His grandmother told him and his brothers a story when they were little about how when she first moved to Arizona, she went on a hike with her friends one evening. She claimed to have run in to either a ghost or an alien. Something spooky undoubtedly. Arizona is a hotbed for both types of encounters.

There have been numerous UFO sightings as well as endless ghost stories about places like the Superstition Mountains or towns like Jerome.

Whenever Jason is alone, he isn't thinking about hockey, or his worries. He may start out that way, but then he drifts off and wonders about what else is out there in the universe. What else exists in the cosmos beyond what he can see and comprehend? He takes another sip of his tequila and heads over to pull the chicken and asparagus from the grill.

"Who won?" Jason asks as he enters the house.

"Nick did, but it was by decision."

"Damnnn G, getting better."

"Hell yeah, I think I can get him next time."

"Where'd he go?"

"I don't know, I think he went into his room."

"YO SLICK! DINNER'S READY!"

Ari chases Jason around hoping that something falls for him to eat. He remains by his owner's side while Jason cuts and plates his food and is more than pleased to get a couple end pieces from the thin side of the breast.

Nick and G plate their food. They take it over to the couch where they sit down to eat and pop on the Formula One show on Netflix. After a couple of episodes, the boys call it a night and head to bed.

5

As THE SUN makes its way over the McDowell Mountains, it lets the golfers warming up on the range know that their tee time is soon approaching. Jason and his buddy from youth hockey, Sosa, had been at the practice range hitting balls and warming up since first light. During the summer months, it is imperative to get early tee-times since the day's pretty much shot from the heat by ten-thirty, and even that can be pushing it. Some people can only afford to play at places like this during the heat of a summer day and once upon a time, Jason Wagner was one of them. But now, he's a professional hockey player and a member at Troon North. So, the measly twenty-dollar cart fee and the nominal guest fee for a *prime tee-timed* round of golf is by no means a big deal.

So far, Jason's career has afforded him more money than he's known what to do with. It's not like he's amassed an exorbitant amount of wealth; there are players in his league that are making more money every year than he has in his entire career. But still, it's way more than he could've expected to make selling insurance like his uncle did or going out to work at the family ranch like his older brother had.

Jason takes a few more swings with his nine iron as Sosa dials in his big-dawg Callaway Rogue ST driver. "She-yew, how far you hitting that thing these days Sos?" Jason asks his friend as he bends down to pick up his alignment stick.

"Ohhh buddy... I usually get about a three-ten carry when I hit it right."

"Just crushin' it, hey?" Jason says as he flashes a jack-o-lantern smile while walking back toward their cart. "How much you wanna go a hole?"

"How about a grand?"

"Fuck me, a grand. Either you signed Auston Matthews or your short game got a lot better." Says Jason as he hops in the driver's seat of cart number twenty-one.

"Oh yeah? We'll see about that one, buddy. You're still waiting to see if you can even afford a stack a hole," Sosa says as he puts the head cover on his driver and sheaths it in his bag attached to the back of the cart.

"How 'bout you sign me and get me a job then?" Jason says from the driver's seat.

"You've got an agent," Sosa says climbing in.

"Man, I sure hope so."

Sosa is from Washington state and played on the same team as Jason for Jason's last season before Juniors. The two remained friends when Sosa went to Washington State University to pursue his law degree so he could follow in his dad's footsteps and become an agent for hockey players.

When Sosa first joined his dad's agency, he had no clients and was not going to just be given a client list either. He had to earn it, and that meant starting out with signing guys that were prospects to play juniors or being "family advisors" to kids with hopes of playing in college and helping them develop from hopefuls to prospects to players. Signed, sealed, and delivered. Currently he's got three kids in the Western Hockey League, one in the O, and one kid at Arizona State University.

He lives in his hometown near Seattle, but regularly makes the rounds to visit his clients. He doesn't usually get out to the desert during the summer months but his client at ASU is a hometown kid and he was just drafted. Sosa's here to meet with the family and talk about the kid's future, but he couldn't miss an opportunity to hang out with one of his closest buddies.

Jason and Sosa drive up to the starter's area to grab their scorecards and get the official go-ahead from the nice older fella known as Jim. Jim runs a tight ship. He's tall, slender, always wears a sunhat, and has eyes and nose like a hawk. His mood is much better early in the day, before all the drunks and jerk-offs start coming in late for their tee-times, throwing off any sense of order. It forces him to improvise and figure it out so everyone still gets out there and has a good time. It's a thankless job for the most part, but he does enjoy getting to know some of the more prompt and respectful club members from time to time.

One of his favorites has just pulled up with a guest and they're clearly eager to get going with their round. "Pinnacle Course is all ready to go for you boys," Jim says. "Have fun out there. Either of you need anything before you get going? Tees? Towels? Got your scorecard. Cart's got the GPS."

"Think we're good, thanks Jim, we appreciate it." Jason says as he reaches into his pocket to hand Jim a twenty. An unneeded but much appreciated gesture that has kept Jason in Jim's good graces for the every once in a while that he's late for a tee-time.

Before heading out, Sosa gets out of the cart, walks over to the water cooler, and pulls out a nice thick clear plastic cup from the sleeve attached. He pulls out a few napkins from the dispenser, then stuffs them into his cup in preparation for his next dip. He gets back into the cart, placing the cup in its holder, and lifts his butt cheek to access his back pocket where he just sat on his can of Copenhagen Wintergreen Long-Cut. He retrieves the can and pops it into the storage in front of him along with his phone and wallet.

"Alright. Let's rip," says Jason, disengaging the parking brake as he stomps on the accelerator and begins cruising up to the first tee box.

The first hole out on the Pinnacle Course at Troon North is a beautiful three hundred-ninety-two yard, par four, that's fairly straight with beautiful desert on each side of the fairway running the entire length of the hole.

Both guys have their driver in hand to get the round kicked off. "You wanna go first?" Jason asks pointing his driver in the direction of the tee-box.

"It's your club," Sosa says with a laugh.

"Yeah, So... be my guest. I insist."

"How about we flip a tee?"

"Fine, we'll flip a tee," says Jason, as he grabs a tee from the front pocket of his Nike Golf shorts. He gives it a good toss with a nice flick of the wrist for style, and it falls pointed at... him.

Sosa laughs and says, "Yes, let's see it. First hole, thousand bucks, who's getting it?"

Jason pulls out a Pro V1 from his pocket and places it on the tee, then sets up to address the ball and take his stance. He likes the Pro V1s because he can customize the number and he always gets them with his jersey number stamped as opposed to the typical one through four found in the sleeves at pro-shops.

Jason takes his time on his back swing, imagining that his left arm is a catapult, which slowly and steadily is ratcheted into position so that in an instant, he can pull the trigger and swing his driver's club head at a speed of one hundred-twenty miles per hour. Not as hard as long bomb, Liv Tour Pro, Bryson DeChambeau, but faster than the PGA Tour average of around one-seventeen.

As soon as Jason gets to the top of his back swing, he engages his core, fires his hips with his legs acting as pistons, and rotates through his shoulders to absolutely smash his ball three hundred-twenty yards. It *just* stays in the fairway on the right-hand side.

"Oh fuck me, I forgot you weren't really in the playoffs last season," Sosa says as he walks up to plant his ball and tee into the ground. "That was unreal."

"Not a bad start, eh?" says Jason while coolly putting his tee back into his pocket, "This is my first real round of the summer. I've been injured."

"Well, you're obviously healed now." Sosa addresses his ball like he means serious business, his stance is just a little wider than it was when he was on the range a few minutes earlier and he's almost aiming a little to the right. He takes a couple of deep breaths, pulls back, and hits the ball so hard, he almost comes out of his shoes. It was a long hard snap-hook that finds its way into the desert on the left side.

"Don't worry about that, it opens up down there. You'll be alright," says Jason knowing that it'll be a pill to find and he'll most likely have to drop.

"Fuck off," Sosa says with another laugh as he loads up into the cart.

They buzz down the cart path toward where they saw Sosa's ball cross over into the unknown. Sosa has already made up his mind that if he can't see the ball from the cart path, he is going to be dropping a new ball, taking a penalty and looking to get it back on the next hole.

Luckily for him, as they drove up to where they saw it had rolled off, there it was, about ten yards into the desert. A little rocky and sandy but, hey, at least he doesn't have to give up a stroke. He gets out with his seven iron in hand, just hoping to make good contact and get it close to the green.

"You're gonna make me hit off this?" he asks.

"You can drop if you want."

"But I gotta give up a stroke?"

Jason nods his head decisively, "Gotta play it as it lies, I'm afraid." An obvious reference to the line in *Happy Gilmore.*

"Hah, fuck off."

As Sosa makes his way toward his ball, he begins to hear something that incites a terror unlike any fear he's ever known, and it sends shivers all the way down his spine. It is the unmistakable sound of a rattlesnake's tail. He looks down and sees the nope-rope coiled up, rattling its little death maraca... and instinctively he just starts bashing the poor bastard's brains in with the toe of his seven iron.

It all happened so fast Jason didn't have time to process what was going on. He thought maybe Sosa realized it wasn't his ball and he was upset about having to drop.

After assessing the damage to his club, Sosa walks over to his ball, lines up and takes his best whack. The ball ends up getting to just before the green, leaving him room still to make par.

"What was that about?" Jason asks Sosa as he makes his way back from the desert.

"Dude..." Sosa says still processing what had just transpired, "I just killed a fucking rattlesnake."

"No you didn't, are you serious?"

"Yeah. I heard it rattling and looked down and started hammering it in the head."

"Well go grab 'em," says Jason with a hint of western in his tone.

"What do you mean go grab him?"

"Go grab 'em. We gotta cut off its head and bury it."

Sosa is back at the cart now and can't believe what's happening, "Are you nuts? Absolutely not. A fuckin' hawk will be by in two minutes." Sosa says with a nervous laugh hoping his friend is joking.

"Rattlesnake's good eatin'. Hardest parts killing one and you've already done that. Come on," Jason says as he gets out of the cart and starts toward the dead snake.

"Wags. We just started a round of golf. People are gonna start catching us. No. Let's go."

Jason stops and turns back as if his dad has just told him he can't go play with the other kids. "Fine... fuckin' pussy." Jason gets back in and slams the pedal to the metal, sending them speeding across the beautifully kempt, lush green fairway toward his ball.

Sosa chuckles at the thought of all this suddenly making him a pussy. "You're a fuckin' nut," Sosa says with a hearty laugh. "What kind of asshole starts a round of golf at Troon North and turns it into a hunting trip?"

"Hey man, you were the one that killed it, not me. I was over here in the fairway."

"That thing was gonna bite me and I panicked, alright?"

"Yeah, yeah, whatever," says Jason, pulling up to his ball.

Jason takes out his fifty-six-degree wedge and puts it seven feet short from the hole with about two feet of backspin.

"Wow," says Sosa. "That was unreal."

"Huh? Who needs hockey? Maybe I'll join the tour? How about that?"

As it turns out, Jason does need hockey. He ends up parring that hole along with many others over the course of the round. He also has a few birds, couple bogeys, a double, and a triple that he'll try to forget about later that night at the Rustler's Rooste.

The two pals load up to hit the road back to Jason's house when he feels his phone vibrate with a text notification. He pulls it out and is surprised to see four missed calls and now three text messages from his French-Canadian agent, Marty:

BIG NEWS! CALL ME ASAP! 2 TEAMS!

WAKE UP!!!

I TAKE THE BIGGER ONE 4 U :-)

Jason shows his friend who laughs and shakes his head as he sets his phone on the wireless charger and puts his Tahoe in gear.

6

JASON AND SOSA continue hypothesizing about who the teams are and what their offers could be as they unload and proceed into Jason and Nick's house. It's a nice house on the edge of DC Ranch, which is a luxury subdivision in North Scottsdale. Nick's usually at the gym this time of day, training, which leaves only G and the world's most ferocious guard dog, Ari.

G is in the kitchen wearing his pajama bottoms preparing some breakfast. It smells like eggs and slightly overcooked bacon. He's currently at the nice, gas-burning stove made by Wolf, heating some raw tortillas so he can make burritos.

The door opens with a chirp from the security system letting anyone in the house know that someone's come in. The noise causes Ari to leap from the L-shaped couch in the living room adjacent to the kitchen. G turns his attention away from his tortillas and toward the door to the garage and is shocked when he sees Jason walking in with his golf bag. "Woah, have you been gone all morning?" G asks.

"Yeah? What do you mean?" Says Jason. Sosa stands there not knowing what to do but amused.

"I thought you were in your room this whole time," G says.

"It's like eleven-thirty bud. No. Remember? Sos was coming in early, I had to pick him up, and we were gonna play golf. Slick was saying how he wanted to go last night but had to train," he tells Sosa.

"Ohhh, that's right. I guess I wasn't even paying attention to the time, my bad."

"You're good, G. Smells good, brother."

"You guys want some? I can make more."

"I'm okay, thanks though. Sos? You want some?"

"I'm good too man, but thanks."

"Suit yourselves."

Jason and Sosa confirm that they haven't slipped into a parallel universe and proceed through the kitchen and into the middle room of the house which is a game room with a bar, ping-pong, air-hockey, and pool table. It also is where the boys keep their golf bags. Jason and his brother have bag storage at the clubhouse but because they also have a TrackMan Golf Simulator set up in this room, they always end up bringing their stuff home.

After dropping their golf bags in the game room, they head back into the living room and kitchen area. Jason pulls out his phone as he and Sosa sit on the couch to make the call back to his agent.

Marty has been Jason's agent ever since he decided he was going to try his hand at Major Juniors, despite what had happened to his older brother. Marty was a new agent at the time, cutting his teeth with young prospects and told Jason he could get him on the Kamloops Blazers of the Western Hockey

League at the age of sixteen. Since Jason was drafted to the NHL, Marty has closed four professional deals on Jason's behalf and has helped him secure millions of dollars in earnings. Why had Jason been so worried?

Marty had a way about him that made it seem like he was Jason's buddy. There was something cool about him. He was a fighter in the Q and used his free ride to college to become a lawyer, then an agent. He rode Harleys, wore a goatee, and always seemed like he could still feed 'em pretty good if needed.

Early on in Jason's career, there was near constant communication between him and his agent. Marty would call and check in. They'd talk about games or talk about the league, even if it wasn't near contract times. It was like Marty was the uncle that Jason never had. In truth, Jason had a couple uncles, but he didn't really know them, other than the fact that neither of them was very much into hockey. Marty was interested in Jason's career, his perspective on the game, and his thoughts as a friend. Their bond reached its pinnacle when Jason signed his biggest contract a few years back.

Since then, the tone's stayed the same, but the frequency and the quality of conversation has gone way, way down. It could be due to Jason's getting older and not being worth as much money as he used to be. It could also be because Marty has signed other fresh young talent to his client list and is hopeful they'll bring higher offers for him to work and negotiate than what Jason currently brings. Either way, Jason can't think these kinds of thoughts too deeply. He taps the messages app, then on Marty's contact at the top of the screen, then call, putting it on speaker. Marty picks up after the first ring.

"Jason! How are you, my friend? I've been trying to reach you."

"Hey Marty, funny, I've been trying to get in touch with you, too. Whatcha got?"

"Ah yes, yes, I've been-eh meaning to get back with you but-eh you know how it can be. Anee-wayz, what we have-uh is some good news. Two team call. Dey both say, 'We want Jason, we want Jason,' I say, 'Okay, I'll speak with Jason and get back.'"

"Which teams?" Jason asks while trying to keep his mounting irritation at bay. He wasn't irritated at the fact that two teams have put in an offer for him. What was irritating was his agent's insistent theatrics. He could never just tell it to him like it is. There's always a presentation and it always has to be a show.

"Minnesota is the only team."

"You just said there were two teams," says Jason, "Who's the other one?"

"Minnesota is offering three point nine million over three years."

Sosa quietly celebrates and puts his hand in a fist up to congratulate Jason.

"Woah. That's a big deal."

"Oui, biggest one yet! They originally came in at two years with one point one million per."

"Damn. How'd you get 'em up?"

"I used the other dog shit offer as leverage."

"Man, well good work, let's do it. I still want to know the other team though."

"Eh?" He says dismissively, "It was Vegas but dey can't pay you, Jason."

Here we go, Jason thinks. He remains silent just looking at Sosa who is also mouthing the words, "How much?"

The line stays silent for a short while longer before Marty checks to make sure he hasn't lost connection, "Jason?"

"Yeah, I'm here. Sorry, how much for Vegas?"

"Jason, it doesn't matter, dey cannot afford you with what Minnesota has offered."

"Marty... Are you fuckin' serious? You're not gonna tell me?"

"Okay, okay, okay, fine. Relax. But Jason. Remember. Three point nine million dollars. Guaranteed."

"Marty tell me the offer or I'm gonna hang up and call them myself."

"Vegas offer is only two years at only one point two per year."

Sosa makes a face that says he knows that Jason is fuming right now and is doing everything in his power not to fire Marty in this instant. Jason remains quiet, partly to do the math and partly to stay calm.

Regardless of the math, *two point four million* for two years close to his hometown on a team that's recently won a cup and is a real contender, at this stage of his career? It was better than anything he could have hoped for a few days ago. The only thing he has left to do is raise the Stanley Cup and get his name etched on it forever.

"Jason?" Says Marty checking again to make sure he hadn't lost connection.

"Yeah," says Jason still processing his emotions. Sosa checks his watch and taps Jason on the arm letting him know he has to split for his meeting. Wags gives Sos a nod and a thumbs up.

"You see? Minnesota is the better offer. It is obvious. More money, longer time, and better team. I'll just send over zee papers for you to sign."

"Just hang on a second Marty. When do they need to know by?"

"I told Minnesota you'd get back to them by the end of the day."

"When did you hear from Vegas?"

"It was just yesterday, then today Minnesota."

"Alright, can I think about it for an hour or so and get back to you?"

"Jason, what is there to think? This is what you pay me for, please Jason."

Jason shakes his head and looks up at his ceiling.

"You know what? I don't wanna go to Minnesota."

"Ahhh, but Jason the deal is much better there."

"Yeah, well. I don't know what to tell ya, if there's an offer to play for Vegas, I'd like to accept it please."

Now it's Marty's turn to be silent.

"You there, Marty?"

"Yes. Sorry, okay Jason, if dat is what you want-eh, then I will send over zeh paperwork right away."

"Alright thanks, I'll let you know when I get it."

Just as Jason ends the call, his brother Nick enters the house from the garage after having just passed Sosa on the way in. "Yo yo, how'd it go?" asks Nick.

Jason tosses his phone to his side and leans back in relaxation, putting his feet on the ottoman. "Good news. Heading to Vegas."

"Right now?" G says.

"No, to play. They offered me a two-year deal at one point two per year."

"Oh hell yeah bro! That's what's up." G says.

"No way, seriously?"

"Yep."

"Congrats bro!" cries Nick who makes his way to Jason for a big hug, "What should we do to celebrate?"

"Thanks dude and I don't know, Sos has never had rattlesnake before, I say we take him to Rustler's Rooste."

"Can I come?" asks G.

"G, of course. Always."

"Hell yeah, I'm down," says Nick.

7

RUSTLER'S ROOSTE sits atop a butte in the foothills of South Mountain in Phoenix, Arizona. It overlooks the Arizona Grand Resort Golf Course and boasts stunning views of the whole city. Every night, patrons arrive in their western themed garb, hoping to get a feel for what life was like in the Old West. The story goes that before it became a legendary cowboy steakhouse, the original structure was a hideout used by cattle rustlers in the area. Cattle rustling was and is a serious offense and led a great many of outlaws to meet their maker either by gun or by rope back then. Now, Rustler's Rooste serves as a place where all kinds of people can go and eat and drink and dance and have fun with the whole family.

Jason and his brother Nick are duded up in their western wear consisting of some blue jeans, plaid button-ups, and boots. Jason took Sos and G to Boot Barn so they could look the part while they were there and wouldn't feel out of place. G wanted to get a hat, so he's rocking a nice, black, wool felt cowboy hat and is buzzing as they walk through the sections to their table.

They're brought to their seats which are pretty close to

where the slide ends. The whole scene triggers old memories for Jason and Nick.

"You remember when you were scared to go down that thing?" says Jason.

"Yeah, when I was like two and didn't wanna go down alone?" asks Nick.

"Yeah, bet you won't go down it tonight."

"Bet I won't."

Sosa looks over at the slide and says, "I'll go down. Fuck it. After a few drinks? Why not?"

The waitress makes her way over to the table to bring waters and take everyone's drink order. They each order a beer and just before she closes her book, Jason says, "Ehm, can we also please get a round of tequila shots as well as an order of rattlesnake to start?"

"Sure thing." She makes her notes, closes her book, and starts back toward the bar.

"I can't get too housed cause, I gotta skate in the morning, but we gotta do at least a couple, hey?" says Jason.

"Sounds good to me." says Sosa.

"Same," agree the other two.

Jason has always had a habit of keeping his head on a swivel. It was something that his coaches told him was important, and so he always worked on it, even off the ice. It's smart to do for general security reasons, but he mostly uses it as a way to scout the area for a potential candidate he can share his bed with. He scans his surroundings when he notices a beautiful blonde woman in her mid-twenties helping a toddler-aged boy off the slide they'd just ridden down. Jason watches as the little boy leads the woman back up the stairs so they can go again.

Jason smiles and rejoins the table's conversation where Nick is explaining that he's trying to get his next fight, but the guy he wants to fight just booked another fight and so Nick feels like everyone's ducking him.

"How many do you have left on your contract?" asks Sosa.

"Two more, but if I become champ again, that re-sign is going to be way bigger. If I win one, it'll be alright. If I lose both, I'm probably getting cut."

"Damn."

G nods his head and says, "Isn't that crazy? Guy's already had the belt and he's worried about not getting re-signed. Not even in his prime yet."

Nick laughs, "Thanks G."

"No doubt," says G, putting up his fist for a bump.

Jason notices the woman and toddler getting off the slide but again turns his attention back to the table and says, "He'll get re-signed. He may be too chicken shit to go down that slide, but he isn't scared of anyone on that roster, and I bet at least a month's pay on it every time he steps into that octagon."

Nick smiles at the kind words from his older brother, just as the waitress brings her tray of drinks and sets them on the table. Each of the boys says thank you as she walks off to another table. They all pick up their shots and hold them out to clink before ceremoniously putting their glass to the table then back to their lips for the sweet distilled Mexican agave juice to go down the hatch.

"Man, that was good," says Sosa who is known for his love of beer. While he was in college, he got after the rum and the vodka a little heavy and grew to dislike the taste of both.

"Tequila's the best, man. Low on calories, gives a nice buzz, and it's got a crisp taste," says Jason.

"Yeah, I always forget about it, being up in fuckin' Seattle."

"You and your tequila dude," says Nick.

"You know, just cause I'm not some sophisticated scotch or whiskey guy doesn't mean I got a problem."

"No, it's just funny that tequila is your go-to."

"I guess," says Jason as he picks up and swigs from his Modelo noticing the blonde from earlier heading back up the slide steps. "Speaking of, I'm gonna go grab us another round." Jason gets up and starts up the stairs to the upstairs bar and hopes to run into her.

There's a platform halfway up the stairs where the band is set up and is currently plucking along and crooning the words to Dwight Yoakam's "Guitars, Cadillacs".

Just as Jason reaches the top of the stairs, he sees the back of the woman and her co-slider, arms in the air as they had just pushed off down the slick stainless-steel slide.

Damn. Missed her.

Jason makes his way over to the bar where he orders four more shots of tequila and realizes he's going to have to go all the way back down the stairs with these four shots.

Maybe she'll see me carrying four shots and we'll meet up on the stairs.

He carefully handles all four little glasses and starts back toward the stairs and the slide, making sure to keep his hands and body still as he walks. He steadily descends the staircase down to where his table is. With only five stairs to go, the toddler and the woman both come marching up the stairs. The little boy clips Jason's leg, which throws off his balance, causing him to spill his shots.

"Oh my gosh, I'm so sorry," the woman says.

"No, I'm sorry. I just spilt tequila all over you guys!"

"Oh, we're fine, I don't think it got on us, but you definitely are gonna need another round of shots. Can we buy them?"

"No, no, that's okay, thank you though," Jason says, "When I was his age, I used to run up these same stairs and go down this same slide."

The boy looks at his mom who smiles and says, "Wow, how cool is that? He's been coming here for a long time!"

"Oh yeah, you guys have a good night and enjoy the slide alright?"

"Thank you and sorry again about the spill," she says.

"Don't worry about it. Who knows, you may see me going down the slide a little later if we ever end up getting the shots back to the table."

This makes the woman laugh, which lets Jason know she's interested. The only question is, who's kid is she with?

By the time Jason returns to the table, the plate of fried rattlesnake is already sitting there. Nick has taken a couple pieces and put them onto his plate along with some of the dipping sauce, but Sosa and G are waiting until Jason forces them to try it.

"Where are the shots?" asks Sosa.

"You guys didn't just see? I was carrying 'em down the stairs and got knocked by a little kid that's got that blonde taking him down the slide. We'll ask the waitress for another round when she comes back."

"I think I'm gonna need another shot if I'm going to be eating this shit," says Sosa.

"Just down your beer and have a couple bites."

"What does it taste like?" G asks.

Nick forks a piece and puts it up for them to see. "Just like chicken," he says before giving it a dip in the sauce and putting it in his mouth.

Jason serves his plate full with bits of rattlesnake and drizzles the dipping sauce over the top of each piece.

"Alright, here it goes," says Sosa as he forks a piece and brings it up to his nose so he can give it a good sniff.

"Just eat it man. Put it in your mouth. You too, G, grab one of them and take it down," says Jason.

They both do as they're told and after a little bit of chewing they realize it does kind of taste like chicken.

The boys drank a few more beers and took a couple more shots while they ate dinner and listened to various popular country songs being sung by the live band. They recap the earlier round of golf and celebrate Jason's new contract.

Jason doesn't end up seeing that girl for the rest of the night, but he does get a helper on a rare score for G. It was always a side-mission to try to get G laid because he was so awkward and shy, but the boys came through at the Rooste.

Jason and Nick both told her they'd be nothing without G and that he was their manager. Sosa stood by at the bar, laughing from afar, as he watched it all go down.

Next thing they knew, G wasn't coming home in the Uber with the boys. He and his chick were taking their own ride to her place.

8

———————

It's still dark out when the rink maintenance guy gets to work, even in the summer. Rick's in his early sixties and played college hockey back in the day. After a couple of marriages went south and a few businesses fell apart, he decided to go back to his first true love: hockey.

He's been at the rink for going on eight years and spends the majority of his days there at AZ Ice Arcadia. He's a former addict and now devotes his life to God and hockey. There is no one that can drive the Zamboni like Rick, the rink guy.

The Zamboni makes its final pass on its way into its corral in the corner of the rink. Jason and Jake catch up on what's happened since their last skate. Rick shuts and locks the boards back into place after setting the nets out on the ice. Jason and his on-ice skills coach wait for a few minutes to let the ice set. The Zamboni leaves a layer of water that will cause pucks to stick to the ice if the water doesn't freeze back over first. Jason and his coach eventually step out from the bench and feel the blades of their skates dig into the hard, glossy, freshly resurfaced sheet of ice. Jason takes his first couple of strides. He gets close enough to the boards for Rick to recognize him and give a friendly wave. Jason smiles nods and shouts, "Morning Rick!" as he continues his first lap.

Jason's skills coach Jake sets his bag of pucks out on the ice near the boards. He attaches his whiteboard to the top of the plexiglass via a hook. He watches Jason take a couple of laps around before skating to the Zamboni doors so he can retrieve the nets and skate them to their places.

The two of these boys played together for a few years growing up, with Jake's dad as the head coach. Jake has somewhat followed in his dad's footsteps, working on developing good players into better players, but rather than coaching his kid's team, he's focusing on the individuals and the skills it takes for them to make it further along in their career.

Jason is at a point in his career where he's as high as he's able to go, and at the same time he's desperate to stay there. It used to be that once the season ended, the off-season would start. Every once in a while, you'd hear stories of guys' freakish workout routines or their wild on-ice activity but for the most part it was pretty tame.

Nowadays, hockey is a year-round sport and players work just as hard in the summer as they do during the season. If Jason doesn't continue working on his game and stay out there during summer months, his play during-season will be too slow to keep up anymore. The speed of the game has increased so drastically over the years and Jason wasn't ever the quickest guy to begin with. His speed and quickness have been his point of emphasis with his training since he was twelve.

He skates over to the unzipped puck bag and tips it on its side to dispense a few pucks. He grabs one on the backhand side of his stick blade and skates up the wall. Becoming one with the puck on his stick, he does a lap around the ice. Cradling and imagining opponents and real game scenarios, he bursts down the ice. When he reaches the top of the face-off circle, he edges to the outside and fires a rocket snapshot that smashes into the underside of the cross bar, stopping the puck's upward progress, and redirects its energy down on a trajectory that finds its way into the back of the net.

He skates around the underside of the face-off circles in front of the net and grabs another puck from the four or five that have spilled out. This time he takes the puck on his fore-hand and really digs into the ice with the steel of his skates as he wheels down the side. When he gets to the top of the circle on the other end, he fires off another laser that finds the empty net.

Jake is now set up at his whiteboard, which he expects is enough to let Jason know that it's time to quit fucking around and get to work. Jason skates around the net he just scored on and comes buzzing up the ice on the opposite side of where Jake and his whiteboard are. "Yeah, yeah, yeah!" Jason yells.

When a hockey player yells "yeah" any amount of times in consecutive fashion, that usually means they want someone to pass them a puck. Jake can't help himself and zips one right on the tape of Jason's forehand as he crosses the red line. This time, instead of a snapper at the circle, Jason winds up and fires a nice and controlled slap-shot no more than two and a half feet off the ice, that would've clocked in at upwards of ninety miles per hour.

"Alright, let's go. Quit fuckin' around, we got shit to do," says Jake.

For the first exercise, Jason is going to be strapping a nylon belt around his waist with a bungee rope attached to one of the belt-loops. Jake is going to hold the other end of the rope and point his toes together, creating drag. At the same time, Jason is going to go from sideboard to sideboard as hard as he can.

After doing this for long enough that Jason wants to puke, Jake decides to bring out his parachute attachment for the belt. It's another drag inducing mechanism that will increase the level of difficulty for Jason as he skates.

"What the fuck is this about?" Jason asks with a sense of irritation.

Jake laughs and says, "Aye, if you were faster, we wouldn't have to do so much of it. Here, strap this on, I gotta set up the next drill."

Jason straps on his parachute and is careful to not skate over it. "Alright, what do I do with this thing?"

"You're gonna use this center circle here. You start out slow, then by the time you get to halfway on the circle, put it in gear and start moving. Just stay on the outside of the circle. After one lap coast around, then go hard again."

"Got it," says Jason as he starts out around the circle with slow and easy strides. As the circle continues to bend, he crosses over with big, exaggerated steps, and by the time he gets to the halfway point, the parachute is full of air. He pumps his legs hard, forcing his own apexes to be greater than that of his guide which is painted under the ice. He eases up and starts to coast and shift the weight of his body to move him in his intended direction. "You want me to change sides ever?"

"Huh? Oh yeah, switch ways after every two hard ones."

"Alright," says Jason as he begins picking up speed again.

By the time Jake has finished setting up the next drill Jason has gone around the center circle a total of four times in each direction. He skates back up to watch Jason perform his last repetition. "Looking good there Wags, real good. You can be done."

"Thanks buddy," says Jason as the two of them skate toward the bench where there are a few water bottles.

"How you feeling?"

"Like it's not the middle of summer," Jason says as he grabs a bottle and takes a sip.

Jake smiles and nods, "Yeah, just cause it's hot out don't mean it's time for vacation."

"I guess not. Good news for you, eh? What's next?"

"Great news for me. Great for the game though, too."

"Yeah unless you're mucking it out hoping it doesn't pass you by cause skills coaches like you keep turning out phenoms every other draft year."

Jake makes a face at his client and buddy. "Get the fuck out of here, you got plenty of time to play still."

"Yeah. At least two more years. What do we got next?"

On the whiteboard Jake draws the cones and barricade as they are on the ice. The barricade is somewhere in between the middle and top of the face-off circle near the boards. Then the cones are set up in a large triangle near the blue line.

Jason and Jake will both start on the wall at the blue line. Jake will fire a puck into the barricade, signaling Jason to start. Jason skates down, picks up the puck as he transitions to backwards skating up to the top cone. Once at the apex of the top cone, he's supposed to start angling in toward the middle of the ice. Stop before the inside cone, fake a shot, go back the other way, and in through the lane for a quick shot on the net. Then, come around the cones and set up for a one-timer at the top of the other face-off circle.

"Got it?" asks Jake.

"Yeah, got it."

Some of the young kids who will be next to take the ice have arrived early for their summer league game when they notice Jason Wagner is out there skating on the same ice they were about to be on. They all watch for as long as they can before they have to start getting dressed for their game.

Jason and Jake do a few other drills that worked on offensive escapes, as well as some redirects where Jake rips clappers from the point and Jason stands in front of the net and makes contact with the majority of the shots, successfully redirecting them into the net.

As soon as the kids are ready to go, they are out of their locker room for another chance to watch a player they look up to, grinding it out, and looking like a machine. It's impossible for the kids to know what Jason was thinking or feeling last week. They can't imagine what he was going through internally. All they can think about is getting their chance someday. They think about what it would be like for them to be the one getting off the ice to greet a group of young kids. Inevitably, some of them will go on to have a real chance at making it. How Jason interacts with them will show them how they ought to act once they get to that level.

Jason starts his cool down and stretches on the ice while Jake packs up all the training gear. He always finishes by picking up pucks. He slides the pucks from the back of the net over to the bag area by the fives. Then he flips them into the bag from the ice with his stick.

Skating over to help with the last couple of pucks, Jason calls for an alley-oop with his stick up as he glides toward the bag, "Yeah!"

Jake uses the toe of his blade to bring a puck back and flip it up, Jason uses his hand-eye coordination and redirects it off his backhand at waist height into the bag.

The kids from both teams next to play are ready and waiting along the glass near the bench that Jason will be coming off the ice from. They all ask for fist bumps which he obliges, then they all ask for autographs which again, he is more than happy to oblige.

He doesn't have a complex, but he knows he's no superstar in the NHL. The fact that kids still look up to him, appreciate him as a player, and want his autograph is something that will always be cool to him. It makes him work harder knowing that the next generation is watching and taking notes. He wants them to be better than he has been, as did the generation before him.

Once he's out of his gear and showered, he puts on his shorts and T-shirt and checks his phone. The email that came through from Marty was Jason's new contract. He taps the document on the attachment and zooms in to do a quick look over. *Are you fucking kidding me?* Jason immediately texts Marty that this was the wrong offer and to send the correct one immediately.

9

So far through his second session with Dr. Sutton, Jason has been recapping the events of the week; they celebrate and talk about the relief of the burden despite still waiting for it to be official on account of Marty's negligent manipulation tactic. Jason admits that he was most afraid because he doesn't have any job skills to speak of. He knows he doesn't have enough money to live on forever and even if he did, he'd be bored to death. He's had no work experience and didn't go to college. "You know, my dad left home and went and got a job when he was only sixteen. He went to college, became an entrepreneur, and here I am, almost thirty, and without hockey, I'm worse off than he was."

"I wouldn't say you guys are exactly comparable."

"I know we aren't, but the net result of my experience on a real job is less than my dad's was at sixteen years old and it's weird to think about that when I'm pushing thirty, you know? I've never even changed a tire."

"I see what you're saying, but the life experiences that

you've accumulated over the course of your hockey career shouldn't be discounted. When the time does come, and the next chapter starts, you may be surprised to see that things are more or less the same no matter where you are. As lame and corny as it sounds, it really is what you make it to be."

"No, it makes sense when it's in context. I see what you mean but I still don't see how that applies to changing a tire."

"You will once you're doing it."

Jason has talked about his parents and his younger brother Nick, though he's hardly mentioned his older brother more than once. Dr. Sutton is curious about the family dynamic and feels that could have been a contributing factor to how Jason was feeling before his contract signing. The contract ensures he will remain employed for another two years, but there will come a day sooner or later, when he is without a contract for an upcoming season. Dr. Sutton feels as though it's his responsibility to arm Jason with the skills and tools so that he can transition to being a "regular guy" when the time comes.

"What does the family think about your new team and being so close to home?" asks Dr. Sutton.

"Oh man. They're so pumped, my mom just started crying when I told her, same thing with my grandma. I think they were just happy I got signed and wouldn't have to retire yet. My dad seemed pretty stoked, and Nick was obviously excited. I haven't told you much about G, but he lives with us at the house, and he's most pumped of anyone, he loves Vegas."

Dr. Sutton laughs, "That's too funny. What about your older brother? You said he worked on the family ranch? Is it close enough for him to make any games?"

"Yeah, my dad's dad's got a ranch up there near Flagstaff. It's been in the family a few generations, but we were never really close with him. He and my dad didn't get along which was what led to my dad leaving at sixteen to go live with his grandparents in Tempe.

"Then when Carl quit playing hockey, it got ugly between him and our dad. Carl was drunk and depressed all the time and wouldn't go get a job, so finally our dad kicked him out. That was when he went up and got a job for our grandpa, working at the ranch. We haven't spoke in a few years. Every now and then he'd send me a text, but I haven't heard from him for a while now. I know he's not dead, so I guess that's enough."

"That's a tough deal man. When did he stop playing hockey?"

"He played until he was nineteen I think. Then he just quit."

"You guys ever talk about it? He ever tell you why he quit?"

"I always heard him telling different people different stories. All just depended who was around is what it seemed like to me."

"I see."

"Like, to one person he'd say he got too many concussions, then to another person he'd say he got traded to a different league and didn't want to go. But the year I got drafted was really tough on Carl, and it was around then that things got bad and he ended up getting the boot from the house."

"Do you feel like it's your fault?"

"I don't know that I feel like it's my fault, but I do feel like me living what he thinks is his dream doesn't help either of us."

"Do you feel like you're living his dream?"

Jason takes a second to ponder the question.

"No, I don't think so. Maybe it would've taken me longer to get into without him leading the way, but I've wanted to play in the NHL since I was six. I feel like for him it was a competition thing, and if he couldn't be the best one in the family, then he wasn't gonna play at all."

"Were you guys competitive growing up?"

"Yeah, we were. But we were also super close. All three of us. Nick was a goalie and Carl was a D-Man so we would all play street hockey in the driveway and not come in until bedtime. We had some older neighborhood kids that played hockey and were close in age to Carl, so they were always over. Other times we'd have some kids from one of our teams over and would always be playing together."

"Does he keep in touch with Nick?"

"He did more so than with me, but not really anymore. It got worse after Nick and I bought the house together. That was pretty much the last either of us heard from him. We invited him out to visit but he just congratulated us and said he'd come out. Hasn't returned calls or texts since."

"That's too bad."

"Yeah, it is what it is though, you know? It'll work itself out."

"Yep, that it will. So long as everyone works at it."

They both laugh.

"That's the hard part."

"Yeah. It definitely can be, but the goal here is to give you the tools and perspective to put yourself in a spot to make things better, wherever it is."

"Well, I appreciate it."

"It's what I'm here for. And what you pay me for."

Jason laughs, "That's right."

"Alright well, this seems like a good point to take a break till next time. What do you think?"

"Yeah, I think so. I feel good." Jason stands up and walks over to shake Dr. Sutton's hand.

"Alright, text me if you need anything between now and then okay? Jessica will get you on the schedule for next time."

"Sounds good, thank you."

10

Jason still hasn't heard anything from Marty and is desperately trying to keep his mind off it. He heads to the Scottsdale Quarter, which can be a stressful affair for people that don't like crowds. The place is always buzzing with activity, whether people are going to a bar or restaurant or just going shopping. It's an outdoor mall that even during the summertime, doesn't die down all that much.

Jason doesn't mind crowds, especially in places where hockey isn't at the forefront of everybody's mind. There are places like Montreal, Toronto, or one of the other cities where hockey comes first. Hockey players in cities like that are recognized instantly, making it difficult to go out and do things without being swarmed in the streets. Jason has primarily played in cities where the people couldn't care less about whether or not he was a professional hockey player.

In Arizona, Jason runs into people he knows more so than he is recognized. The hockey community in the desert is a tight one. Everyone knows everyone from one thing or another. The people he runs into knew him before he became a professional hockey player, save for the few kids every now and then who know of him from TV. For the most part, though, people leave him to himself and have no idea who he is or what he does.

Since playing in the WHL, Jason's had a discount at Lululemon so it's where he always finds himself shopping for new clothes. He knows his sizes, he knows they're going to fit well, and he knows they're going to last a long time. It's easy for him to walk in, grab some stuff, and get out.

While Jason looks over the new t-shirts he spots out of the corner of his eye his old coach, Mark. Sensing that someone is looking at him, Mark turns his head to see Jason.

"Coach!"

"What's up Wags? How you doing? Getting anything done for next year?"

They clasp hands and do a bro hug.

"Seems like it. Vegas if my soon to be ex-agent ever sends over the paperwork."

"Nice. That's sick. Congrats. They're gonna need you this year. Better be ready to go."

"Oh, I will be, don't worry, I've been scraping and wrapping all summer."

"Heh. God knows you need it. Tell Jake more bungees."

Jason nods his head and laughs, "It's good to see you."

"You too, Wags, tell your mother and father I say hello. How is your mother by the way? I heard about her surgery."

"She's good, it went well. Doctor said he got it all so she's just been recovering and trying to keep it all under control, so it doesn't come back."

"Give them my best. Tell Slick I said what up." Mark was the one who originally gave Nick his nickname. It stuck and became the one that was loudly chanted before the start of each fight.

"I will."

Mark was Jason's high school hockey coach for a couple years before they parted ways. He was also the skating coach for the Coyotes at the time and being that Jason's weakest part of his game was his skating, he'd been the perfect fit.

Jason went to Colorado, and Mark ended up with the Rangers as their skating coach where he and Jason linked back up for a fun couple of seasons. Mark had felt terrible about Jason being traded at the deadline the year before. He didn't have anything to do with it, and knew there was nothing he could do about it except call Jason and give him his best.

After Jason finishes picking out a few new shirts and a couple pairs of shorts, he checks out at the register and then makes his way over to the bookstore on the southeast side of the outdoor mall.

Jason loves all forms of entertainment. Books, films, TV shows, stand-up comedy, it doesn't matter. Lately he's been really into reading as he finds it to be the best escape. It's not that his life is bad, he is simply curious about other people's lives and the stuff they have to go through. Even if they aren't real people and are just figments of an author's imagination. He feels that if a character has been created and thought up in a world that tells a complete story, that is more of a real person than a lot of the people he sees walking around.

The question of which was better, film or book, always annoyed Jason. He felt like both were almost always great. The question for him was how much time did he have? If he had time to watch a whole movie or TV show, he'd watch a whole movie or TV show. If he had time to read a whole book, he'd read a whole book. If there's not time to watch a whole movie or TV show, he reads the book. He finds it a lot easier to pause a book and start it back up than a film or series. There are also a lot more good books that never make it to screen than there are good screen projects that didn't start out on the pages of a novel. He's realized that there's so much more a writer can do in a novel than one can do in a screenplay. The freedom is something easily felt through the pages. Films and television series can only go so far. In a book, it can go as far and as long as the author wants.

Jason's two favorite genres to read are westerns and spy thrillers and usually he alternates in buying one of each whenever he comes in to the bookstore. This week, he's in to pick up a copy of *Only The Dead* by Jack Carr. Jason's hooked on the series and that's next in line for him to read. Starting *The Terminal List* series was what made Jason realize that not only could he read for fun, but he liked to.

When he arrives at the thriller section, he heads to find the authors whose last names start with a C. He finds who he's looking for but not what he's looking for, *Terminal List* through *In the Blood* and those are each sitting on his shelf all having been read at various points over the last few years.

He makes his way over to the western section to see if they've got a copy of *The Crossing* by Cormac McCarthy. Luckily, they do, so he plucks it from the shelf and starts toward the registers.

"Aloha!" says the friendly older hippie gentleman that sports a ponytail and glasses.

"Hi there, how's it going?"

"Oh. Pretty good. Pretty good. Are you a member?" He says before scanning the book.

Jason pulls out his phone and taps the store's app which has his member barcode, "Yep, here's that."

"Hey wait. Do I know you from somewhere?"

"Uhm, I come in here pretty often during the summer."

"No, no, not from here," he looks back up at Jason and really uses his thick glasses to focus on his subject.

"I play hockey," he says hoping that's it and he can move the interaction along as the line is starting to get longer.

"Naw, nope," he looks back to the register to complete the transaction, "Ah well, either way, you save five bucks!"

"Hey! Alright! Sweet."

"Have a good one."

"You, too."

Jason started reading when he noticed how much time he was spending on his phone while waiting to do stuff. Reading is also a great way to pass the time for him on plane rides and away trips during the season. Before, it was that he would just sit around and play games on his phone or scroll on social media. Now, his phone is the last thing he wants or needs during his leisure time. Nick started reading first, after seeing how cool John Travolta looked in *Pulp Fiction,* always walking around with his novel. Not long after that, Jason joined in and started bringing one around. It made them feel cool and smart.

* * *

BY THE TIME Jason makes it home from his day, it's deep into the afternoon and he still hasn't heard from his agent. He calls his buddy Sosa, who agrees to sign him and finalize the deal with Vegas. He taps the messages app and composes a text to Marty that reads: I've hired a new agent. Thanks for everything.

11

THE NEXT DAY is an off day for Wags. He's out playing golf again, this time with his buddy, Dallas. Dallas lives out in Gilbert and they always take turns on whose course they are going to play.

Like many from Jason's network, Dallas is another former teammate. They have been playing golf together since they were ten. Started out playing little par three nine holers and just played as much as they could. Dallas was always better at golf than Jason but Jason could always outdrive his buddy, so it kept him going out there. Every now and then Jason would win the round by more than one hole and when he did, it took his best and Dallas' worst to make it happen.

On this lovely summer morning, the boys are both having a decent round as they make their way down the stretch of the last hole at Longbow. Jason's on his second shot after Dallas put his second shot to within four feet. Jason lines up over the ball and sets his arms and legs. He looks up and sees the flag. After already having checked the distance to the pin with his rangefinder, he knows that a nice and easy pitching wedge shot should do the trick in getting the ball somewhat close to the hole.

Dallas watches from their cart as Jason flushes the face of his pitching wedge against the ball and slightly sweeps the tips of the blades of grass, just beyond where the ball had been laying.

The two buddies watch the ball as it soars through the air.

"Sounded good," says Dallas.

"Yeah, we'll see," says Jason squinting his eyes to follow the ball along its path.

"Looks good. No way. No way."

The ball gets fringe boosted and takes a couple of skipping bounces onto the green and drops straight into the cup.

Jason stands silent with both arms in the air like he's just scored a goal in front of twenty thousand people. Putting down an eagle secures the victory for Jason, but Dallas still putts out for birdie like a gentleman. They both had a solid round and were right near par.

Jason's first time playing this course was with Dallas. They were playing in a tournament for their youth hockey organization as boys. The dads and kids teamed up to play against one another and had a blast all day long.

Jason still has flashbacks to the first time a prairie dog darted out from the brush, onto the cart path, and directly under the wheel. They could both hear and feel the bones of the tiny rodent smush under the weight of their cart. His dad felt terrible, probably still does. Anytime it's been brought up, he's always said, "Damned thing just ran right out in front of me. Wasn't anything I could do. Little fucker just got smushed."

After Jason and Dallas finish their round without having

killed a single animal, they head to the clubhouse for an early lunch and a couple of beers.

"Still can't believe you're gonna play for the Knights," says Dallas.

"It's pretty unreal, hopefully we'll get to make another run for the Cup. God knows you don't need me playing more golf," says Jason as he takes a sip from his beer.

"Yeah, no shit. Go back to sandbagging like you did before you got to the show."

Jason laughs, "Oh, fuck off, you know how it is when you're not playing every day."

"I know how it is when you do play every day."

Jason laughs again, "How's married life?"

"Best thing I ever did. Hands down."

"No shit?"

"Dude. It's the best. Plus, she lets me play golf whenever I want."

"I always hear about guys getting read the riot act if they even bring up playing a round of golf. God forbid going out to hit some balls."

"Nah, you know Kara, she knows what's up."

"That's a good set up there."

"You got anything going on?"

"Nothing serious, you know how it is. We're going to Vegas next week, so maybe I'll meet the one out there. That'd be something, hey?"

"Yeah good luck with that."

"Hah, thanks. Hey you guys wanna come?"

"Man I wish. I'm swamped with work this week then we've gotta go to a wedding in California. Next time though."

"Well, if you guys get there and it sucks, just jet on over to Vegas and we'll have fun."

They both laugh and continue on with their meals before settling up to head their separate ways. A couple months later when they played next, Dallas would win by four holes.

PART II

12

―――――――

By the time the boys finally load the Tahoe, it's almost eleven in the morning. Jason had wanted to get an earlier start but between himself, Nick, and G it just wasn't going to happen. None of them had started packing until the morning, and Jason is the only one who is an early riser and doesn't have to set an obnoxious number of alarms.

Vegas is a short jaunt from Scottsdale when traveling by private jet out of KSDL but to drive it is still pretty short and a lot, *lot* cheaper. On the levels of rich, Jason and his brother are on the one just beneath that which would allow them to painlessly partake private air travel. Yes, they can and yes, they have... once. But with the strain it had put on the trip, they vowed to not do it again unless someone else pays. Sure, there are always commercial flights available but those are a pain in the ass and G is always trying to bring his pot and only God knows what else.

"Hey are we stopping to eat at all by chance?" G asks.

"Yeah, we'll stop at a Jack or McD's," says Jason.

"Alright, cool."

"Best part of the trip right there," says Nick.

They get in and buckle up. Jason puts his SUV in reverse, backs out of the driveway, and starts on the road to Vegas.

The boys loaded up on four items each at McDonald's and are heading west on the 101 until they hit the I-17. Then they go north, through the desert toward Kingman, via Wickenburg. They stop once they get to Kingman for gas and a piss break.

"How much longer is the drive?" asks G.

"About an hour and half, maybe a little more," says Jason. "Why, you got somewhere you gotta be?"

"No, I'm just wondering. I'm gonna stay in here and wait for you guys."

While Jason and Nick head inside to relieve their bladders, G retrieves his vape pen which is filled with cannabis oil. He puts it up to his lips while depressing the button on the battery and takes a big drag then he lets out some big deep coughs. He repeats this a few times. In between each puff, he flails his arms and hands around like a wacky-wavy-inflatable-arm-guy from a used car lot in an effort to help dissipate the smoke.

Before long, the Wagner brothers rejoin G and resume their journey. They set out on Highway Ninety-Three, and within a few miles, Jason checks the speedometer, and sees they're doing about ninety-three. The radio is set to Jason's playlist which typically means either psychedelic rock or old-sounding country music and not much in between. Nick has a broader taste in music, though he enjoys his brother's favorites well enough. G's always listening to his own music in his head. Sometimes he puts his earbuds in and other times he just sits there, air drumming along to a track that only he can hear.

Nick turns to Jason and asks, "What do you think Carl's up to?"

"Who knows. Probably birthing a calf or some shit."

"Yeah... Probably. Too bad Sos couldn't make it. Guy loves Vegas," says Nick.

"That he does. He had to get back though and I'm sure he'll join us on the next one. We'll still have fun with just us three."

Sosa was always a maybe for the Vegas trips. Sometimes he'd make them, sometimes he couldn't. Nick goes back to reading his book which is a copy of James Dickey's novel *Deliverance*. G holds his Nintendo Switch and plays Super Mario Bros in the back seat. Jason nods his head to his music and silently sings along as they continue to cruise toward the dam.

It used to be that, when driving to Las Vegas, you'd have to do the whole Hoover Dam experience. It is a long and winding road that has views down into Lake Mead. People are always walking around, taking helicopter tours, and making it a whole ordeal to drive through. One time when Jason was younger, his team had a tournament in Las Vegas and the traffic at the dam was so bad it added an extra two hours on to the trip and he almost missed his first game.

Nowadays, the highway goes right over the Colorado River and turns into Interstate Eleven. That takes them right up to Henderson. From there, they just hop on the 215, take that to the Fifteen and boom. Off at Tropicana, left onto Las Vegas Boulevard, then finally left into the Aria Resort and Casino.

G had started silently dropping ass just after those first casinos near the dam, but it almost smelled like... beef jerky?

"Yo G, when did you get the jerky?" Nick says while reading his book.

Jason looks in the rearview mirror and can see G can't hear on account of the fact that he's playing his game and has his earbuds in. "He can't hear you bro. I don't think he's got any jerky either."

"What's that smell then?"

"G!" yells Nick, now turned around.

A startled G pulls out an ear bud which reveals the blaring of an electronic dance beat, "What's up?"

"When'd you get the jerky?"

"What jerky?"

"I told you he didn't have any jerky."

"What's that smell then?"

"Huh? Oh, I gotta deuce."

Jason rolls down the window and starts cracking up. G joins in. Nick puts his shirt over his nose and gags.

It's just after sunset when the boys pull up to the valet stand at their hotel. A member of the valet team opens the front and rear passenger door then makes his way around to the driver's side.

"Are you staying with us at the hotel sir?" asks the valet.

"Yep, under Wagner," Jason says as he hands the guy a twenty.

"Sounds good. Thank you very much. Do you guys need help with your bags at all?"

"No thanks, we got 'em," Jason hands the guy a second twenty so that he will treat his vehicle extra nicely. The boys grab their duffel bags and head inside.

13

THE WAGNER BROTHERS have been going to Vegas almost all of Jason's life. When they were babies, their dad had an environmental business out there and so the whole family would trek back and forth from Phoenix nearly every weekend.

When they started playing hockey, Las Vegas served as a great watering hole where all the teams from the southwest would converge for weekend tournaments. Almost every major holiday had a hockey tournament in Las Vegas attached to it and the parents loved it. So did the kids. They always stayed at a place like the Monte Carlo and would always try to see a Lance Burton show and the parents (mainly the dads) tried their luck in the casinos. The first naked woman Jason ever saw was on a baseball card given to him by some guy slapping the deck against itself on the strip.

Since he turned pro, it's been a place for him and his buddies to blow off a little steam in the summertime. Another old hockey buddy of Jason's named Daylan lives there and works in the clubs. He's worked his way up and is now one of the top guys to know. He always hooks up Jason with tables at the club and VIP privileges like dinners and rooms.

He's got a hookup for a suite at the Aria which is where Jason usually stays. It's a two-bedroom penthouse that overlooks the strip. G sleeps in the living room and Jason and Nick each get a bedroom. They usually stay three nights and only have to pay for the first two.

The suite itself is immaculate. There is a wall-mounted tablet which controls virtually everything in the room from drawing the shades to controlling the TV. They've got custom mattresses, plush robes, and a fully stocked mini-bar.

The team had booked him a stay at the JW Marriott, but he politely declined as he already had this trip planned and paid for before the signing. Mostly though, he didn't want to be watched like a hawk while he was in Vegas. He knew that if he stayed on the team's bill, they'd be keeping tabs on him somehow. Plus, as nice as it is, he prefers the JW's in Phoenix and Scottsdale. He and his boys are here to have a good time and be close to the action. Not play golf and get spa treatments. They could do that at home.

Once they check in at the private registration desk and take the private elevator, they arrive at their suite and each claim their sleeping quarters. Jason drops his black and gray Louis Vuitton duffel bag on the foot of his bed and begins to unpack his toiletries and items he wants to hang up before plopping onto the plush and luxurious mattress. He pulls out his book and begins to read while Nick and G get situated.

Nick decides to hop in the shower and G uses his time to get more stoned and play more Mario. G had tuned the TV to ESPN where they were breaking down the upcoming fights for the weekend. When Nick surfaces from his shower, he joins

G on one of the chairs in the living room to watch the coverage.

"Man, I would love to fight these guys for my last two fights."

"Bro, you'd starch 'em, no doubt," G says as he takes a hit and offers his weed pen to Nick.

Nick takes it and gives it a good rip, "Guys keep ducking me and I don't have a fight, so fuck it."

"It'll come. Just gotta stay positive."

"Hell yeah, G."

"Hell yeah. So, what's the plan for tonight?"

"I don't know, you seen Jason?"

"Not since we came in."

Nick gets up and heads to Jason's room. When he arrives, Jason is laying on his stomach horizontally across his bed with his book in hand.

"Yo, what's the plan for tonight?" Nick asks.

Jason takes a second to finish his page before answering, "I'm down for whatever. I know my boy Daylan will have something set up for us somewhere either tomorrow or the next night. I just have to meet with the team tomorrow."

"Alright."

"We gotta hit the tables too for a bit. See if G can't bring us any more luck like last time."

"Oh yeah."

"Know what I mean? Try to get this trip paid for."

"Definitely. Should we do that tonight?"

"Sounds good to me. You guys hungry?"

"I could eat... G, YOU HUNGRY?"

"YEAH," G yells from the living room.

"Should we eat here or go somewhere else?"

"I don't know but can we continue this conversation in the living room... where I'm not standing here like a jerk-off while you lay there with your book in your hands, facing the other direction?"

Jason laughs and marks his place in his book then sets it aside and gets off the bed starting towards the door.

They join G and each take a chair, leaving G alone on the couch.

"Alright so the game plan for tonight is we're gonna grab some food and then we're gonna hit the tables," says Nick.

"Sounds good to me. What're we eating?"

"What sounds good, G? You want a steak? Sushi?" asks Jason.

"I'm cool with whatever."

"How about Jean-Georges'?" Says Jason.

"I'm always down for that," says G.

It always amused the boys how much G loves getting dressed up and going to fancy dinners or theme restaurants. Especially with, in his daily life, how long he can spend in one outfit and how many days he's comfortable going without a shower. The first time they all went out to a nice dinner, G spent half the day getting himself ready and by the time he was, he looked like he was ready to go to homecoming. Jason and Nick kindly instructed him to lose the tie and undo his top two buttons. Now he keeps his hair short, and it doesn't take him nearly the time it used to for preening. Also, thanks to his newly abundant wardrobe since moving in with the brothers and becoming the recipient of their hand-me-downs, he spends much less time trying to figure out what to wear.

"How do you smell though? Do you need a shower? How long's it been?" asks Nick.

"I should probably hop in and rinse off real quick," says G.

Jason sniffs his armpits and says, "Yeah, I was going back and forth myself, I'm gonna take one as well. Know what I mean?

While Jason and G take their showers, Nick retreats to his room where he grabs his own book then comes back out to the living room. He turns the volume on the TV down so that it was still audible but not loud enough to distract him from his reading.

Nick hears his name on the TV and stops his reading to listen. The reporters were questioning whether or not Nick still had what it took to be the champion. They're going on about how they feel he would fare against the top ranked guys.

"It's all about activity. Activity. Activity. Activity. As soon as fighters start doing that one or two fight a year thing... you know? It starts to take a little bit of time for them to get back going once that next fight starts. That's all I'm really saying."

The co-analyst agreed and went on to say, "Obviously he was the champ before and was one of the youngest to ever do so, but that was a couple years ago and the guys he beat back in the day have come a long way since then. It seems like his foot's off the gas, comparatively speaking."

"Well he's got two fights left so we'll see what he can do with them."

Nick turns off the TV and reopens his book, "Yeah you mother fuckin' will see as a matter of fact."

Within half an hour, the boys are dressed and ready to go. They each sport the business casual attire required for the reservation that they booked via the tablet in the suite. Jason and G both have sport coats on while Nick goes with a classic black button-up.

14

Jean-Georges Vongerichten is one of the world's most renowned chefs. He has restaurants all over the world and is intimately involved with each one to ensure top level quality. His steakhouse at the Aria is one of the boys' favorites and they would be remiss to not indulge at least one night. Upon arriving, they are taken to their table and handed large thick one-sided menus. The menus are a formality on account of the fact that they each already know what they want.

After a few minutes to settle, Chef Robert comes out to visit. "Hey there fellas, how you been?"

"We've been good Chef, it's great to see you!" says Jason.

Nick and G say, "What's up, Chef, good to see you."

"You guys, too. I won't take much time, I just wanted to come out and say hello, I already know you guys know the menu!"

"We appreciate you."

"Hey, did I see something about you signing to come play for the Golden Knights?" he says before leaving the table.

"Yeah, I just did. I'm going to meet with them while we're here."

"Hey man. Congratulations. I love going to those games with my family."

"Thanks, Chef. Let me know when you want to come to a game, and I'll get you some tickets. Maybe come down and meet the team afterwards or something."

"That would be unbelievable. My kids would love that."

"Cool. We'll set it up."

"Alright, well you fellas enjoy your meal. Wait, yo, Nick, when's your next fight?" Chef asks.

"We were actually just talking about that. I don't know. Whenever I get the call."

"I know when you get it, you're gonna put that fool to sleep."

"Yes sir. You know it."

"Alright, have a good night and let me know if you need anything."

They each say thanks and Chef Robert heads back into the kitchen where he resumes his magic. It takes a full crew to run a kitchen, but with Chef Robert at the helm things get done right and prompt. There's no dillydallying in Chef Robert's kitchen but there isn't hostility either. He's a sweet and talented chef who loves making flavors come to life for his guests.

The waiter brings over the complimentary bread and the bottle of Caymus that the boys ordered to kick the night off. He pours some into each of the boys' glasses and sets the bottle on the table. "You three ready to order?"

They order the carpaccio and grilled octopus to start and the waiter heads back to pass along the requests to the kitchen. Jason, Nick, and G raise their glasses and clink before they take their first sips. "Little vino with the boys. Classin' it up, hey?" says Jason.

"Oh yeah," says G.

"It's good huh?"

"I like wine at a place like this, but I usually am more of a whiskey guy myself," says Nick.

"Yeah, we know," Jason says.

Nick and G laugh and take another sip of wine while Jason applies butter to the bread on his plate.

"Anyways, we gotta figure out our numbers here," says Jason.

Nick nods and gets serious, "Yeah, what's your limit?"

"I think I'm going twenty."

"Twenty?"

Jason nods his head.

"I was thinking twenty also," says G.

"I don't think you guys are talking about the same kind of twenty there G."

G reads the table and realizes Jason intends to risk twenty grand tonight, "Oh. Ohhh. Yeah no, I was thinking I could start with twenty dollars."

Jason and Nick bust out laughing.

"Buddy, you're gonna get like, one hand. I think the tables are at least twenty-dollar minimums."

G just shrugs his shoulders, "Then I'll just watch and say I only lost one hand."

"If you're going up to twenty you better bank G some cred-it," says Nick.

"I will, I will. What're you putting up?"

"I'm gonna stick to my usual ten and see how it goes."

"That's fair enough. I just signed a nice contract and I'm feeling lucky."

The waiter brings by the appetizers for the table and the boys dive in. The grilled octopus is exquisite and is served with the most perfectly cooked crispy potato wedges.

For the main course, Nick and G both get a sixteen-ounce F1 Wagyu ribeye cooked medium-rare, while Jason puts down one of his favorite dishes, Chilean sea bass. The food is supreme. The experience, as phenomenal as it had been so many times in the past. By the end of dinner, they had finished three bottles of Caymus and were ready to go hit the tables.

15

After walking the floor a few times to scout the best table, they finally had to settle on the only one that had three open seats. Ideally, they'd have been able to find their favorite dealer, Harold, but more on that later. The boys take their seats in the middle three chairs. G sits in between Jason and Nick. On the far left next to Jason, is a suited, zooted, and booted, businessman who looks to be on a real good run of bad luck. His tie is loosened, shirt unbuttoned, and there is a profuse amount of sweat dripping from his forehead. The man hardly even noticed Jason as he sat down. It wasn't until Jason hit blackjack on his first hand that the man even acknowledged him.

"Oh what the fuck is that? Fuckin' guy just sits down."

The dealer just looks at the man with disgust and knows it won't be long before a pit-boss comes around and handles this maniac. Jason wins twelve-hundred-fifty on the first hand and can feel it's going to be a good night.

The next hand, however, is a complete clusterfuck. G has thirteen between his two cards and the dealer is showing a six. The fat drunk idiot on the far right starts telling him to hit.

Jason urges G to stay. G looks to Nick who shrugs. Nick is a lot looser when it comes to playing blackjack so if the call were his, he might hit. The stressed-out businessman starts berating G for even contemplating the decision which only fuels G's desire to take the risk. "Hit," says G with a shit-eating grin, wanting to see what will happen.

The suit blows his lid and starts screaming and cussing and even reaches over Jason for G. Obviously Jason blocks his arm from getting to G, but the commotion and the melee ensures that a pit-boss and security come over pronto. The dealer tells him what happened, and they kindly escort the hot head from the table.

After that, Jason went on a hellacious losing streak. Something from that unkind fella had seemed to rub off on him, causing the balance of the table to be tipped in some sort of way. In an effort to minimize any catastrophic loss, Jason reduced his bets down to a few hundred and hoped the tides would soon turn. Nick was holding steady, even up some, and G was skipping every other hand to conserve his money. Gambling isn't really his thing.

The dealer change brought no new luck. Jason went down five grand an hour for three hours. The worst luck he's ever had, and he just keeps going. "It'll come around, we'll be okay," he says even though he was the only one that was really down.

Nick is up five grand somehow with his loose playing and questionable blackjack IQ. A stark contrast to his brother, who almost always plays the book move and has found himself down to his last five grand from his marker. Just then, there was another dealer change.

A six-foot-six tall man with a skinny neck and a large bulbous nose, meanders over to his post at the table and sits down. He monotonously shows his hands over the tables. He acts as if he's preparing to do a magic trick, like to make something disappear but really, it's so the eye in the sky can see he's not hiding any cards anywhere. All of the dealers are required to do it, but this one has such a calm and cool swagger about the way he executes the movement.

"Oh here we go," says Nick excitedly.

"ROLDIE!" Says Jason, "Finally! Now we have a chance. Fuckin' rights."

"What's up Harold?" asks G.

"I'm good. How are you boys? Long time no see," Harold says coolly, like they're in a jazz club.

"We're alright Harold, we need for you to bring us a little luck though. We need that Harold hookup for some good cards, you know what I mean?"

"I'll see what I can do. Who wants to cut the deck?"

It was Nick's turn to cut so he takes the plastic card and inserts it a third of the way in and the dealer does his thing. Next thing they know, they're playing Blackjack. Nick's made nineteen, G's at seventeen, both stay and Jason has a four and a seven. Harold's showing an eight. "Double," Jason says as he pushes forward the requisite chips before Harold can turn over Jason's next card which is a jack of spades. The boys celebrate.

Harold flips over his nine of hearts giving him a seventeen and pounds the table in front of G before paying out the winnings for Jason and Nick.

"Alright, here we go now," says Jason as he stacks all his winnings on top of each other and places them in the betting area. The fat, drunk idiot had bailed just before Harold showed up so now it was just the three boys and their preferred dealer.

Jason won the next few hands and kept doubling up on his

winnings. Before he even had time to realize, he was up thirty grand over the initial marker for twenty and Nick was up twenty over his ten. Even G was starting to sniff five figures, albeit with a little help from Jason here and there via some free rolls.

When Harold departed from the table, he left with almost twelve hundred dollars in tips from the three of them, which is a lot. Way more than average. The next dealer didn't bring as much luck and Jason was ready for it. As soon as Harold left the table, he reduced his bets to five hundred. "Always better to take it easy when feeling out a new dealer. Who knows what kind of vibes they're bringing to the table," he warned.

After some wishy-washy luck and making out about even on the new dealer, the boys decide to call it for the night and head up while up. They ask to be colored in, which means to have all their chips condensed into less larger markers making it easier for transport. Then make their way through the casino; toward their private elevators.

On the walk, they notice a bachelorette party at the bar next to the casino. The girls take notice of the boys, too, particularly Jason and Nick, and invite them to join.

They let the girls know that they need to run up to the room quick to stash their winnings from the night and would be right back down. But they also let them know they were more than welcome to join the boys upstairs in their penthouse suite, where they could continue their party.

16

IT TOOK VERY minimal arm twisting for the bride-to-be to want to join but she wanted assurances that no one would attempt to "try anything" with her. Everyone swore. Jason paid for the girls' tab with a couple of his smaller chips and they strolled toward the elevator. The three single girls of the group made themselves known and the other three figured they'd tag along for free drinks and entertainment.

The girl that had taken to Jason was very touchy and had interlocked arms with him in the elevator. She stayed that way even as they got into the suite. Nick's woman walked close by his side, and their touches were intentionally unintentional. G's girl was a little less hot and was a little bummed she wasn't going to get one of the brothers. She was visibly less enthusiastic. Ultimately, she accepts the fact that the brothers would be nothing if not for G's managing (wink, wink) and that was enough. Plus, *It had been a while,* she thought.

Luckily it's the first night, which means the suite is in stellar condition. G's hide-a-bed is even still hidden. They used the tablet on the wall to order up more booze for the night. They got three bottles of champagne, a bottle of tequila, a bottle of whiskey, and a couple buckets of beer.

It doesn't take long for hotel staff to bring a roller cart full of liquor up to their suite. Jason thanks the guy and gives him a twenty before closing the door. "Alright. Who's ready to party?"

Nick is quick with the whiskey and pours himself a glass. Jason begins uncorking the first bottle of champagne and does it silently which is quite impressive to the girls when they see it. They were used to seeing people make a big scene about popping a bottle of champagne and even if they don't, there's usually an unavoidable *POP* that goes along with the removal of the cork. Jason pours a glass for everyone and holds up the remaining swig in the bottle for his brief toast.

"To Vegas!"

"To Vegas!" They all shout and take a drink.

Jason slams what was left in the bottle, pours himself a glass of tequila and leads everyone over to the living room area.

"Which room's yours?" Jason's girl asks him.

"The one back there," he says pointing over his shoulder with his thumb.

"Can I see it? I've never been in one of these big suites."

"Sure, yeah." He stands up and leads her into his room.

He opens his door and gestures toward the room and says, "Here it is. Got a nice little chair over there, the bed is unreal."

"Oh, I'm sure."

He leads her toward the attached bathroom when she grabs him, turns him around, and pulls his face toward hers to start making out with him. She aggressively flicks her tongue around on the inside of his mouth for long enough that he is starting to draw wood. The girl starts to put her hand down Jason's pants when, from the living room, one of the girls, probably G's, calls out for her to come back.

They both smile and laugh quietly.

"Maybe I can stay after my friends leave and we can have a sleepover," she says seductively.

"Sounds good to me."

They kiss and go back out into the party and join in the conversation, but it doesn't take long for the girls in relationships to head down to their rooms. The first two to leave were the girls in relationships. The bride-to-be would have left sooner had she not been enthralled by Jason's talk of aliens and ghosts. Nick and his girl laughed at him while G and the bride-to-be were intently listening. Jason and G's chicks were in the dining room talking about their own problems from back home. G's girl is really going through it, it seems.

Jason chats about the infamous Phoenix Lights incident which was said to have been of extraterrestrial origin. Then he went on telling stories about how when he was at Lake Powell with his family, they could see what his uncle said was the ghost of an old Native American Chief on horseback.

"He would come up to the edge of the cliff that was above the beach where we had the houseboat parked and just look over the whole area."

"I don't remember that," says Nick.

"Well either you blocked it out cause it scared you, or weren't there when we saw it. But it definitely happened, multiple nights."

"Did he ever do anything?" asks the bride-to-be.

"Who Chief? No, he just sat there on his horse and looked out over the lake. On the last night it felt like he was watching and pointing at us though."

"Oh my God, that's so scary." she says.

"Yeah. I guess. I don't know, I don't mind 'em."

"What ghosts or Native Americans?" she says with a laugh.

"Ghosts. Obviously, I don't mind the natives, they're great. They invented hockey. Wait... you know what? Maybe it was lacrosse. Actually, I think they came up with both, and either way, I love 'em. But ghosts. I don't mind ghosts," he says casually before taking a big swig of his glass of tequila. "They've never bothered me before."

"You know, I guess I've never thought of it like that."

"Well think of it! You never know when a ghost might help you out."

She takes a second to ponder his wisdom, "You're right."

Nick and his girl laugh and touch which leads to kissing. The bride-to-be takes this as her cue to head back to her room. She goes into the dining room to check on the other girls and let them know. G's girl walks back with her to their room where they are met by the snores of the girls that had boyfriends or fiancés.

Jason's girl refills her champagne and is drawing a bath for her and Jason. Jason refills his tequila and helps G with his bed, "Yo, sorry about your girl dude."

"Oh, it's all good bro. I just wasn't attracted to her at all."

Jason laughs at the thought of G being so unaware of the girl's lack of interest in him. "We'll find you a nice little mamacita tomorrow, G, don't you worry."

"Hell yeah."

They give each other a fist bump and Jason heads into his room.

He arrives to the bathroom just in time to watch the girl

drop the robe that she had presumably changed into before starting the bath.

"Wow," says Jason as he takes in her naked body. Her hips sway as she walks up to him and begins helping him to get undressed. Kissing him and teasing him up and down his neck. They get into the bath, drink, giggle and rub their warm wet hands all over each other's chests. Most of their conversation is trivial, but the depth of their physical connection is ragingly deep.

Soon they were out of the bath and into the bed where they ruffled the double sheeted three hundred thread count linens for a total of three minutes and twenty-six seconds (thank God for the booze or it'd have probably been under two).

Not long after that, they pass out naked on each other and sleep a few hours. Until the sun comes up and fills the bedroom with vibrant rays that beam into Jason's eyes, causing him to roll over and curse in anger that he'd forgotten to shut the curtains. His coital partner from the night before stirred to see what the matter was, and almost startled Jason. He either had forgotten about her or assumed she would be gone by now. Soon she was up and out, doing the walk of shame back to their room so she could get ready for the brunch her group had planned, but not before another quick romp for the road.

Jason walked her through the suite to the door to see if anyone else was up yet. The shades were drawn all through the common areas which told Jason he'd been the lone dummy that night and meant, who knew when the others would be up? *Hopefully Nick's girl makes it to their brunch,* Jason thinks before he opens the door and kisses his new friend on the lips and sends her down the hall.

She doesn't make an effort to stay in contact and they don't exchange numbers or social media handles. She just sashays down the hall and out of his life. To most guys, that would be the dream. That is, until they have too much of it. Then it becomes a nightmare. Not an actual nightmare, Jason will surely be over his feelings before long, but there is that brief moment of thought, the brief discomfort where Jason wonders, what is the point?

17

JASON GETS BACK to his room and checks his phone and sees that he has texts from his old agent Marty, then from Sosa, two missed calls, a voicemail, and a text that said: Don't worry about that French fuck. I'm coming to Vegas.

Jason reads his texts from Marty which read: U try to fuck me and hire ur friend? Then: I block the deal with the league. And lastly: It would be wise for you to come back under me if you want to play in the NHL next year.

Jason calls Sosa and it immediately goes to voicemail. He hangs up. *Fuck.*

After an hour of traveling along with the kid and his wolf in the book he's reading, G wakes up and starts rustling around. Nick and his girl are soon to follow. The boys head down to the pool for a brunch of their own, putting their last night into the past. They start discussing onto Jason's new dilemma. If Jason's contract becomes void, that means he's back to not having a job.

Suddenly the trip turned bad. The carelessness that flowed through their veins the night before was replaced with great amounts of dread and anxiety. Jason hardly touches his eggs Benedict due to the giant knot he has inflating like a balloon in the place where his appetite should be.

Not long into the meal, Sosa comes huffing and puffing through the doors. He's wearing golf pants and a polo and he's wearing the same oversized backpack he used during college. He stops and scopes the area to spot his new client. Jason and Sosa make eye contact and nod heads as Sos trudges over to the table.

Sosa comes up, already in the war zone. He's got a game face on that shows he means serious business. It's unlike anything the boys had experienced from him thus far as friend, agent, or teammate. Maybe this was a persona that he adopted sometime during his years of studying law in college. Nevertheless, he's in rare form indeed, full of piss and vinegar. He has the utmost of Jason's attention and his confidence.

Directing his energy toward his newest and highest earning client Sosa says, "Alright, so here's the deal. Marty filed a complaint with the league and bitched about how he did all the work to get everything lined up and then you pulled the rug out from underneath him and hired me with his money... That's essentially what he's saying."

Jason's face says that he's confused by the accusation, "Well, that's bullshit. You were there when I talked to him. I hadn't talked to him for weeks before and haven't talked to him since."

"I know, I know, it's bullshit. But when he found out who I am and who my dad is, I think it set him off. Because that was mentioned in the complaint too, which is absurd."

"So what do we do?"

"What'd he send to you?"

"Yeah, show him the texts J," says G.

"Wait till you get a load of these," says Nick.

Jason opens the messages and hands his phone over to Sosa before taking a bite of his food.

Sosa scoffs at each text and says, "Ridiculous. We obviously need to fight it. And the way we're gonna fight it is you're gonna write a letter to the league that just tells the story of what happened."

"So, it's my word against his?"

"It's currently his word against nothing. Your word doesn't count for anything until you get it out there."

"Okay, so I gotta write a letter to the league that says what? After however long of me reaching out with no response from my agent, he came to me with two offers, one of which was kept secret from me?"

"Yeah exactly, and you can write about how he said he only used the Vegas offer as leverage and didn't even do any work on the deal and also, that he sent you the wrong offer to sign after you'd made your choice clear. Either way don't worry about it, we will figure it out. I already talked to the team here and we've got a little bit of time. Let's just have some fun while we're here, hey?" Sosa says.

"So am I still going to meet with them today?"

"They said they would hold off on that until everything with the league is straightened out. You know how it is, they don't want to lose a draft pick."

The boys feel good enough for now and are happy Sosa ended up making the trip after all, although they wished it were under different circumstances. The waitress comes by and takes Sosa's order. Sos hadn't eaten whatever it was they tried passing off as breakfast on his first-class flight from Seattle and is eager to dive into one of his favorite aspects of Vegas: the cuisine. Sosa isn't a glutton, but he appreciates good food, showmanship, and attention to detail.

"I was pretty bummed that I wasn't gonna be coming out here with you guys, I gotta be honest," he says.

"Us too. It's not the same without you man," says Jason.

"Yeah we were talking about it on the way up, you missed a good run last night," says Nick.

"No shit?"

"Yep, then we hosted a bachelorette party." says G with a smirk.

"Get the fuck out of here, no you guys didn't."

"I wouldn't say we hosted a party," says Nick.

"Yeah it was more like a kickback," says Jason, who swallows his bite. "There were some girls at the bar near the casino and when we were heading up to put away our chips. They stopped us and wanted us to join them."

"So instead, you had them join you upstairs in your guys' penthouse?" Sosa asks.

"Pretty much. Yeah, just ordered some booze up and hung out and talked for a while."

"No one bagged the—"

"No. God no! We were perfect gentlemen with her."

"Yeah, she made us swear no one would try to make a move on her."

"Oh shit. That's incredible. How were the bridesmaids?"

"Mine was... great, very nice, very pretty. I don't think I ever got her name but, you know, great girl all around, I'd say. I think Nick's girl missed their brunch today from sleeping in. Didn't she?"

Nick laughs, "I don't know if she missed it, but she did

wake up in a panic then got out of there pretty quick, so who knows. Hopefully she made it."

"No morning after action, Slick?"

"Nope, sadly not."

"What about you, G?"

G shakes his head and uses his hand to cut his neck, "Nah, my chick was beat."

The boys laugh.

"Well today's a new day, G. Maybe we can find one for me and you," says Sosa.

"You're gonna stick around?" Says Jason.

"Why not, I'm already here. Fuck it. As long as you guys are cool with it."

"Of course! We can move some stuff around upstairs. Get you a cot or something, it'll be great."

"I'll probably get my own room just in case, but will obviously hang with you guys 'til then."

"Either way, we're happy to have ya, buddy."

They finish their breakfast and are handed the bill. Sosa grabs it and fills it with enough cash to cover their food, drinks, and a twenty-five percent tip. Then they head up to the suite to game plan the rest of their day and forget about their Marty problem.

18

Sosa knows it's going to be a battle to get everything smoothed over with Jason's contract, but he made it his mission to keep that solely to himself. There was no sense in Jason being panicked, that wasn't going to do anyone any good.

It was on Jason to write his letter when they got back to their suite, even though they had some time. Sosa agreed that it was better to do it sooner but didn't want to add undue stress.

"If I let the situation linger… that will add undue stress. The sooner I can write my side of the story down, the sooner we can get it over and dealt with," says Jason as he walks to the mini fridge to retrieve one of the leftover beers from the night before.

"Do you want any help writing it?" asks Sosa.

"No, thanks man. You guys can do whatever, I'm gonna go onto this dining room table and knock it out. Daylan's got a table set up for us at Zouk for tonight. Then I've gotta do my workout at some point today down at the gym."

"Cool. I'll be in here if you need me."

"Alright sounds good. I'm probably just gonna hang out

and read a little. I'm pretty tired honestly, I'll join you in the gym though if that's cool," says Nick.

"For sure."

After about five minutes of sitting in the living room with G and listening to him laugh out loud at the various Reels and clips he was watching, Sosa started to think, *How can Wags write with this going on?*

"G, let's go gamble, come down with me."

Sosa and G head out of the suite so Jason can work in peace. The first thing they do is stroll around the grounds of the hotel. They take a hot lap to scope the scene and get an idea for what people were getting into. Who knows? Maybe they'll stumble upon another bachelorette party and be their *male entertainment.*

After the lap around the casino, they decide that they'll also do a quick lap around the pool and see what's going on there. The energy from the casino was a bit low for the boys with Sosa just getting in and all. He doesn't like gambling enough to pop down next to the guy who needs a second seat for his oxygen tank and there certainly were no bachelorette parties going on down here at this time of day.

The Aria has three pools including the one on the roof, a regular resort style pool with the wet bar, and a party pool. The boys make their way through the crowd of conservative couples and older people toward LIQUID Pool Lounge. There's music bumping which lets them know there's something good going on.

The moment they get in there, they're greeted by a sea of people in and around the pool, jumping and dancing to the beat. There are women with perfectly shaped bodies walking around in scant little bathing suits that hardly cover their nipples and none of their behinds. If there were any modest looking women on site, Sos and G couldn't see them. Gaggles of people line the lounge in the cabanas. G and Sos don't know where to start.

Sosa leans over and raises his voice, "How about any of these broads, G? You see any here that would work?"

G looks at Sos and says, "I think we could find one here."

"Let's go grab a drink and then we'll see what's what."

G's bouncing and bopping his head like he's at the Roxbury, "Alright! Yeah! Sounds good!"

They walk through the sea of smoke-shows and to the bar, paying no attention to anyone that wasn't a female and didn't register as at least a seven on their scale. They both order screwdrivers and down them feverishly, like shots. They order two more and take them casually over to a couple of open lounge chairs near the pool just as the former dwellers grab their stuff and leave.

Neither of the boys have their shirt off yet and they aren't really even talking to each other. Instead, they sit and stare, fixating on all the different bodies of women without even realizing it, drifting away into a dream state where the only people that exist are them and the girls they're eyeing. There are boobs of all shapes and sizes and all the women have great asses. Each glance sparks new fantasies for G and Sos that had never existed before. Sosa is the first to snap back to reality and tries to mutter something to G, but it was no use. G is in a trance, like he stared into the eyes of a giant, hypnotic serpent and could hear nothing. The serpent was wrapped around poor G so tight that Sos had to shake him out of his creepy trance. "Hey... yo, G. Snap out of it, let's get in the pool and talk to some of them."

G blinks for the first time in a while and shakes his head, "Y-y-yeah, you're right. We can get chicks without the Wagner brothers."

"Buddy, trust me. Got all the way through college and never even had to drop his name."

G looks at Sosa in awe. G has never been with a girl that he pursued on his own, save for the one he met on a gaming forum that turned out to be a dude. Since then, he finds himself looming in the obscurity of the crowd and spending more time wondering whether or not any of these girls would even give him the time of day in a conversation.

"You go in there!" G says. Then talks very quietly and completely inaudible over the music and noise of the party, "I'm gonna see what's up with this one," nodding in the direction of the girl he wanted to approach.

Sosa nods his head and takes off his shirt, exposing a very white barrel chest which is contrasted by a forest of black chest hair, and struts toward the pool steps.

On the lounge chair beside the boys' is a beautiful woman in her twenties, wearing a slightly more modest looking bathing suit than the rest. She seems to be in a state of melancholy which triggered G to want to help from the second they sat down. Not because he thought he could use her sadness as an in, but because he never liked seeing people sad. He felt like there was too much fun going on all around for a girl as pretty as her to look so down. After rehearsing a couple of lines in his head and chugging the rest of his screwdriver, G finally gets up and walks the couple of steps and stands over her, "Hi! I'm Grant! My friends call me G!"

The girl forces a smile, "McKenzie."

"What?"

"McKenzie!

"Nice to meet you McKenzie. You seem sad. Can I get you a drink?"

"Oh. That's okay. Thanks."

Remember what Jason and Nick say: Be confident and give it a couple of tries. "Are you sure? It's really not a problem, I just finished mine and was getting ready to go grab another."

She takes a second before answering, "What are you drinking?"

"Screwdriver I think is what my friend said! It's just vodka and orange juice... pretty good!" He says while bobbing his head again.

She giggles and thinks G's awkwardness is cute. She figures he probably won't try to drug her and after the fight she just had with her now ex-boyfriend, she figures she could use a drink.

She smiles and says, "Alright. I'll take one of those, please."

G returns a smile, "I'll be right back!" Then heads back toward the bar.

While in line, he scans the pool to see what kind of progress Sosa has been making. G could see Sos bouncing up and down in the pool with his arms wrapped tightly around the hips of a very friendly looking Latina woman. He orders the screwdrivers and brings them back to the lounge seat where there's now a very large and well-built man with a razor sharp beard, faded tattoos, and a deep dark tan sitting next to McKenzie.

G decides that this big fella's disposition is a hostile one and moves to intervene. G puts his arm out toward McKenzie with her drink in his hand as she tries to give him a look that says, "Please don't do this," but it doesn't register.

"What's the problem here?" G says with authority.

"I don't think that's any of your business there, bud," says the angry muscle man.

Just then, Sosa looks back to check on G and their stuff at the lounge chair. When he sees tensions rising, he realizes that he is going to need to step in.

Sosa books it out of the pool and over to the chairs and is calling out for G, "G! G! You good?"

G gives the thumbs up with his drink hand which causes the overly aggressive bodybuilder to turn around and see Sosa closing in on them. The guy smashes G's arm without warning, causing him to spill his drink.

Sosa rushes in, "Woah, woah, woah, I'm sure this is a misunderstanding let's all just chill out."

McKenzie is fuming. She grabs her things and hightails it out of LIQUID, toward the general pool, and presumably back to her room. The two of them had been in a toxic off and on type of relationship since high school. Today's breakup happened because he was letting other girls feel his arms while they were at the pool. McKenzie was at the bar when this was going on and saw it from a distance. She had already taken him back after he cheated on her multiple times with multiple women, one of which, was McKenzie's best friend.

Roid Rage growls and grits his teeth menacingly, his eyes start to twitch as they gaze into G's soul, "I better not see you guys again! You hear that?! Huh?! Fuckin' got it?!"

Sosa's hands are up on account of he has no desire to trade blows with a guy of this size. G on the other hand had been doing some training in mixed martial arts, particularly in the discipline of jiu-jitsu. He's a one stripe white belt and has a couple of tricks up his sleeve. Unfortunately for G, this guy would prove to be too much for his slick transition to back from the double leg stuff that was probably coming and would never be able to get his arms around the behemoth's neck. Sosa manages to peel G away and they split.

On their way back to the suite, Sos wouldn't stop talking about how awesome it was to see G man up like that, and almost wishes he would have let it go down. He was buzzed enough to convince himself and G on the walk back that if that guy would have tried anything, G would've choked his ass out. Sos had a newfound respect for G after that incident. He wasn't just a morale guy for the Wagner brothers, he was turning into one of them in his own way. Slowly but surely.

19

Before the second night gets underway, Jason and Nick need to do the workout that Jason's strength and conditioning coach Ryan Banning sent along for the trip. Whenever Jason goes out of town during the summer, he's given workouts that he's expected to execute and log his performance. Over the years, Jason has only lied on three or four workouts, and those all had valid reasons. Banning didn't think there was ever a good excuse for missing a workout. Hence the fibbing. Given the current contract situation, Jason wouldn't dare miss this trip's session and is always glad to have his little brother in the gym with him.

The fitness center at the Aria is beautiful and state of the art. They have every type of machine imaginable, a big open space for the dumbbells with a crystal clean mirror that spans the entire wall. The crowd level is low to moderate. There are a couple of well-built, middle-aged guys who don't look like they miss many workouts. They all perform repetitions with real tenacity. Using the weights almost as a portal to their youth, where they channel youthful strength and energy. Seeing them makes the boys think of when they were younger and would workout with their dad on the weekends. They used to marvel at their dad who can still to this day lift just as heavy as they can while maintaining stellar form.

Jason and Nick warm up on the bikes to start. Out of the corner of their eyes they notice but don't look at the beautiful girl in her twenties, with dark hair and tanned skin, wearing a grey sports bra, and tight black short shorts. She's sitting on a bench in front of the dumbbells. She's performing shoulder presses with fifteen-pound weights, and stares intimately into her own soul so as not to accidentally make eye contact with anyone but herself.

After their warm-up, Jason opens his phone which has the workout saved on a spreadsheet. "Alright, so, were gonna start with dumbbell goblet squats and then superset squat jumps for one minute."

"Got it."

They each pack their earbuds into their ears and turn on their respective playlists.

"Let's get it," says Jason, who then walks up to the heavier section of dumbbells on the opposite side of the mat from where the fitness model is, and retrieves a sixty pounder. He brings it back to the open area in front of the mirror and grips the weight with both hands then brings it up to his chest just below his chin. He sets his feet and cranks out his warmup set of ten repetitions in a nice bouncy rhythm.

"Ten?" says Nick.

Jason nods his head yes as Nick picks up the dumbbell and performs his ten while Jason does his squat jumps for a full minute. He uses the clock on the wall above the mirror to keep track of time.

The sets go down in repetitions of two, but the weights need to increase accordingly. After each set, Nick puts the weight away and Jason grabs a heavier one for them. They continue this and their squat jumps until they're using the heaviest weight for four repetitions.

For the next exercise, the boys will be doing lunges while holding dumbbells in each hand. This time super-setting with burpees for a minute. Some of the men at the gym were starting to take longer than usual breaks in between their sets so they could watch the two athletes training.

The Wagner boys were used to the looks whenever they trained together in public and never minded it. It always made them push harder, knowing that they were being watched. Even the girl snuck a couple of peaks over the course of her time in the vicinity, but the boys were too focused to care anymore, and she wouldn't dare approach them.

Less can be said for the guy in his fifties who is wearing bike shorts and some local marathon t-shirt. He has no problem coming right up to the boys and standing next to them for a front row seat. Nick is on his second to last set of lunges and Jason is doing his burpees, so they don't notice his proximity until they finish. They both notice the guy at the same time and pause their music so they can hear what he's saying.

"Wow. You guys are impressive," he says.

"Oh, thanks." says Jason.

"Yeah, what do you guys do? You athletes or something?"

"Yeah, I play hockey and my brother is a fighter."

Nick gives a nod, "How are ya?"

The guy turns to Nick, "Like UFC?"

"Yep."

"No shit? Hey who do you think is gonna win the fight tomorrow?"

"I'm not really sure but I'd like to fight either of them next."

"Well after seeing you in here, I got my money on you, that's for sure." The guy turns back to Jason, "You play for the Golden-Knights or something?" The way he said Golden Knights was almost like he said it as one word.

Jason nods, "I just signed last week actually."

"Get outta here, do you live here?"

Nick offers an awkward laugh, "I don't know if they'd let guys do that, would they? Live at a hotel on the strip?"

"You know, I don't know. I'll have to ask. But in my case at least, no, we're just visiting now, then I'll move out here as it gets closer to the season."

"Ah well, either way, it's cool to watch you guys in here. Keep it up."

"Hey we appreciate that, have a good workout," says Jason.

"Yeah, take care," says Nick.

"Thanks, what are your names? My kids would kill me if I didn't ask."

"I'm Jason."

"I'm Nick."

"And our last name is Wagner."

"Cool thanks guys. Hey, you know what, if I'm not being too much of a heel, could I get a picture?"

"No problem."

The guy gets set up for a nice selfie with the brothers and walks off so they can all resume their workouts. It only tacked on a few extra minutes and now the guy had a cool story to go tell his kids. It also gave Nick and Jason a longer break from their brutal sets, which they were not displeased about.

After the lunges, they had a few other exercises that focused on strengthening their legs and improving their fast twitch muscle activation. The gym dies down and they are pretty much the only two in there, except for a younger kid who is on one of the chest machines.

Jason and Nick close out their workout with another bike ride to cool down.

"Good shit," says Nick.

"Good shit."

20

ZOUK NIGHTCLUB IS POPPING tonight with one of their residents performing one of his newest sets. It's a giant open room with a stage platform at the front where the DJ booth sits. The club features some of the absolute best when it comes to local talent.

The stage is filled with girls wearing minimal clothing along with some other VIPs of the male variety. Along the outskirts of the club are some VIP tables, one of which is currently occupied by the Wagner brothers, G, and Sosa. Their buddy Daylan keeps popping by to check on them and to make sure everything is good. The boys have access to the stage and would get there eventually but they want to settle in and get a little buzz going before heading up.

The beat is bumping, the vibe at the table is good, and they start to get after the tequila that Jason just had the bottle girls bring instead of vodka. As the night goes on and they start incorporating some women into the group, they'll add champagne and get some of that going, but until then, tequila will be the drink of choice.

Daylan comes by for a quick shot and to check in, "Yo, you gotta get up to the booth, these chicks up there are in-sane!"

They all agree to down their drinks and head up. The entire club is a madhouse, full of beings that look human but are behaving more like bees and the DJ is queen bee leading the hive. Some of these kids are so whacked out on zips, trips, coke, and molly, they wouldn't be able to tell you what planet they live on. But still, they are dancing and bopping up and down, almost in unison... looking like a freak hive of human bees.

There was no lie, these chicks are all so unbelievably hot and they're all bouncing and doing their own version of a mating ritual in which interested men will seek the dancer they most like. Jason quickly makes eyes with a girl in a tight, cut-up designer dress. Some magnetic force brings them closer toward each other as they dance, never breaking eye contact, and already moving in synchronization. That or they were controlled by string, like a couple of marionettes being worked by one puppeteer.

"How does he just do that?" G asks.

"He's a wizard, always has been," Nick says leaning over so G could hear.

The boys all dance and pair up with a girl and after a break in the set, they take their girls back to their table where they order a couple bottles of champagne, which the bottle girls always bring out in great extravagant style.

They all try to communicate with each other over the next set of music, some more effectively than others. G and his chick are very respectful of each other's personal space which makes it difficult for them to understand each other. They both just kind of awkwardly nod and bounce up and down like they know what the other person is saying, but neither does. Jason and his girl have no problem talking into each other's ears, the usual type of club interaction where the girl asks name, what does he do? Why is he here? All of that. Nick and his girl are still dancing up in the booth. Nick loves to dance. Sosa's voice booms in his girl's ear as he feels the need to compensate for the noise with volume and that closeness in proximity isn't sufficient.

Sosa's girl is the first to go, she has to go back to her friends or something. G's chick took that as a sign she should bounce, too. Sosa's girl probably was trying to save whatever was left of her hearing. Then as Sosa watches G's girl leave, he notices the girl from the pool that G was talking to earlier walking by the table. He nudges G to make him aware.

"That's McKenzie!" Says G, "MCKENZIE!" He yells while waving his hand around like a lunatic. She can't hear and continues to walk with her friends, three equally attractive girls, dressed for a night on the Strip. G slumps down and looks at Sos. "Should we go talk to her?"

"Do you see that dude?" Sosa yells.

G looks around and can't find the walking billboard for toxic masculinity and shakes his head no. The two of them get up while keeping an eye on the girls to make sure they aren't going to meet up with a bunch of dudes. Instead, the girls find a spot on the dance floor and join the rest of the bees.

Once G and Sos decide the coast is clear, they head out to join. Rather than abruptly walking up to the girl from across a crowded club, they jump on the dance floor and will "accidentally" bump into them while dancing.

McKenzie is dancing with one of her friends when she notices G, who's staying tight in his box. He shifts his weight from one side to the other, trying to keep his shoulders loose, with his head and eyes up, looked toward the heavens, as if asking God for strength and or guidance to make a move.

She walks up to G and sticks her finger in his chest, "Hey, I remember you!"

That makes G's entire trip. "I remember you, too!" he says with a proud smile. "You wanna dance?"

She smiles and turns around and glues her whole backside to his front. Then, she wraps her arm around his neck and turns to purr on his chest like a cat and whispers something in his ear. Blood starts moving for G, quick. She leans forward and starts grinding on him. The young man grabs hold and tries to stay in rhythm, now fully torqued.

Sosa and McKenzie's friend look each other over and decide they should also be grinding on one another. And why not? The conditions are set, the mood is right, so they go for it. The other two girls dance with each other and keep an eye out for guys.

Back at the table, Jason and his girl are sat down, cuddle dancing, and sipping on champagne. Nick and his girl are finally making their way back to the table for a little bit of a much-needed rest as well as some refreshments. Nick looks like he just got done with another workout, but his chick seems to be into it.

Back on the dance floor, G is thinking about animals, trucks, trees, that job he had as a roofer, anything to keep him from having a pipe bomb explode in his pants. He yells in her ear, asking if she and her friends want to come to their table for some drinks.

Sosa was starting to sweat himself, so he was relieved when G gestured that they were headed to the table and for them to come along. He and the three girls follow G and McKenzie and are warmly greeted by the Wagner brothers.

They all try to introduce each other, but it's more for show since the music takes up the majority of what is hearable and no one can hear anything anyone's saying. But who cares? They sure don't.

Another bottle of champagne is delivered and they stay put for a while. Or that was the plan. Not long into this last bottle, the big fella shows up, and he's not alone. Neither he nor his buddy seem to be happy. Who knew what this menace had been up to since his last interaction at the pool party? What had he taken that fueled the burning fire inside of him? Is this just how he is? How can a guy like that get along in the world? Screaming and cussing and bursting out of his clothes all the time.

"Oh fuck!" says McKenzie.

"What? What is it?" G looks to where McKenzie is looking and sees that a fully grown rhinoceros is set and readying a charge to kill.

Sosa looks over by chance and quickly alerts Jason and Nick. They both stand and look to size up the man that's threatening their friends now for a second time in one day. They point at the guy and Jason scrunches his face like, "Him? That guy?" Which only makes the guy angrier. He's now fuming. Screaming and cussing and pointing. His veins on his neck look like they're gonna burst. The buttons are clinging to the placket of his two sizes too small, shiny black dress shirt. His friend, who must be his workout partner, starts getting wild and joins in on the aggression.

Nick watches as a smirk begins to form over his face. He's like a predator in the wild. These poor souls don't know they're prey. Daylan walks up to check on the boys when he sees the hopped-up bodybuilders in their painted on clothes harassing not only club VIPs, but his personal friends. He uses his secret service style communications device on his wrist to get security over ASAP.

The big boys in black make excellent time and have a quick conversation with the assailants. One can only guess what was said in their brief big-bodied huddle but sure enough, they leave without protest.

The Wagners are a little bummed that security had to step in, but being as they are both professionals, they figure they should act like it. Daylan stuck around to get the story of what happened and comped the boys another bottle. After that, they all decide to take the party back to their suite at the Aria and maybe going for a swim in the pool on the roof. Daylan would be by when he was done working to see if he could make it with one of the girls that wasn't already taken.

* * *

RATHER THAN GETTING into a cab or Uber, they all decide to walk the two miles back down Las Vegas Boulevard and take in all the Strip has for the night. Unfortunately, it's nothing good. Not long into their walk, G is sent flying forward by a violent push.

"What the—" says Jason who turns around to see the pair of raging freaks from inside the club.

"What? What's up?" he demands.

Jason raises his eyebrows and grabs the guys' arms as they advance toward him, then lowers the arms by pure strength and grabs both of the bigger man's wrists with his left hand. They struggle for a second before Jason loads up and coldcocks his adversary right on the cheek, causing him to do a little wobble. The buddy tries to grab Jason but not before Nick grabs him and feeds him a stiff right jab (he's a southpaw), then another, followed by a quick and snappy straight left that buckles his opponent.

Jason's guy goes for some sad attempt at a headlock, which Jason uses as a way to create leverage on the bigger man. He forces the guy to choose between releasing his grip or bending over as Jason straightens his back. He doesn't release and tries to squeeze even harder, doing nothing but exerting strength and energy. Jason is now fully upright and lands a barrage of punches on the guy before cops show and break everything up.

G was slow to get up with the help of McKenzie. Sosa stands by with the other girls making sure they are out of the way. Sos wasn't shy to fight back in the day, but it had been a while and he was more than certain the brothers didn't need his help. At least not during the fight. His time to help would come.

No charges are pressed, probably thanks to the assailants' heightened egos, and the cops continue their beat up the street, going in the same direction they'd ordered the men to go. Jason, Nick, G, Sosa, and their gaggle of girls press on to the Aria in the opposite direction. McKenzie and her friends are locals and explain the situation of her lunatic ex-boyfriend on the way. She apologizes incessantly but they tell her that they will always stick up for G and would deal with whatever was to come.

The whole rest of the night, as they drank, danced, talked, and partied, Jason could only think one thought: *I'm fucked.*

Nick is also concerned. His hands aren't technically registered as lethal weapons (despite the popular myths). But it's not a good look, especially with an actual fight the next night and him only having two fights left on his contract, neither of which are scheduled. He could easily be put on preliminary fights against the next up-and-comers and be used as a stepping-stone. Win or lose, it wouldn't matter in that scenario.

The brothers could only hope and pray that none of the bystanders videoed it or uploaded anything to social media.

21

Unfortunately for them, the video never shows the start of the fight and there are multiple videos. It's not long before Jason and Nick are ID'd as being the ones whopping ass on the Strip. They wake up, tagged in various posts the next day along with another text from Marty that reads: Come back with me and I'll smooth everything out.

He scrolled with his thumb and saw a hack written article about the situation, but the site is relatively unknown and doesn't get much traffic by the look of it. It was always so frustrating how people could make up whatever they wanted about any player and never face consequences.

"Fuck, boys. This is not good," says Jason.

"No it's not," says Sosa, "but it's also not the first time for either sport where something like this has happened."

"Not like this though," says Nick, "I'm surprised we're not getting calls from Triple H to join the WWE."

"You know what, I actually have a missed call from a number in Stamford, Connecticut. Maybe that's them. I'm kidding. Though you guys would be unreal at that."

"If this all blows up, that's not a bad route," says Jason. "We could be tag team champs."

"What would your name be?" asks G.

"I don't know, we'd figure out something good though, I'll tell you that. Work out some sick finishers, too," says Jason.

"We'd just be ourselves wouldn't we?" Says Nick.

"I think he means the tag team name, right G? Like: The Brothers of Destruction."

"Yeah. Well that was Undertaker and Kane but—"

"You guys aren't going to the WWE," says Sosa.

"You started it man. And G I know, it was just an example."

"Okay, well I was joking," Sosa says to regain the seriousness of the situation.

"Alright, so how bad is it?" It's like he's asking a doctor about a muscle tear.

"I can't say for Slick, but the videos show at least that he didn't start it and was protecting you."

"What're they saying in the comments?" Says Nick.

"Everyone knows that Wags wasn't out there picking fights. They're loving it actually, people are going nuts."

"I read some article where the guy was trying to pin it on concussions and alcohol abuse," says Jason.

"Well that's lunacy and I can't imagine living in a world where something as gutless as that would stick," says Sosa.

"Fuck, you and me both. Have you heard from the team or anyone from the league yet?" Jason asks.

"Not yet. On top of everything from before with Marty, they've now gotta review everything from the incident and meet about it and all of that nonsense."

"Well, what do you think?"

"I think you have a defendable, even commendable position, and I was there as a witness. I still think we can beat the Marty problem once we get your side out there."

"I know, I'm working on it."

"Hey not to interrupt, but are we staying tonight?" asks G.

"I'd probably prefer to head back," says Nick.

Just then, Nick's phone buzzes with a text from his boss that says: You guys are coming to the fights tonight. Don't punch anyone.

"I guess Slick's in the clear," says Sosa.

Nick chuckles, "I guess so."

"And I guess that means we're staying tonight, G."

"Wait, we're going to the fights?"

"Yeah, Dana texted Nick and told us to come."

"Alright, sick!"

THAT NIGHT, they go to the fights and are featured on the screen during the break. They get to go back to the fighter's area afterward and meet a bunch of the fighters. For Nick these are just people from work, but to Jason, Sosa, and G especially, it's cool to meet them and talk with them after a big win or even a tough loss.

They also talk briefly with Dana after the card and he doesn't seem to be very upset with his fighter, more so with his brother, Jason, but not too seriously. He gives Jason and his agent some advice for how to get ahead of the incident and make it so it works in their favor. They thank him for his advice and generosity, and he says to let him know if they need anything and to get home safe.

All in all, the night is a good one. The only bummer is that

Jason had lost virtually all the bets he put down on the fights and ended up giving back every cent of his winnings from the night before, down to his original twenty grand. He thought about putting it all on black but decided with everything he had going on, that he better not risk it.

22

THEY WERE out before eleven the next day and had one last poolside brunch. The just under five-hour trip that lay ahead was uneventful save for the tire that went flat on Jason's Tahoe just outside of Kingman. Sosa had caught a flight back to Seattle and said he would keep Jason updated.

The car hobbles over on the spare tire to pick up Ari at the boutique pet hotel where Ari is treated like royalty anytime Jason and the boys are out of town.

They arrive back at the house, which was cleaned by their cleaning lady while they were away, and immediately sink into the couch in the living room and turn on the TV.

Nick's fate had somewhat eased Jason's thoughts, though he couldn't help but worry still. Hockey is different than other sports and the players are held to such a high standard. Who knows how this will impact him. It all depends on what the guys at the league see in the video.

The next call was from Jason and Nick's dad. He asked if they were together and then started with the disciplining about how they're professionals and they ought to act like it, and yada,

yada, yada. It doesn't even sound like he believes it himself, but he's saying it because he feels like he has to since he's the dad. He gives himself away when he gets excited at the retelling of the story, relishing in every gory detail and says, "I bet those guys looked pretty rough after, huh? You boys fucked 'em up pretty good it looked like," starting to sound proud of his boys.

"Pretty much," says Jason.

"Have you heard anything from the team?"

"No, Sos said we'll hear something sometime this week."

"Mm. Alright."

"Guess what though?"

"What's that?"

"Changed my first tire today."

"Good for you. Did you tighten the lugs in a star?"

"Yeah. It was pretty easy and just seemed like common sense, even the stars."

"Yeah, if you tighten in a circle, it can mess up the alignment of the wheel on the axel when the lugs get tight. Anyways, well hey, the other reason I called you boys was to let you know... your grandpa passed away last night."

Jason and Nick are shocked and look at each other.

"Wait, what?" Nick asks.

"Yeah I guess he went to sleep last night, didn't wake up this morning."

"Sheesh, that's kind of sad."

"Yeah."

There's a brief pause before their dad says, "So anyways funeral's on Friday, Mom and I are gonna go."

"Is it at the ranch?" Says Nick.

"Of course."

"Alright, well we'll see you up there then, I guess," says Jason.

"Yeah, are you guys just going up for the funeral?" says Nick.

"Probably. Who knows what your mom will wanna do."

"How's she doing by the way?" Jason asks.

"She's been good. She's been going to this blood doctor that's able to draw her blood and analyze it somehow. He says her blood shows absolutely no cancer in her."

"Well, that's good," they both agree.

After the call ends, they are still so in shock they can hardly process the news. Especially with how the conversation started out. They're happy about their mom but shocked at their parents' plan to attend the funeral.

"I guess we're going to the ranch," says Jason.

"I guess so. Kinda sad though, isn't it?

"Yeah, sad that he and Dad never got their shit worked out."

"Wonder how Carl's doing."

"I'm sure he's fine. Uncle Matt's been running the ranch for a while anyways. Grandpa hasn't been working a few years."

"Yeah, I know, but still."

"I don't know how he's doing man. I'm sure he'll be there, and we can ask him then."

Jason, Nick, and G order take out for dinner and just hang out at the house for a nice peaceful easy night in. Jason could feel the weight of everything piling on him but is powerless as he has no control at this point.

23

WITH THE FUNERAL later in the week, Jason decides it's time to get himself cleaned up a little bit. Summer mange in full effect, he strolls into the luxury men's barbershop for a quick cut and a little masculine pampering. The shop has eight stations and a common area for shampooing and conditioning. The ambiance is very dark, with most of the walls and furnishings in black. There are rope lights which give off a warm-yellow, almost orange glow and candles everywhere.

The barbers are all women except for a couple of guys that probably would have a hard time fitting in with the culture at a traditional barbershop. They'd probably fare better at a women's salon culture-wise, but they can't stand cutting women's hair and are damn good barbers. With all the women sharing that notion, it's a great barbershop with a luxury salon feel.

Jason's brother Nick always gets his hair cut by what he teases as being a "real barber", but Jason knows women and gay guys are just as qualified to cut men's hair as anyone. Probably more so, and if it had to be done, he wanted it done by the best.

Haircuts are so infrequent for Jason and he hadn't really ever gotten one during his summer break, so he doesn't have a regular barber in town and just walked in to the one by his house, willing to trust whoever was next available. He only got his hair cut a couple times a year and hated it every single time. It was a necessary evil, and it always ate at him no matter how good the barber or stylist thought they did.

When he played in LA, he grew accustomed to the bougie barbershops that served drinks, gave head massages, and did all the stuff with his face, like the beard trim and the masks and serums or whatever they use.

This was his first time at this new shop, and he let the apprentice at the counter know that he was a walk-in and was good with who ever before plopping down and whipping out his phone. He opens Instagram and begins scrolling through his feed which is full of hockey news and highlights, golf news and highlights, MMA news and highlights, sprinkled with some posts from old friends sharing cutely captioned photos while on vacation with their fiancés, wives, and families.

Then, into the foyer walks the beautiful blonde woman he had seen at Rustler's Rooste, wearing a barber's apron, eager to meet her next client. She's the first to recognize that they had already met but doesn't assume he remembers her, so she plays it cool. She checks the computer for his name. "Jason?"

Jason stands up and puts his phone away before looking in the direction of his barber. *Holy shit. No way.* "Hi, yeah."

"Welcome in, my name's Hannah," she says as she leads him back to her station.

"Hi Hannah, weird question but were you at Rustler's Rooste a couple weeks ago?"

"I was, I wasn't sure if you remembered me or not when I walked up."

"Of course I remember. I spilt shots all over you guys on the stairs, how could I forget?"

She laughs at him as they arrive to her station then gestures toward her chair as Jason takes his seat. She drapes the cape over his shoulders and secures the buttons at the back of his neck. Next, she lifts her head for her eyes to meet her subject's in the mirror. Taking in his head like a sculptor before a block of marble, she visualizes exactly what she would do before asking her client what he wants.

This was standard practice for the ever-professional Hannah, however what was not standard practice were the dirty thoughts flashing through her mind as she studied the man in her chair through the looking glass. "Ahem, so how do you usually like your hair cut?"

"Honestly, I don't. I don't like getting it cut all but it just is starting to get out of control and I've got a funeral on Wednesday."

"Oh no, I'm sorry. Okay, so do you want to go short? Or just a trim?"

"Could we start with a trim and have an option for going short once I see it? Maybe just make it so it looks a little less mangey."

"Sure, we can do that. You have really good hair, so I don't want to cut it unless you're super sure."

"Okay, cool. Thanks."

"No problem. You know what, I almost forgot, let's actually get you shampooed and conditioned before we start," Hannah says while leading him to an open washing station.

She begins by running the water over his head, coating each

strand of hair with warm jetted water, and uses her nails gently to get the roots in a way that sends chills all the way down Jason's body into his toes. Normally this part felt good, but Hannah's touch was pure serenity. Her fingers ran through his locks and rubbed his scalp with a tender but firm touch. He could feel the hairs on his arms raise.

They didn't do much talking during this part; Jason's eyes were closed, his mind adrift. Hannah continued to fight off her sinful thoughts and reminded herself that she was in no place to be getting involved with anyone, let alone someone as put together as he seems to be.

I mean he's wearing a Rolex, she thinks.

Back at her station, she goes to work with her scissors, "So what do you do for work?"

"I play hockey."

"Like professionally?"

"Yep."

"No way, that's so cool. I don't know very much about sports, and I just moved here from Orange County. But I have been to a Ducks game once."

"Oh there you go. I just signed to play in Vegas, so when we come to play here, I'll get my hair cut and you can come watch."

"Yeah, that'd be fun."

This stalled the conversation and left each to their thoughts and the artist to her work. *Is he hitting on me?* she wonders.

He watches in the mirror as she meticulously makes her cuts. *Maybe she doesn't like athletes,* he thinks.

Her eyes never look up though she can feel the presence of his stare as she circumnavigates her subject's head.

At her first checkpoint, she stands up and looks over her work. "Alright, how's this?"

Jason always has a hard time gauging the length when it's wet. His last haircut was at a weird in-between length that made him want to shave his head, but he usually just went with the first stop. If it wasn't terrible, get up and go. If it was, get up and go, fix it once he's home.

"It looks good. How much would you say you took off?"

"About an inch and a half maybe, just the ends that were a little dry and starting to split. You want me to go shorter?"

Jason tilts his head continuing to examine his hair in the mirror, "No, if you think it'll dry good, then I'm good."

"Alright, easy enough. Do you want your beard trimmed and a charcoal mask?"

"Yes, please."

Hannah is just about to start on Jason's beard when he asks, "Hey, can I take you to dinner sometime?"

Hannah is shocked and doesn't know how to respond, so she just starts trimming his beard with her clippers. Eventually though, she nods her head, subtly answering yes to his question but not wanting to be loud about it.

Jason plays it cool and stays casual all throughout the rest of his time in the chair, as she lined up and trimmed his beard, and finished by lathering his open face with a charcoal mask.

At the end of the visit, she writes down her cell phone number, still with the nine-four-nine area code on the back of her business card that has her name, the shop's logo, phone number, and address.

He smiles taking the card and puts it into his Louis Vuitton wallet, "Do I pay with you or up front?"

"They handle all of that up front. But you're all set. Hopefully I'll see you soon," thinking there was no chance she'd hear from him for a date. He'd probably never even come back to get his hair cut.

"Sounds good, thank you, and it was great seeing you again."

"You too." she says.

At the end of her shift, she was more than pleased to have doubled the cash she prayed for earlier that morning thanks to Jason's generous tip. When she took the job and was forced to put her son in daycare, she made it her mission that her time away from him would not be remotely wasted. She figured that each day should be worth a certain amount of dollars, almost like a daily goal. She would pray to hit that amount so that she could take care of her and her son alone, which is what she'd committed to doing. Some days the amounts were the exact amount that was prayed for. Other days, it was much more.

24

THE PUBLIC NEED for a speakeasy hasn't existed for almost a hundred years. They came to prominence in America during the years in which the country prohibited alcohol. The Prohibition Era was one that outlawed the sale, production, consumption, transportation, and importation of booze in any form.

It was a divisive time in the country's history. Droves of people that weren't criminals suddenly became such when the Eighteenth Amendment was put into effect. Gangsters like Al Capone bootlegged alcohol from Canada, while rum runners like Bill McCoy brought it in via the Bahamas. In between were the people in Appalachia, making their own high-powered whiskey that would go on to be known as *moonshine*. All the illegal alcoholic beverages were sold at these underground establishments called: speakeasies.

Nowadays they're just hip bars that come up with crafty concoctions and are located in obscure places like behind a barber shop or in the basement of a restaurant. The one Hannah recommended for their late, Wednesday night date is at

Desert Ridge in Phoenix, and it's underground. Jason walks up to his date who is dressed in a blue jumper. She has the biggest and most beautiful smile when she sees him wearing a Grateful Dead T-shirt. They have a quick hug and head down the stairs.

"This is so cool. You said you've never been here?" asks Jason as they walk toward the entrance.

"I know, and no I haven't. I just saw it on Instagram and have been wanting to come ever since."

The friendly hipster at the front door welcomes them in and shows them over to a pair of vintage, oversized chairs with a small coffee table in between.

"Have you guys been in before?"

"Nope, this is our first time," says Jason.

"Alright, well I'll give you guys some time to check out the cocktails, let me know if either of you have any questions."

"Sounds good, thanks."

Jason and Hannah both look at each other and smile. Hannah takes a deep breath.

"You look beautiful."

"Thanks," she says with a blushed smile. "You look very handsome."

Jason starts to look at the menu to try and figure out what he wants to order. The cocktails are all a lot more involved than what he typically drinks, but after enough deliberation, he decides to go with the *Raising Arizona,* undoubtedly named after the classic Coen Brothers film of the same name.

"Great choice," says the waiter.

"I'll just do the same please."

"I'll be right back. Did you guys want to put in for any appetizers or anything?"

Jason looks at Hannah who nods and says, "I'm okay thank you."

"Be right back."

Hannah has only been on a few dates since her last relationship ended. Most of them turned out to be therapy sessions for her to vent about her ex, or else the guys were weirdos, and she tried to get out of there as quick as possible. Lately she's just been focusing on herself and her son, accepting she'd be raising him on her own.

"So, how long have you been a barber?"

She laughs at his attempt to break the ice, "Well I've been doing hair for three years but the first year was as an apprentice at a salon in Orange County."

"Oh nice, did you like that? Obviously not if you're a barber now."

"Yeah, not really. Women are just so picky with their hair and can be a real pain to deal with, especially at those types of salons, so when we moved out here I just decided I was gonna be a barber."

"Have you ever worked in a regular barbershop?"

She laughs again, "What do you mean a regular barbershop?"

The waiter is back with the drinks and sets them down on the table. They thank him as he heads to another table. The drinks are served in a cyclone glass which happens to be one of Jason's least favorite glasses. Hannah picks hers up and lifts it to cheers with Jason, they do so while maintaining eye contact.

"You know where it's just one big room and there's like four or five chairs and all the barbers just give it to each other and the customers?"

"No, I never did that, but I worked at a Great Clips for a little when we first moved."

"Oh, nice."

"Yeah my son and I moved a little over a year ago so."

"Was that who was taking you down the slide?"

"Yeah, his name is Jeffery and he's just about to turn two. He's the sweetest little guy."

"I figured he was yours, he looks just like you." Truth was, Jason was shocked to learn she had a son, but being a man of quick wits, he figured that was the best thing he could say.

"He does, everyone says that. But yeah, my parents moved out with us and we're living together in Cave Creek for the time being."

"I haven't been up there much but I hear it's a cool place."

"Oh yeah, if you're a biker or a cowboy."

Jason laughs, "Well my family's got a ranch up near Flagstaff, so I guess if I didn't have hockey, I could be a cowboy. And I have always wanted a Harley."

"There you go, you'd fit right in."

They both laugh and take more sips of their drinks.

"So are you from here, then?" she asks.

"Yep. I am."

"Wow. I feel like that's so rare."

"Yeah, I'm a fourth or fifth generation Arizonian, which is pretty cool."

"That is cool. Most people I meet here are like me, from somewhere else."

The waiter strolls back and Jason switches to a drink called the Jalisco Vacation while Hannah sticks with the Raising Arizona that she said she really liked. Jason felt like it was a little sweet and fruity for him despite the jalapeño infused gin. Maybe it was the glass that threw him.

Jason plays it cool but inside is wondering all kinds of different questions and he doesn't know whether or not they're appropriate to start asking. *How freshly single is this chick that the kid's not even two yet?* "So, what made you pick Arizona?"

"Honestly, I just needed a change. Jeffery's dad died when Jeffery was only eight months old, and I was just finishing my first year with that salon and absolutely hated it."

"Oh wow. I'm sorry to hear that."

"It's okay, I'm sorry to put you on the spot with that."

"No, no, don't worry about it. But dang, that's tough."

Jason automatically assumes that since she's from Southern California, the dad must have been in the military or something.

"Yeah, but his parents actually live here. You have to meet them before you meet Jeffery, but don't worry, they're really cool."

After Jeffery's dad, Jeff died, Jeff's parent's, Jeff Senior and his wife bought Hannah a brand-new car and paid for it with cash. They also kept her on their phone plan for a while to help out. They were crushed when their son died, but were relieved for Hannah and little Jeffery's sake.

"Oh, for sure."

"If you want to, obviously," feeling like she may have gotten a little ahead of herself.

Jason's starting to feel quite hot as the sweat starts to bead on his back. "Of course. I'd love to meet them all," he says as the first drip rolls down each of his vertebrae, even following his spine where it's crooked near the bottom from his scoliosis.

"Good," she says with a smile. This is the first time she's enjoyed herself on a date in a long time.

The waiter is back with the drinks. They toast again with locked eyes and take big sips.

Jason feels comfortable enough and has a good enough buzz on to ask, "So what-uh you know..."

"Happened with Jeffery's dad?"

"Yeah."

She chuckles darkly, "Well," then pauses to think of which sugar-coated version of the story she was going to go with, "He had a bit of a drug problem and killed himself."

Jason's eyebrows raise, "Like he overdosed?"

"No. Well, a couple times he did, but that wasn't what did it. We were in a fight and technically not even together when it happened. He said he was gonna do it and I didn't believe him, because he constantly threatened it. You know? I didn't think he'd actually do it."

"But this time, he did it?" Jason's eyebrows raised almost to his hairline.

Hannah nods her head solemnly, "Hanged himself while we were on the phone, the day before my first Mother's Day being a mom."

"Woah. That's heavy."

She looks worried that she's scared him off, "I know, I'm sorry. I just feel like it's better to be upfront about everything."

On all her previous dates leading up to this one, she told this story in a way that almost made it seem like she wasn't accepting of the facts and was in denial about the whole thing. Not of him being dead but how he died and what their relationship was like when it happened. With Jason, she felt like he'd be able to take hearing it and she was tired of being afraid to tell the truth.

"Yeah, no, totally, I appreciate it. What a situation though."

"Yeah, it sure was. But like I said, we were broken up and he had threatened it all the time. Like, we had bullet holes in our closet from him saying he was going to shoot himself."

"But he never did?"

"No, just shot the wall and made me think he'd done it."

"Sheesh. Was Jeffery in the house?"

Hannah nods her head, "That was when we first moved out."

"But then you went back?"

She grimaces and nods her head, "There were just a lot of bad situations that should've made me leave. Like the cheating, the beating, the sneaking around, the emotional abuse, but I just kept feeling like I could force it to change you know?"

"Yeah, I know what you mean."

Jason had no idea what Hannah meant. He'd never been through anything near as bad as this. His older brother Carl had flown off the rails a time or two and made some pretty rash claims, but ultimately, he was all talk compared to this. What this woman is talking about is some real deep stuff.

"Anyways, enough about all that. Let's talk about you," she says.

The waiter comes by and gets their order for another round of the same drinks.

Jason sits back, "What do you wanna know?"

"Did you always want to be a hockey player?"

"Pretty much. It's all I ever remember actually wanting to do."

"Do you have any siblings?

"I do, I have two brothers. You?"

"I have a brother but we were both adopted and we have different birth parents."

"Have you ever met your birth parents?"

"I've only talked to my birth mom on the phone. We follow each other on social media and stuff but we don't talk regularly or anything."

The waiter comes by to let them know they were closing up soon and this was last call. They both forego the final drink and just enjoy each other's company, continuing to talk about all kinds of things. At one point during the conversation, there was no talking and they just gazed into each other's eyes and communicated that way.

When Jason paid the bill, Hannah couldn't help but compliment his signature. As she should, he's only been perfecting it since third grade. It has a real nice flow to it with both his first and last name being legible.

* * *

JUST AS JASON and Hannah arrived at her car, Hannah admitted to Jason that she was hungry.

"I could eat. What's open?" he asks.

"I think In-N-Out's open 'til one."

"Let's do it. You wanna drive us over there?"

"Sure, but don't judge my car. Remember, I have an almost two-year-old."

"Oh, I won't."

Jason climbs into her fully paid off Jetta and there is trash, Cheerios, Jeffery's coloring pages from day-care, and a long hose hooked up to the air conditioning unit, that stretches all the way to the backseats so that Jeffery can get cool air. When she turns her key and fires up her people's wagon, her music comes on and is halfway through Tupac's "Hail Mary". They laugh about the state of her car, and she explains that she wasn't expecting anyone other than her son in anytime soon.

They both order Animal Fries and continue their date until they close down yet another establishment. At that time, they say their good-byes and planned to see each other again soon.

25

STARFIRE Ranch has been in the Wagner family for three generations. Just over five thousand acres of land outside of town was given to the family as payment for the well drilling that Jason's great-great-grandfather did to provide water for basically all of Flagstaff. Soon after, they got out of the water business and started ranching. It's a full-scale operation that raises cattle and produces top quality beef.

Jason's uncle has been running the ranch for about ten years and sees that the day-to-day is executed. All of his kids work on the ranch in some way or another. A few of the other cousins are there doing something. The rest of the employees are just men and women that've been there so long that their sons, daughters, and grandkids are now working alongside them. The whole ranch is one big family. Everyone that works there also lives there. It's where they raise their families, it's where they celebrate holidays, it's where they do everything. For Jason and his immediate family, they are outside of that, only having been to the ranch a couple times when they were really young. The last time ended in a drunken quarrel that made

Jason's dad swear the next time he came would be for his dad's funeral.

Jason's dad has two brothers, one sells insurance (his biggest client being the ranch) and the other's at the ranch working with the cattle. He doesn't really get along with either. He was quite a bit older and had a different mom. He was close with a few of the ranch hands back when he was young and felt they were much more father figures to him than his actual dad ever was. He kept loosely in touch with them over the years, but after that big falling out, had never again spoken to his dad. Now, he would never get the chance to again, not on Earth anyway.

To this day, the boys have no idea what actually went down, but they figured it was a lot of stuff combined that ended up being too much and it all came out that night. When the brothers were young, they all vowed to each other that they wouldn't end up like that. Now the only one not holding up on his end of the deal is Carl, or so the other two feel.

Carl wouldn't have ever admitted it to anyone, and probably hadn't even actually realized until recently, but he's happy with who he is and the life he gets to live. The anger and depression that fueled his negativity has turned into something new, something good. His lack of communication with his brothers isn't because he's got a grudge held over them. It's not even because he's bitter toward them for living lives he could've only wished of. Instead, it's the self-consumption that comes from hard days of doing back breaking labor on the ranch. He loves it. Not to mention he's fallen deeply in love with one of the women at the ranch and she loves him back.

He stands on the porch nervously awaiting his family's arrival, with his fiancé Maria standing beside him. Nick springs out of the backseat of his dad's Escalade and walks up to Carl with arms wide open. Nick always looked up to his oldest brother, even when times were dark for him. Carl is just a little bit taller than Jason, but Nick is the tallest.

"Long time," says Nick.

"Long time," says Carl.

They hug while their parents get out and come walking up. Their mom rushes up to Carl and wraps him up in a giant smothering embrace, clutching tightly for all the years that she'd not seen or heard from her oldest son. Carl had no idea about his mom's cancer surgery and so when he finds out that day at the funeral, he's just glad the doctor was able to get it all out.

"Hi Mom."

She sobs and clings tighter. The most difficult thing she's ever had to do was kick Carl out of the house. In fact, she fought it a great deal, almost to the end of her marriage. Ultimately, she decided her husband was right about them enabling his destructive behavior.

Unlike with his brothers, Carl hasn't kept in touch with his parents at all. A couple times a year, his mother phones the ranch and speaks to whoever answers. It's killed her to not be able to see or talk to her first born and despite his progress, the whole situation made her grow resentful toward her husband. Not outwardly, but somewhere deep down in a place she didn't like to think about, she hated him for it. Or was it that she hated that it had needed to be done? All of these thoughts and emotions come rushing through her mind as they hug. Their dad awkwardly stands by awaiting his turn.

Maria leads Nick and their mom inside the main house to see who all is there. Maria's father Ernesto has been at the ranch since he was sixteen years old. He's been one of the most loyal and hard-working ranch hands at Starfire. His wife died while giving birth to Maria. It was a miracle that Maria made it. She was hard on Carl when he first come to the ranch. There was no time in her day for his self-loathing and she made sure he knew it. Once she broke him, that about broke her, and now they're just putty in each other's hands.

Carl puts out his hand which makes his dad start to get red in the eyes. He grabs his son in a big bear hug and says, "I love you, and I'm proud of you"

"Thanks, Dad. I love you, too."

The healing was instant. They had both come to acknowledge their own faults in their own time but neither wanted to make the first step for fear that the other would not forgive. They go inside to join the rest of the family which is comprised of everyone on the ranch and all the others. All the cousins, uncles, aunts, employees, people from town, and even the ex-wife of the dead patriarch (probably to make sure he's really dead); the only one still missing from the bunch is Jason. Nick walks around the open floor plan of the main house taking it all in. He was still in diapers the last time they all were there, unable to remember any of it. The only recollection comes from photos he's seen of himself there when he was a baby. He walks up to the back door that leads into beautiful vast country.

"Sure's pretty innit?" says Carl as he walks up behind his youngest but biggest brother.

"Yeah. Sure is."

"Long way from the bright lights on the Strip, tell ya that."

Nick turns to face his brother, "You saw the video?"

"Of course I saw the video, you two assholes coulda really hurt them guys," he says, half-kidding.

"Well they made it seem like they knew what they were doing when the one shoved G from behind. Launched his ass."

Carl starts laughing as he remembers G from when they were young, "No way Jace's still got Grant Taylor hanging out with you guys."

"Oh yeah, he lives with us now."

"Oh shit."

"Oh yeah. I think you knew and that's why you haven't come down and visit."

"That's exactly why I haven't been to visit. I don't need him trying to cast a spell on me or anything again."

"That was only one time."

"Once is more than enough."

They both turn their gaze back toward the country to laugh and stand there for a minute.

"Speaking of, where is Jason?"

"I don't know, he said he was leaving pretty soon after us."

"He's not coming is he?"

Nick stays tight-lipped.

"Fuckin' weasel."

"He's just got a lot going on. You know how he is. Plus, he and Grandpa weren't close and he probably thinks you hate him and don't want to see him. I mean, even I thought that."

Carl frowns, "Man. I don't hate you guys. I never even hated Dad or Mom. Definitely been angry but if anything, I've hated myself. Every time I'd reach out to you guys, thinking I was ready to rejoin the family or whatever, but then stuff would come up around here and I'd just get busy."

Nick nods but doesn't say anything.

"When you guys bought your house down there, I just doubled down around here and figured I should do something

with my life. It wasn't as much jealousy as it was embarrassment, you know what I mean? You two used to look up to me
and all that. Fast forward a few years later, you two are buying a
big house and living the dream together. I'm flat on my ass out
here, mopin' around feeling sorry for myself."

"Looks like you're doing pretty good now though."

"I am. Thank God for Maria. Don't know where I'd be
without her. I found my purpose, I guess you could say. Each
day just got easier and easier to deal with my own shit. The
harder part is facing it all, and you guys. It's always just been
easier to be settled into my new life and just... you know."

"Forget about us?"

"Yeah. I guess. But not 'cause I don't love you guys, I just
don't wanna bug any of y'all. You all have your thing going on
and I didn't wanna keep bumming everyone out. I figured the
better move'd be to just keep working on my stuff. Hope our
paths would cross again and the timing would be better."

Nick is conflicted on how he feels in the moment. He
thought this whole time that his brother hated him, Jason, and
their parents. To find out that he's happy and loves life and has a
purpose makes him wonder, why does he still act like none of
them exist?

Their grandfather had Alzheimer's and as his condition
worsened over time, he would constantly mistake Carl for his
first son, the boys' dad. At first it bothered Carl greatly because
of the anger he felt toward his father, but little by little he came
to understand why his father was the way he was. One night a
few weeks back, Grandpa and Carl were sitting around talking
when suddenly the old man broke down. He started crying and
saying how sorry he was for the way he treated Carl's dad when
he was a kid and went on and on about how grateful he was to

have the second chance to make it right. Carl didn't know whether or not the old man knew who he was talking to, but he appreciated it nonetheless. Watching his grandfather die slowly as that horrible disease ate away his brain made him realize that life was entirely too short for harboring frustration and anger. It also made him see the fragile being that he had become. A once curt man who had been softened by his condition. To the point where he didn't know where he was or who he'd been talking to.

"Well I'm happy for you," says Nick.

"Thanks. I'm sorry I've been a shit brother."

"That's alright, we got time to make it up."

"Yep, that we do. You and Jace will have to come up and do some work one of these summers."

Nick laughs, "Yeah, sure. You gotta visit us first though."

"What do you think Jason's doing if he's not coming?"

"Who knows? He still hasn't heard from the team about the fight on the strip, then his old agent tried to block his deal because he was butt-hurt about getting fired. So, I think he's just trying to figure out what's gonna happen. He really was gonna come, even got his hair cut a little for it and everything."

The funeral was under way in the next hour or so, then they went back into the main house for a celebration of life party for the family and all the employees of the ranch. Carl and his dad talked for hours while Nick kept the cousins entertained with tales of glory in the octagon. It was a nice day for the Wagner family; it was too bad Jason wasn't there to be a part of it.

26

WHILE THE FUNERAL was going on, Jason was sitting on his couch, reading his latest purchase from the bookstore and was waiting for Sosa to call. G's been out and about doing G things, so Jason and Ari have the house to themselves which is rare during the offseason. Normally it's at least the three guys and the dog, but there are always people coming by or something going on.

As he sits looking at the pages of his book, he finds himself realizing that he isn't reading. The words on the page could say anything. He's only thinking about his job. Over trying to concentrate, he marks his page and sets the book down. He picks up his phone and heads into the black hole that is social media. There he tries to fill his thoughts with anything other than the stress of what is to come.

He sees a few stories right away about guys getting signed, re-signed, and traded, including multiple transactions by Vegas, which sets him off into a real panic. The one that scares him the most is the free agency signing of Nikolas Karlov. Karlov's a few years younger, and a little taller than Wagner. Wags is only six foot one and Karlov is six-three.

When he first came to the league, people had been touting him around as the next Ovechkin, Malkin, or Kucherov, but that was based on his international play. By the end of his first season, people knew he would not be the next Russian phenom, but he would be a solid and reliable third- or fourth-line winger on a high-end team. His specialty is meat and potatoes, hard, gritty play, everywhere on the ice. When he's in the defensive zone, he gets the puck out. When he's in the offensive zone, he's battling in the corners or in front of the net. In the neutral zones, he gets it deep.

Jason and Nikolas have gone up against each other multiple times over the years and were well aware of the other's similar play. When their teams faced off against one another, they were always matched up to be at each other's throat the entire game. The two of them have never formerly fought, despite there being numerous scuffles after whistles. Each of which were interrupted by linesmen and allowed the tensions to continue to rise.

The chances that the Golden Knights are going to be going with two players that fit this kind of role are not great. What was more likely was that they were going to be dumping Jason in favor of the Russian.

Jason checks the comments on the post. He sees a few that are to the effect of: See ya Wags!

"FUCK!" He exits the app and slams his phone into the cushion next to him on the couch.

He picks his phone back up and calls Sosa.

"Wags. I was just getting ready to call you," says Sosa.

"Any news?"

"Yeah, Vegas just signed Karlov."

"I saw that."

"I think the league is blocking the deal, or Vegas is going to rescind their offer."

"Fuck."

"I know, I'm sorry Wags. I'm still doing everything I can."

"I know you are buddy, it's not your fault."

"Who knows for sure though until it's official, right?"

"Yeah, I guess. What else can we do?"

"Just keep training and working. Now that they've signed Karlov, I'm sure they'll wanna get you figured out as to what they're gonna do."

"Alright, just keep me posted I guess."

"I will Wags, we'll be alright."

"Yeah. Let's hope."

They hang up the call and Jason can feel his heart sink. His mind starts racing a million miles an hour. All of the fear and anxiety of his career being over are suddenly back at the forefront. His whole identity is tied to his career and without it, he's just a guy that's almost thirty, lives with two other guys, no wife, no kids, no responsibilities, no purpose. Sure, he has a new girlfriend, and she has a kid, but would they still be there if he stopped playing hockey? Of course, she seemed like a nice girl that wouldn't be with him purely for his status but how can he be sure? He thinks to call Dr. Sutton to schedule an impromptu session but decides he doesn't feel like talking more about how scared he is or complaining about his problems. He's already started to feel weird about even doing the sessions at all. Sitting there complaining about problems while at the same time living out his childhood dreams feels like slapping God in the face a little bit.

He walks over to the kitchen, grabs his bottle of tequila and fills a lowball glass and starts drinking. He sits back on the couch and scours each of the streaming platforms for what's currently available. He mindlessly takes account of all the movies that he's seen juxtaposed to the ones he wants to see. After about twenty minutes spent looking for something to watch, Jason decides to go with one of his favorites, *The Dark Knight*.

G gets home as the film is starting and joins Jason in watching one of his favorite films as well. When it first came out in theaters, he saw it sixteen times. He was enamored by the sound design above everything else. To this day, anytime the subject of *The Dark Knight* comes up, he talks about how enhanced the experience was as a result of the attention to detail in the sounds that came bursting through the speakers at the theater.

By the time Nick is dropped off, Jason and G are at the climax of the film and Jason's hammered. Nick changes and joins for the ending.

Jason raises his glass to Nick as he walks by, "How was the fyurural?"

"The what? How much have you had to drink?"

"The fuckin' funeral, how was the funeral? Fuck off."

"We can talk about it tomorrow."

Nick is able to piece together that Jason's not in any mood to talk and his half-hearted attempt to do so was only a ploy to make it seem like there wasn't something wrong. He also knows that he is the last person his brother would be confiding in. Not because of any reason other than for his pride of being the older between the two. Nick doesn't take it personally. He just watches the ending of the film and heads to bed when it ends.

27

JASON WAS SO busy being upset and drunk that he forgot about and missed his workout with Ryan Banning. He knew he wasn't going to the funeral, but he figured he'd still get to the gym to complete his workout that was scheduled for later that day. That was until he spoke with Sosa. After that, all bets were off.

Jason's phone dances on the arm of the couch as the vibration is attempting to let him know that he has an incoming call. The noise and the feeling jolt him awake. It's strange how when someone is drunk, it can seem as if they are in the deepest of sleeps, but then at other points of the sleep, the faintest sound can snap them back into consciousness, albeit a spinning one. The reason, of course, is because drinking alcohol close to the time of going to bed has been said to disrupt a person's sleep cycle. It will indubitably wreak havoc on the whole experience, switching around patterns and shortening REM windows. It's never high-quality sleep when a person's drunk themself to it.

Jason reaches his arm for where he can feel the phone's

vibration and brings it up to his face. SOS Emoji is what the caller reads.

"Hello," Jason says with a gravely tone.

"Oh shit, are you alright? You sound awful."

"Yeah, yeah. I just got in one yesterday after we talked last."

"Did you get it out of your system?"

"Like puke?" Jason says while he removes the blanket that G must have draped over him in his sleep and sits upright.

"Pity drinking."

"Depends if you've got more bad news."

"It's not great."

"It's official?"

"It's official," Sosa says in a solemn tone.

"Fuck, man," Jason says sounding like he's been defeated and then kicked in the nuts.

"I know Wags, but listen, the Strip thing didn't have anything to do with it. That fuckin' pigeon Marty was out for blood and had everyone on his side before it even started. I also found out through everything that he went out and signed Karlov after you fired him, so just a double fuck you."

"How gutless is that?"

"Beyond."

"I mean we gotta file a complaint now right? With the union?"

"We can, obviously we have the right, but that's just money. Do you really think we won't be able to find you a team with you being a free agent? Someone's gonna need you, Wags."

"Who? I doubt Minnesota will take me after I said no to them. God only knows how Marty told them. Now we've also got the Strip thing."

"I don't think anyone really cares about that. Especially

since you weren't even arrested. If anything, it just made you more popular and now more people will want to buy your jersey."

"I just always remember as kids, everyone would always be like, 'You better not get into trouble on the streets and get caught on video otherwise, there goes your career.'"

"Right but you didn't get in trouble. It's not like you were doing some racist rant that's gonna have you get canceled or anything."

"No I know, but still. You really don't think it's a big deal?"

"I don't think it is. I think there's a lot worse things professional athletes have done or could do than stick up for their friends who were viscously attacked on the street."

"Alright, if you and everyone else thinks it's no big deal, then we should be getting some offers, right?"

"We will be, obviously the league's kind of slow right now just because of the time of year and everyone was under the impression that you would be playing for the Golden Knights. So unfortunately, no one was thinking about you."

"What about the Devils, where Karlov was?"

"I've done some looking around and there's definitely a few teams that missed out on a guy like you."

"Like who?"

"Arizona's one that could use you, but I'm not sure if they can pay you what you want."

"Buddy, if it's even remotely close and they'd be willing to bring me in, that's where I want to play. Fuck, I don't care if it's league minimum."

"I'll make some calls and see what we can come up with. In the meantime don't get too hammered, you need to stay in shape."

"Alright, dad."

"Fuck off, I'll let you know if I hear anything."

"Thanks brother."

"Later."

Jason hangs up this call feeling much better than the last one. Physically though, his head feels like it's a hundred pounds and the spins have taken hold. He closes his eyes and nods his head back and tries to concentrate. Soon, he's calibrated enough to blink open and slowly attempt to stand up. The morning after a bad night of drinking always seems to hit harder than the mornings after a fun night of drinking, and last night was no fun. He walks stiffly into his room where he has the thought of crashing onto his plush and freshly made bed that got no use the night before. Instead, he makes his way into the bathroom and turns on his steam shower.

After his shower, Jason feels like a new man. He feels great and is ready to take on the day, although the spins are still slightly present. He's reminded of them when he goes into his messages with Hannah where she's sent him three messages to his none. Their way of communicating with each other is almost like sending checkpoints in their day. Since their first date, there were usually about four long messages that they sent each other every day. They check in, share exciting moments, and express their excitement for when they're able to be back to each other's arms.

He's now missed three of her messages and her tone doesn't seem to suggest she's insecure, which is reassuring to Jason. They were just her usual messages with usual updates, and she just hoped that all was well.

He vigorously types out a response apologizing and briefly explains the events of his last twenty-four hours then hits send.

He closes his eyes to recalibrate again. *I need some food,* he thinks. He knows that the right thing to do would be to make himself a nutritious breakfast with what he has at the house, but that's not what he wants to do. He wants to go to Jack in the Box. He texts Nick and G to see if they're awake and want anything. Neither of them reply, so he heads out to procure the greasy sustenance he needs to soak up his bad decisions from the night before.

His journey makes him think back to when the boys lived in Denver, right on the border of Centennial and Aurora. The closest Jack in the Box to where they lived then was at least thirty minutes away and he and his brothers would make the journey out to Parker at least every other month. He knows that fast food is terrible for him, but it's a guilty pleasure that he allows himself every now and then when he really needs it.

28

LATER THAT DAY, Jason's back on the ice with his skills coach Jake. They are working on breaking the puck out of the defensive zone as a winger. The strong side winger's job is to stand on the boards somewhere near the hashmarks on the outside of the face-off circle and be ready for a pass.

In a game, there are five skaters on each team and it's all moving very fast. The winger that receives the pass from their defenseman will have only a couple of options for what they'll be able to do, but the choice has to be made immediately. The reason is, there is an opposing team's defender that is trying to keep the puck in their offensive zone and will be coming to attack.

One option for the winger is to pass the puck to the winger on the other side that is cutting across the middle with momentum. The trouble with that, is the other defender sitting in the middle, ready to step up and intercept the pass, then skate in casually for a clean shot on goal. The other option is to use the glass or the boards on the side they're on to bank the puck off the wall, and around the attacking defense.

In that case, it becomes a foot race between the weak side winger and the weak side defender and in most cases, the winger is going to win the race. Mainly because the defender can't abandon their whole side of the ice to try to chase a puck. They'll have to use other means like angles and coordination to stop the attack.

Jake is having Jason work on both sides as he plays both right and left side winger. It all depends on what the team needs that night. He favors playing on the left wing for a couple main reasons. One is that it allows him to break the puck out high and out off the glass, using his forehand, being that he's a right-handed shooter. The other is that it's nice to be in a good position for a sweet one-timer.

Right now, he's working the left side where Jake poses as his team's D-man, comes around the net and snaps a hard crisp pass onto Jason's tape. Jason fumbles the puck.

"What's the problem sweetheart? Was that too hard a pass? Don't guys still pass hard in the NHL?"

Jason laughs it off and credits it to the hangover. Jake comes around the net again and fires another pass on the tape. This one Jason handles and quickly turns around 180 degrees and flips the puck high up off the top part of the glass, and out of the defensive zone.

"There you go!"

Jason nods and gets back into the starting position to go again.

"Aye, this time, after you chip it out, skate hard through the imaginary D-man. In a game, try and make the guy take an interference penalty."

Jason nods his head and Jake starts the drill, this time he

rims the puck around the boards which forces Jason to turn and face his backside to the board and press up against it tight, heels and all. This will stop the pucks progress around the boards and it should be in Jason's feet. He turns his body, scoops up the puck on the blade of his stick and makes a small move off the board. Then he flips the puck high off the glass and out of the zone. He skates hard through the imaginary D-man and into the neutral zone where he picks the puck back up on the blade of his stick, skates into the offensive zone, and snaps a shot in the top right corner of the empty net on the other end of the ice.

After a few more repetitions on the left side, they switch over to the right. The trick on the right side is for Jason to be quick with it and get the puck out using the back hand. For this side, the height of the chip-out isn't as important as the charge that comes with it. The defender is forced to take said charge into account and start to back up. If he's beat, he'll have no chance to stop the winger, and the attackers are off on an odd man rush.

Jake comes around the net from the other side and zips a pass to Jason who receives the puck on his forehand and only has to turn maybe thirty degrees to the right so that he would be facing the imaginary D-man. He takes two powerful strides and chips the puck off the boards and out of the zone then skates hard to retrieve the puck and take it in for a shot.

"Do you usually like going higher or lower from your back-hand?" asks Jake as Jason skates back toward the start of the drill.

"I'd probably say lower."

"Lower?"

"Yeah I'd say so, why?"

"Just curious, you were going high on all the ones for the other side."

"Yeah, when I get the puck on the right side, I'm just worrying about moving my boots and getting going."

"That makes sense, get him backing up then you just do a little chip around the D-man and just skate through. Even if he blocks the chip, you can bury him."

"Yeah which is what we're doing on the other side, too, but there's the turn which takes that half a second where the D-man can get that little jump, and especially if I get it in my feet."

"Right, okay, let's do a few more on this side."

They do five more on the right side and call it after that. They had gotten some good skating and on ice conditioning work in before the drills. Jake's never had sympathy for Jason being hungover. "Feel free to visit the bucket if you want, but we got shit to do," is what he always says.

Jason's Jack in the Box breakfast actually did a pretty decent job at soaking up the poison and fueling his skate, considering he didn't end up puking at all. He did feel like his sweat was coming out as salty tequila by mid-way, but he made it through the session without vomiting.

After the skate, Jason and Jake hung around and caught up with Rick, the rink guy. Jason tells them about his trip to Vegas as well as where his contract stands. By now, Jason's more than tired of talking about his fight on the Strip and all he wants is a new contract so that people like Rick won't have to look at him like they've been. Like they feel bad for him. Jason hates it when people look at him like they feel bad for him. What should they feel bad about? It's his dream that's potentially coming to an end, not theirs. But maybe it's their own long-lost dreams that draws the look of sadness in their eyes. Maybe it's that life has awoken them during their most precious dreams, and they know exactly how Jason feels, despite never having been in his shoes.

29

Back at the house, the boys are all hanging out, doing their own thing. Nick's in his room doing something. It sounds like he's talking to someone on the phone. G's on the couch playing GTA and Jason's on their TrackMan golf simulator.

It's set up so that he can play a bunch of different courses and there's a projector that casts the images onto the white screen that he hits at. He's currently playing at Pebble Beach, a course he's only had the pleasure of playing once in real life. It was for a charity tournament he and Nick had played a few summers back and they haven't done it since. On video games though, he's scored hundreds of simulated rounds there. It's his favorite course to play, if he can control the wind that is. The time he played there in real life, it was gusting almost thirty miles per hour and really difficult to play in. It was one of his worst scored rounds and killed his handicap for a whole summer. Today he plays in the comfort of his game room, and he has the wind set to calm. He's currently having a very good round and is wishing that he weren't playing alone on a screen in his game room.

Pretty soon, Nick comes storming out of his bedroom, but he's clearly in no mood to play golf. He looks excited, eager to share some good news.

"I got the fight," Nick says.

"Hell yeah," Jason says while putting up a fist for a bump. "Who against?"

"Lemko."

Bryan Lemko had just lost the belt in his fight against Derrick Culver. Early on in their careers, they had both lost to Nick Wagner. With everything that had just went on in Vegas, it made sense for the UFC to run with the storyline.

"Nice dude, when is it?"

"Three months."

Jason sheaths his seven iron and gives his brother a hug. "Sick, dude. Congrats."

"Thanks bro. You hear anything for your stuff yet?"

Jason looks at his brother solemnly, "Not yet. It'll come though. Sos said he was looking around for teams that could use a guy like me."

"He'll find one."

"He said something about the Coyotes."

"That would be sick," Nick says coolly, though he fails to mask his excitement.

"Obviously it'd be nice to win a cup, but they had a good year last year and are buzzing with the news of the new arena."

"Oh yeah I was seeing that, they're putting it up here right?"

"Yeah, not too far."

"So crazy, I remember the first time we went to that arena out in Glendale."

"I know, same. It was so far."

"Yeah, hopefully this one does well. If the team is good, people will get into it."

"Oh yeah, remember when they were making the playoffs and got pretty close to going to the Cup?"

"Hell yeah, they were so fun to watch."

"Yeah, so who knows? Either way, pumped for your fight. Congrats man."

"Thanks bro, same."

"Hey you wanna play some golf?"

"I wish. Gotta head to the gym in a little to train and sign the paperwork and all that. I was gonna make some food quick before I head out."

"Alright, have fun."

"You too, aye, see if G wants to play."

Jason looks over at the golf ball sized hole in the wall to the right of where they hit and shakes his head no.

"We gotta get G out to the range more, maybe have him see our swing coach there at the club."

"Hah. Yeah, no doubt. Alright, see you later."

"Later."

Nick heads into the kitchen where he shares the news with G and goes about making his food before he heads to his gym. Jason continues his virtual round and scores his course best of two under par. The sense of accomplishment is tempered by the reminder that he is again facing the potential end of his NHL career.

He could continue to play professionally in some capacity for many years to come if that's what he wanted to do, but if he's not signed by a NHL team for this season, it will probably be the end of the road. He could go play in any of the European leagues and get paid to live a life of leisure and play some pretty competitive hockey, but that's not what he wants. He isn't interested in playing hockey just for the sake of it. He wants to play for a chance to win the Stanley Cup. It's difficult to put into words just how much every young hockey player grows up wanting to see their names inscribed on that trophy someday. For some players, it's easy to play just because they love the game. Some are eager to get back to their homes on other continents and continue playing there because to them, the Stanley Cup is just another trophy. They play hockey because they love it and are happy to be able to do it as long as they can, wherever they can.

For Jason, he feels like there is no point unless it's at the highest level. His body hurts from all his years of playing the style of game he's played. He's had numerous concussions, most of which were undocumented. Nowadays they have guys whose job it is to watch the game for players that look concussed and alert the team so that they can get the players in what they call *concussion protocol*.

That's where they evaluate the player and try to make the determination whether or not they're good to go. Concussions are a sticky topic because there's a lot of ambiguity for how they've been diagnosed and treated. A baseline cognitive test is given at the beginning of the year and almost all of the players will miss a few extra here or there to make it so that when they are actually concussed, it'll seem as if they're alright. Hockey players will play through just about any injury imaginable and that especially includes a minor brain injury.

Jason has always been one of those players and has gotten over more than a few times when it's come to head injuries. He knows that unless he's playing at the highest level, he can't justify the continuation of putting his body and his brain through the stress of a hockey season, especially in some foreign country where he doesn't speak the language. As much as Jason had put the idea of a wife and family on the back burner, he can't avoid that it's there and he wants it. He's suddenly thinking about Hannah and it's as if he already decided she's the one.

30

<hr>

JASON MEETS up with Hannah and her son Jeffery at the Phoenix Zoo. They park in the same section and all walk in together holding hands. It's Jason's first time meeting Jeffery but he's great with kids and doesn't expect there to be any problems. As they cross the bridge toward the entrance, Jason looks down at all the bricks. One of his favorite parts of coming to this same zoo as a kid was looking down and seeing his name on one of the bricks. His grandmother had donated the money so that everyone in the family would have a brick. He keeps it to himself unless he happens to spot it.

"Hey Jeffery, you wanna see some turtles?"

"Yeah!"

Jason scoops up Jeffery and brings him to the side where he can look down at the little lake underneath them. Sitting on the top of a log are four turtles.

"See 'em?"

"Mhm."

"Cool huh?" Hannah says.

"Mhm."

Jason sets Jeffery down and they continue to walk across the bridge to the entrance. Just before admissions, there is a photographer with a green screen who makes it seem like the photo is a requirement to pass.

"Right this way and I'll just have you stop in front of this green screen here."

Before either of them could say no thanks, they are posing for their first family photo together and go on through the gate. Once they're in, Jeffery lets go of his mom's hand and books it. Starts running as fast as his little toddler legs will let him run, straight toward Stingray Bay.

"He loves the stingrays," Hannah says as she picks up the pace to keep up.

"Who doesn't? Do they let you pet 'em?"

"Yep, we usually do a cup of food, too."

Hannah corrals Jeffery and pays for their tickets to do the stingray experience. It costs a few bucks, then a couple more for the food. They go to the part of the tank where Jeffery can get his arm in the water enough to pet the stingrays.

"Stingrays listen to your heart," says Jeffery.

"Oh yeah?"

"They do, they sense your pulse and can tell if you're cool or not," says Hannah.

"That's pretty awesome," says Jason.

"Try and remember to use two fingers buddy," she says.

Jeffery has a blast petting them as they come by and jumps up and down with a big smile every time they splash him with water. When he gets his cup of food, the instructions are to grip the little frozen fish in a way that leaves the head exposed, for it to look like a fish ice cream cone. The stingray then comes over top and sucks it up like a vacuum. Jeffrey ignores that, and just drops each piece into the tank and lets it float down to the bottom. The stingrays don't mind and none of it goes to waste. After the stingrays, Jeffery is soaked. Could be worse, considering it's already ninety degrees out.

Next up are the birds and reptiles. Jason is dumbfounded at Jeffery's knowledge of all the various species of reptiles especially for only being two years old. He himself only knows of the more popular species. This kid could barely talk, and he knows more than Jason. They continue around the grounds of the zoo, doing their best to stick to shaded areas.

Midway through, Jeffery finds a kid sized tunnel that leads to a higher leveled walkway. Once he spots it, he storms toward it.

"Oh my gosh. He loves this tunnel," says Hannah.

"I'll say."

"I'm gonna go up to where he comes out," she says.

"Okay, I'll stay here."

Jeffery is on the top side hiding behind a wall. Jason starts to peer into the tunnel and try to spot him.

"BOO!"

"WOAH!"

Jason actually was a little startled but played it up like he was really, *really* startled for Jeffery's amusement. Jeffery takes back off into the tunnel. Less than twenty seconds later, he's back for another jump scare.

"BOO!"

Jason plays it up even bigger this time. Jeffery giggles so hard he almost falls over and then takes back off into the tunnel. The two of them repeat their bit eighteen times at least before moving on to the next attraction. After the tunnel, they go hang out with the goats at the petting zoo for a while. The sun is high and there is no shade at the petting zoo, not for people that is. Hannah decides it's time to go and Jeffery drops into a fit of rage and protest.

"You want me to pick him up?"

Hannah nods yes.

Jason walks over to Jeffery and says, "Sorry buddy, you can go for a ride on my shoulders though."

Jason picks up Jeffery and plops him up onto his shoulders and they start walking toward the exit. After a few feet of walking, Jason looks down and notices something on his shoe. "Hey, he didn't poop did he?"

"No, you'd be able to smell it," Hannah says as she stops to check the back of Jason, "Oh shit," she says to herself quietly before continuing. "Oh no. He did, I got him, I'm so sorry," she says as she lifts him off Jason's back.

Jason doesn't know how to react, but thankfully manages to laugh. Hannah gets Jeffery cleaned up and changed while Jason decides he's just going to take his clothes off before he gets in his Tahoe and drives home in his boxers. Thankfully, he was wearing a pair. Had he been seventeen or eighteen years old, he might not have been so lucky, considering that was during his *commando era*. Hannah bags up his clothes and says that she will wash them and make sure they are clean by the next time she sees him. They give a long kiss goodbye and say they will see each other soon.

31

Later that afternoon, Jason pulls into his usual spot at Ryan Banning's gym and gets out of his Tahoe. He performs his pre-entrance routine and heads inside to see what sort of hell he'd be facing to pay for missing the other day. There's no one there and the lights are off in the lobby. The only light on is in Ryan Banning's office. Jason walks timidly toward his door. He peers through the threshold to see his coach sitting at his desk, typing on his computer, pretending that Jason doesn't exist.

Jason knocks, "Hey Coach."

Banning continues to type for a few seconds as if still, Jason doesn't exist. Finally, he gets to the end of his thought, and he looks up slowly.

"What's going on?"

Ryan looks at Jason with a desperate pain, "Have a seat, Wags."

Jason approaches the chair in front of the desk and sits down, "Sorry about the other day, I—"

Ryan shakes his head, "No, this isn't about that." They both sit in silence. Banning continues to look into Jason's eyes.

His own eyes are getting redder by the second, starting to glass over. "I gotta shut it down."

"What do you mean you've gotta shut it down? Like training with me?"

The look on Ryan's face is sorrowful but he composes himself before stoically saying, "The gym. Erin's mom had a stroke back in Indiana and they don't have anyone there except Erin's mom and dad and her junkie brother."

"Fuck man. I'm sorry to hear that, what're you going to do?"

"Well, I'm gonna sell all the equipment and see if I can find someone to take over the lease. Gotta go be there to help out the fam, you know what I mean?"

Jason takes a second to brainstorm a way to help out his mentor and coach, "Why don't you just bring everything over and start a new spot over there?"

"Wags. I appreciate it but that's just not how it works. I have no clientele out there, I've gotta start completely over. But it's okay, I'll be fine."

"What about me? Can we still train over video or something? At least still create the workouts? Like you do when I go out of town?"

"Yeah for sure, if you're okay with that. I'd love to still be able to work with you."

"This is unreal. You know, I still have no idea if I'm even gonna be playing next year." Jason can't help but feel that this is a sign coming from God, the universe, or whoever that his world would be next to get flipped upside down.

"You'll find a team, someone will take you. Don't know for how long or where, but you've still got some gas in the tank. I've made damn sure of that."

"Thanks Coach, I appreciate you."

"I know, I appreciate you, too."

"So what about today? Are we still training?"

"Up to you. I didn't even know if you'd show up or not after the other day."

Jason chuckles, "Fuck I know. I fucked up."

Ryan stands up and smiles a real genuine smile, "Come on, let's go for one last session. I start packing and selling tomorrow."

Jason follows Ryan into the gym for the last workout that would ever take place there.

"You gonna join?" Jason asks.

Every now and then, Banning would join Jason for the workout, but most times he trained late at night, long after the last client has left. He takes a moment to contemplate whether or not he wants to save his workout for himself later that night. He had thought about using his final two hours in the gym to take out all his anger and frustrations about everything that is unfair and unjust. Then he realizes that he didn't start this gym alone. Wags has been with him since before this gym existed. The last workout at Banning's *Fortress of Pain* wouldn't be a pity party for one. Instead, it would be a badass celebration where two warriors battle against their inner-quit and overcome triumphantly together.

The show that was put on in that weight room was one that was only for themselves and for those in the spiritual realm who surely gazed in awe at the two men as they ferociously attacked their movements with strength, grit, and tenacity. It reminded the ghosts of a time long since passed. A time from when they existed on the other side, where grit and mental fortitude were prerequisites of existence. Bearing witness to the show of these two surely gives the spirits a sense of hope, that the traits for survival are not dead or gone like their bodies and former identities, but only becoming less common. Which in turn, makes them rarer and more beautiful.

As Wags and Banning cool down and stretch afterwards, it dawns on Jason that he wouldn't have a gym anymore and he would have to get a membership somewhere. That was when he hatched an idea to buy as much equipment as he could fit in his garage and convert that into his gym. He figures that in the event his career is over, he's going to want to stay in shape, but he won't want to have to go places and see people. Especially the gym where he already knows they're all going to ask him what he does, who he is, and all the stuff he usually gets when he goes to a regular public gym.

The thought of it now irked him in a way he couldn't fully explain. Possibly because that's just it, he can't fully explain anything. He doesn't know where he stands in his career, and he can't bear the thought to look at someone and try to explain to them what he does and why it's complicated. They're just going to give him the same look that Rick the rink guy does. Like they feel bad for him. He feels like he'll never understand how people can feel bad for him. He's made millions of dollars by playing a game and living out his childhood dreams. He doesn't feel entitled to have people feeling bad for him.

Jason has lived the majority of his life as one who's attained whatever it's been that he's set out for. He knows that most people don't ever become who they wanted to be. He knows that most people despise their lives, their spouses, their kids, their jobs, and most of all themselves. He has always been in a place of being the one who feels sorry for others. It's always been him that's given the look. The look that says,

"Sorry kiddo, sometimes things just don't work out the way you want it to, that's life." Easy to say when things are going well.

Now, he's on the receiving end of that pity and can't figure out why. It was as if they knew something he didn't, but what? What were his thoughts as he had given the look? Why couldn't he remember? It was probably because he had no thoughts going through his mind when people told their tales of woe. He had nothing to relate it to from his own life. It's not that he's not sympathetic, he just lacks the ability to connect the dots. Everything has always worked out for him and so he feels like it will too for others.

* * *

THE NEXT DAY JASON, Nick, and G come to the gym with a trailer and load up as much gear as they're able to make fit. G had met Banning a couple of times and even tried to workout with Jason when they were in high school. It didn't last long and he ended up preferring his mixed martial arts training over traditional strength training. Nevertheless, he was helpful in the retrieval of the equipment, except for he forgot to latch the back gate and it flipped down as the boys started driving off.

Jason stops his Tahoe and puts it in park before exiting to see what happened, "G. You didn't lock the fuckin' thing, ya meathead."

"Oh shit, my bad."

Jason hops out and walks around the back to flip up the gate secure it shut. He shakes his head at Ryan, whose face suggests he's amused.

"Fuckin' guy," Jason says while shaking his head in comedic

disgust. "We'll get this stuff back to the house and drop it off then see if we can fit any more."

"Sounds good. Try to get it there safe, huh?"

"Yeah, I'll try," Jason says with a nod, then plops onto the driver's seat and puts his Tahoe in gear. They drive out of the industrial complex and start out on the road back to their house. Normally, Jason hops on the 101, but because of the cargo he decides to take the side streets. It only tacks on an extra ten minutes and those were spent sitting at red lights. They spend the whole morning getting everything unloaded and set up.

After a quick lunch, the boys head back to Banning's to pick up a second load of equipment. During their break, they talked about having someone come out to install air conditioning for the garage since it was going to be miserable in there if they don't, even with a swamp-cooler. Heating too. The winters could be unruly if anyone were to do an early or late workout. Jason had skated at a summer camp one year and the rink they did it at had a gym that wasn't heated. It was an absolute nightmare to lift any serious weight, since their hands were nearly frozen on account of the cold. It made him shiver to just think about it.

When they picked up their second haul, that was when Jason and Ryan would say their goodbyes. It was an emotional moment for both of them, although neither showed it too much. Plus, they still had work to do together. The sadness just comes from the fact that all good things come to an end and this gym represented a really good thing.

32

A COUPLE DAYS LATER, Jason had just sat through a business proposition with his buddy Dallas, who has a cool startup idea. Dallas and his co-worker have come up with an app that is designed to compete against the banking system. Jason told Dallas that he'd need a little time to think and see what happens with a contract but was very into the concept. He also mentioned that he'd have to run it by his financial advisor and all of that, but he was intrigued. More than anything, he was impressed by the way Dallas and his co-worker were able to unveil the magic of how the economy works. He never knew that taxes were invented so that the country could justify printing money, and that the purpose of tax dollars was to offset the national debts. He knew almost nothing about the economy or how it worked, but he suddenly felt deeply fascinated. Dallas' co-worker promised to send over some videos that go deeper into the stuff that he was talking about.

Jason's now at home on his couch watching the videos. He's roped G into joining him and now G is also sucked in. At first, he was reluctant but when the videos started talking about how the system uses people and makes money on them, he couldn't help but get into it.

"You know, I've been thinking a lot of this stuff for years bro," G says then takes a big puff off his weed pen.

"Man. I've never even once thought about any of it like this at all. Like, it's always made sense to me to have everything the way it is."

"Yeah but bro... you don't know any other way. Imagine if someone came here from a place that doesn't have taxes or money at all."

Jason feels like he just got contact high from G's thought, "That'd be pretty wild. But the system of making money and paying taxes and keeping money at a bank has just been around for so long. Way longer than America's even been around."

"True," G shrugs and takes another hit.

They continue to watch the video and pretend to understand it, though it will take them both a few rewatches to fully grasp what's being said.

Just as the last video is starting to wrap up, Jason's phone, which is in his lap, starts to vibrate, "Woah-ho," he says as he checks the caller and lifts the phone to his ear, "Yellow."

"Yo, Wags, you free?" Says Sosa.

"Yeah buddy, always, what's up?"

"Alright so, I've got three teams that are interested."

Jason's relief is euphoric, "Fuckin' rights, Sos. Fuckin' rights. Who do we got?"

"Dallas, Pittsburgh, and, Arizona."

"Get the fuck out of here, no way."

"I swear to God."

"You're not fucking with me?"

"Wags, I would never lie about something like this."

"Man. Thank you so much."

"Don't you wanna know how much from each team?"

"Honestly, I don't care. I'm just happy to have a job and to be able to stay here."

"It's gonna be a good thing buddy, I'm happy for you."

"Thanks Sos, I really appreciate you getting it done for me, it means more than you know."

"No, I know. But it'll really mean something when you get re-signed and you guys win the Cup one of these years."

"Hah. Yeah, let's just take it one deal at a time, ah?"

Sosa chuckles, "Fair enough."

Jason can't believe he's got a contract to play in his hometown, despite everything that's just gone on this summer, "Unreal buddy, you're getting something sick."

"Haha, I'm pretty proud of myself too, not gonna lie. It feels good."

"You should be man, this is good shit. You should come out to celebrate."

"You know what, I'm down."

Just like that, Jason is back. He fills G in who has switched over from the economics video to his normal video games. Nick is still at the gym, but would be home any minute. Jason pulls out some steaks from the fridge along with some asparagus and fresh rolls. "What do you think about some steak sandwiches for lunch? Huh, G?"

"Sounds good to me."

Jason has a surge of energy and excitement, a notion to be romantic. He goes for his phone and calls Hannah but gets her voicemail. Instead of leaving a message, he hangs up and sends her a text inviting her over for lunch. After waiting with no reply for a couple minutes, Jason decides to pour a glass of tequila. While Jason preps the food, his phone buzzes with a message from Hannah that tells him she was working, but wants to get together soon. He responds asking for a date whenever she could arrange it. There goes his romantic spirit. Back to prepping the food when in walks Nick.

"Yo yo," says Jason.

"What's going on here?" asks Nick.

"Little celebration steaks for the boys."

"You got a new deal?"

Jason smiles and nods, "Tell him the best part, G."

"He's signing with the Yotes baby."

Nick drops his bag and wraps his older but smaller brother in a bear hug and lifts him up as he hoots and hollers his excitement.

"Right? How sick is that?"

"Very sick. Congrats dude."

"Thanks, Sos did unreal."

"I'll say, now you just gotta bring home a Cup."

"Hah! That's what he said, we'll see. You want a drink?"

"Yeah, just gimme a sec. I'm gonna go put my stuff away and settle in."

"Alright, take your time."

"G, how's your day been?" Says Nick.

"Pretty good I'd say, J and I were learning about money before Sos called. That was pretty cool."

"Oh yeah?"

Jason nods, "Dallas and his buddy have some kind of app they're making and its gonna disrupt the banking system or something, I don't know. We're learning about it."

Nick looks at his brother inquisitively, "Does he want you to invest or something?"

"Yeah but you gotta hear these guys talk, it's super interesting. Maybe there's something there for you."

"Maybe, who knows? You know I'm always trying to beef up my portfolio."

Jason laughs as Nick heads back to his room.

"Hey, how long 'til food's gonna be ready?" asks G.

"I don't know, whenever it's done, why? You got somewhere you gotta be?"

"No, I was just wondering."

"I'm firing up the grill now."

Jason walks through the living room and gets in the way of G. He's currently in the middle of a one versus one death-match in GTA, "Sorry G."

"You're good," says G.

Jason exits through the sliding door with Ari following behind. The thirty-two-pound tank quickly changes his mind when he feels the scorching hot ground beneath his paws and asks to be let back in. His owner obliges and takes a few steps over to the grill. He presses the starter and engages the flame by turning each of the three dials. *It is hot,* thinks Jason as he takes a sip from his tequila.

Without thought, his next move is to set down his glass, take off his shirt and walk over to the pool. He slips out of his sandals and jumps in. The water feels like a warm bath or a cool pool where someone has just peed, only the whole pool was that way. He swims a couple of laps noticing a couple patches of what he would consider cool water. He wonders what causes brief columns of water to be cool while the rest feels like a hot tub, but then he's over it by the time he's out and back at the grill, cooking the food.

✳ ✳ ✳

SOSA ARRIVES a few hours later and they go to the Ocean Club to celebrate. Paul Bissonnette is there having dinner with a couple of other former NHL players who are in town for an alumni event.

"Woah-ho-ho, look at this crew," says Biz who notices them as they're walking by.

Jason turns and sees the table, "Hey what's up Biz? What's up boys?"

They all nod what's up back as Biz says, "Ah you know, just havin' some dinner with the boys, how 'bout you? How you doing? Saw your guys' little scrum out there in Vegas."

Jason looks at his crew, "Same thing. And that was brutal. Those guys kept coming after our boy G here."

"At least you pumped 'em good, eh? And hey bro, sorry to hear about what happened with your contract, that's a tough go."

"Yeah, they had it coming. And it's all good. I actually just signed with the Yotes, so we're here to celebrate."

"Oh fuck, congrats buddy. Let's get you on the pod. I'll hit you up and we'll chat about it later."

"For sure. Sounds good, thanks."

All the rest of the guys congratulate Jason before he and his crew continue following the hostess to their table.

The boys have a great night and eat spectacular food. The guys from the Coyotes table had a bottle of Caymus brought over, which the boys made quick work of, following it swiftly with another. They wash it all down with a couple of butter cakes for the table before hitting the lounge for a drink and to see if there were any women for Sosa and G. Nick is kind of sort of back with his ex and is trying to see how it goes, and Jason's got his thing going with Hannah so they're both just there to wingman and watch.

After a couple of stiff conversations and stuffy drinks, the boys decide to head back to the house. Sosa struck out with a foxy middle-aged cougar with naturally red hair and an unnaturally gigantic rack. He watched a guy her age swing and miss, so he thought himself a good suitor for her evening. After Sosa got back to the boys, they saw a man that had to be in his late eighties struggle and shake with each step as he approached to make his move on the woman who ended up not being a cougar at all. The boys watched the first few minutes of the interaction and after they finished their drinks, they got in their ride home, joking the whole way about the not cougar.

PART III

33

By the first week of September, all the players will have arrived and reported to the team for training camp. Rookie camp starts a day early and is for all the hopeful prospects that have been drafted, are under contract with the organization, or were invited to show up and grind for their shot at the main camp.

This year, the main camp consists of forty-one forwards, twenty-one defensemen and seven goalies. By the start of regular season, the Coyotes roster size needs to be down to a maximum of twenty-three and a minimum of twenty. The rest of the guys will find their way to Tucson to play with the AHL affiliate Roadrunners and some will head back to their college or junior teams for another year of development.

Every new season, at least one guy who played in a development league will really shine during camp and put himself in a good position to make the opening roster for the start of the season. But most guys have the goal of going out there, making a good impression, and hoping that the coaches will remember them if they end up needing to call anyone up throughout the season.

Jason doesn't dread training camp like a lot of the veterans do, especially when he's just been traded to a new team. He finds it the perfect time to really get to know everyone and get a gauge for how the year would go. There were always fitness tests, bag skates, new drills, team bonding workouts, and of course, preseason scraps. It was a way for the guys to get acquainted or reacquainted in some cases, and get back to the task at hand, which is to be a team to win the Stanley Cup.

This wasn't Jason's first trip to the Ice Den in North Scottsdale, though it was his first as a member of the Arizona Coyotes. His first time to the Alltel Ice Den, as it was called then, was when he was on his first mite travel team.

Blue pucks had just come out and they were being used in games for the mites. The idea is that, because they are lighter, they're easier for six- and seven-year-old kids to get up and down the ice with, or have their shots be able to get up in the air with than the regular black pucks.

When Jason first started, he played defense. He wanted to play offense but being one of the bigger kids, his coaches always wanted him on the back end. That would change later on, but during his first trip to the Den, he was on the point.

Late in the third, with his team being down three to four, Jason was passed the puck by his defensive partner. He took a couple of strides into the open ice in front of him and eased the puck back so that he was in position to fire a wrist shot on net. Because of the reduction in its weight, the puck was airborne by the top of the face off circles and continued on a trajectory that stopped its momentum when it pinged off the back cross bar inside the net. He took a couple strides, dropped to a knee, and performed a windmill celebration, just like he'd seen in the NHL games he watched every single night during the week.

Unbeknownst to Jason, on the other sheet of ice was where the Coyotes were on the ice for a practice. Jason's brothers had chosen to watch the Coyotes practice instead of his game and so they missed his goal. However, their dad got it on video and Jason wouldn't stop talking about it for a week.

After the game, Jason and his team rushed to get their equipment off and get into their game-day attire, which in those days consisted of dress pants, a white polo with the team's logo stitched on left chest and the player's number on the right, and a pair of dress shoes.

All the kids took turns meeting the Coyotes players, taking pictures, and getting autographs. Shane Doan was gracious enough to sign and give Nick his orange Easton Synergy Si-Core. While Jason's older brother Carl sought out one of Teppo Numminen's wooden sticks made by Montreal. This was right on the edge of an era when some guys used wood sticks, some guys went composite, and some guys like Mike Johnson, went with a two-piece. It was a composite shaft and a wooden blade that they basically glued together. The argument for them was that they had the benefits of being light like the composites but have the feel and customization of the wood.

Jason was using a two-piece for a back-up at the time and that was what he used as a canvas for the players to sign their autographs. Each player had their own version, their own style. Some signed with their full name, some went initials only, and some went first letter of first name and full last. The thing that all players did, and all their signatures had in common, was the inscription of their jersey number somewhere among the scribbling.

Fast forward twenty years and Jason is among them. He's on the ice as a member of the pack and at the same rink from all those years ago. It doesn't take long for Jason to get the rhythm and flow of the practice. Current head coach Jacques Levesque is in his third full season as such after having been an assistant coach for the two before that.

Before coaching professionally, Jacques Levesque helped out as an assistant coach for his son's Bantam AAA team in Arizona, a team that Jason was also on. Before that, he had an illustrious NHL career that lasted almost twenty years.

While watching players perform the drill awaiting his next turn in line, Jason senses his coach coming toward him. Just as Jason turns to look at his coach, Jacques sticks him in the gut with the blade end of his new Bauer stick.

"Ahhh Jason! It's good to see you. I was very happy to see we got you. Can you come by the office after practice?"

Jason nods his head, "Yeah, sure. Thanks. Happy to be here, good to see you too." *Fuck that hurt. I forgot he does that.*

Jacques came from a different era of hockey. Sticking guys was just part of the game when he played. He wasn't a goon by any means, but he had to deal with them nightly and used his stick well (still does, apparently). He blows his whistle for everyone to take off and start skating as hard as they can in a clockwise direction before meeting up at center ice for a quick huddle to wrap up the practice and start their team stretch. Jacques takes it upon himself to lead the team in the post practice stretches for the first few days of training camp to show that he's still got it.

Once they're off the ice, Jason gets changed out of his gear and takes a quick shower before heading over to the meeting room that Jacques uses as his office for practice days. On his way, he takes note of all the changes that the rink has made over the years and since he'd last been there. Jason knocks on the open door as he makes his way up to his coach with his arm extended.

"Come in," says Jacques as he takes off his reading glasses, stands up, and extends his arm to shake hands and give a hug.

"How's it been?"

"It's been good, it's been good. And you? How does it feel to be home?"

"It's unreal. I really appreciate the team bringing me on."

"Please. We appreciate you coming. We all know what you can bring to this team. I know what you bring to the team. It will be a perfect fit."

"I'm looking forward to it."

"As are we. For preseason I'm going to have you work up and down the lines, try you everywhere and just trust you to know who you need to be and when. But I need a physical body that's difficult to play against, got it?"

Jason nods his head.

"I know you can score. How is your hand? You didn't hurt it more by getting in that street fight in Vegas, did you?"

"No, no, he was like a stuffed animal. Hand's fully healed, skated all summer. Good as new."

"Very good. I'm gonna play you a lot this preseason. We gotta make sure those legs and lungs can still take it, ah?"

"Oh yeah, coach, I'm good."

"That's good, that's good. I also want you to be a leader with the young guys, you know, keep them focused."

"I can do that."

"I know it. Also I heard you on that podcast. That was a pretty funny story."

Jason laughs in shock that his coach listened to it let alone enjoyed it, "Glad you liked it, Coach."

The meeting continues for a little while, the two men catching up after all these years. Jason asks about Jacques' son and Jason's former teammate who is enjoying a fruitful career in luxury real estate sales after he lit it up in European leagues for more than a decade. They talk about Tampa and then they end the meeting. Jason leaves feeling more excited than he's ever been to start a new season. Pure elation is the only way to describe how it feels for Jason to have this opportunity to play for his hometown and for one of his favorite coaches.

34

EVER SINCE HANNAH got her own apartment for her and Jeffery, Jason's been spending a lot of his free time over there. He hasn't missed any workouts, practices, or tee-times, but he doesn't spend much time gaming with Nick or G these days. Nick and his ex are still trying to make things work, which means in all his free time, he's been over at her place.

G is basically living alone in a house that's not even his. "Poor G" is what some might think, but not G. He hardly even notices that the Wagner brothers aren't around. Time works differently for him. It could be on account of the drugs, or it could just be how he is, but he usually doesn't even realize that Jason brings Ari with him.

Rather than playing video games, however, G has gotten really into the economics stuff. He's spending most of his time down the rabbit hole, filling his brain with all kinds of wild conspiracy theories that he believes, without a shadow of doubt, are true. Whether they are true or not, it's probably a good thing to have him start to get into something other than video games. Jason hasn't gotten much more into it since that first day. There had been another meeting scheduled for earlier in the week, but Jason had forgot to reschedule when the camp schedule came out and they still haven't met.

Right now, Jason's at Hannah's apartment, which is a nice little two-bedroom in North Scottsdale, only about ten minutes away from his house. He and Jeffery are watching a Disney show on Jeffery's iPad while Hannah cleans up the kitchen and the toys in the living room. Next is bedtime for the little man. Jeffery had slept in his mom's bed every night until they moved into this apartment, so the transition requires Hannah to lay in Jeffery's bed until he's asleep, and once he starts snoring, then she can make her escape.

During the thirty- to forty-five-minute wait, Jason usually either reads the book he brings or mindlessly scrolls on social media. Anything to keep him from observing all the dead fiancé's belongings, like his bandana which is tied around the bed post, his Grateful Dead stash box, which was repurposed as an urn to contain his ashes, and most of all, the cute photo immortalizing the time he serenaded her with his acoustic guitar while she sat on his lap, arms wrapped around him, under the stars.

Anytime Hannah is with Jason, Jason feels like it's right and things are good. But whenever they're apart, Jason's mind becomes twisted with doubts that she's not ready and she's not over Jeffrey's dad. He finds himself struggling to understand how she could be so sure about her relationship with him, yet she's got all her ex's stuff on display. It's like she still loves the guy. It's hard for Jason to understand because he's never had death end a relationship. In his mind, he feels like Hannah and Jeff would still be together if Jeff hadn't done what he did. Jason doesn't feel like he's got the right to say anything about how it makes him feel because, how he feels is nothing compared to how she must have felt or still does. Rather than saying anything, he just figures she will eventually feel "healed" enough to take the stuff down and move on.

Once Jeffery's asleep, she quietly opens the door to her bedroom and is awestruck at Jason's presence. She smiles and closes her eyes and takes a deep breath. "Hmmm."

Jason sets his book on the side table and accepts her as she turns out the lights and crawls on top of him. For now, he puts aside all his prior thoughts of insecurity. Their lips join as Jason gropes her butt cheeks and brings her tight to his body. He puts his hands inside her oversized T-shirt and rubs them all over her back. Their mouths are open, and their tongues are joined together in a kind of inter-mouth dance battle. Jason starts to pull off her short shorts which prompts her to hop off and strip. Jason does the same. They rejoin their now naked bodies and begin to passionately and loudly go at each other multiple times.

After the last go, they lay there next to each other, both seemingly deep in thought, yet they both simply wonder what the other is thinking. "It's still pretty early, you wanna watch a movie or something?" asks Jason.

"How about let's just talk."

"Okay, what do you wanna talk about?"

"I don't know, what do you wanna talk about?"

Jason laughs, "How about on the count of three we both say something and who ever's got the better topic, that's what we go with."

"Deal."

"Alright. One... two... three."

As if it were written and rehearsed, they both say, "Aliens."

The two of them go back and forth talking about everything they know on the subject and enjoy every second of it. Jason loves their conversations and for the first time in his life, feels like he can freely and openly get into things with the woman he's with. His past relationships were different. The conversations were always monotonous and much like a news broadcast of reporting the day's events with that being as far as the conversation ever reached. With Hannah, their talks are anything but boring or mundane.

This conversation serves as an intermission and after they run out of alien stuff, they were back at each other for another couple rounds. After that, Jason gets dressed, grabs Ari from the couch in the living room, and heads home.

35

———————

Today is Jason's first preseason game. His first game in a Coyotes uniform. Camp had gone well for him. The team was all very welcoming and happy to have him aboard. There's an optional morning skate that he doesn't plan to participate in. Instead, he goes to the aquarium with Hannah and Jeffery.

Afterwards, he heads home to rest. The doorbell rings just as he's contemplating a pregame nap. Jason gets out of his bed and saunters up to the front door. He peeps through the eye hole and sees a guy in his early thirties wearing wranglers, boots, and a plaid shirt standing on his doorstep. The cowboy gives a wave to the peephole. *What the...*

Jason opens the door and Carl gives another wave and gives a half smile.

"Hey man, Nick said it was cool if I came by. I sent you a few texts too but haven't heard anything back. You still got the same number?"

"Yeah I do, sorry I've just had a lot going on. Come in, I don't know where Nick's at, I was just in my room for a pregame nap." Carl enters the house and Jason shuts the door.

"Shit, sorry about that. I can come back a different time. I forgot about pregame naps."

"No, no, you're good, I wasn't asleep yet. What're you doing down here?"

"I actually came for your game tonight and figured I'd come a little early and see you before since you keep duckin' my calls and texts."

"I'm not ducking you, I've just had a lot going on."

"Yeah, Nick tells me you had a kid, congrats."

Jason laughs, "Yeah, I guess. Hockey stuff though, too. Heard you and Maria got married. Congrats."

"Well, not yet, but I appreciate that. To be honest, I just figured you didn't wanna talk to me, which I could understand."

"Clearly," Jason says under his breath though it still registered with Carl.

"Look man, I don't expect you to just forgive me and forget about everything I've done to hurt you. Hell, I wish I could just let you beat the shit out of me 'til you do, but I know that won't help anything. I just wanted to see you and apologize in person and tell you to have a good game tonight."

"What're you doing until the game?"

"I was just gonna head over to Mom and Dad's then I think we're all going to the game together."

"Is Maria with you?"

"She's at Mom and Dad's, why?"

"I just wanted to make sure you didn't have her waiting in your truck."

"No. I told her she'd see you later."

Jason nods coolly. The interaction is a lot to process. He had an idea that it would be coming at some point, but he wasn't exactly expecting it would come hours before a game. Luckily, it's just a preseason game. "Well you wanna see the house while you're here?"

"Yeah, sure, if you don't need to take your nap."

"Nah, I don't usually actually nap, I just like to hang around. Come on." Jason leads him into the first room which is the game room.

"Wow, this is pretty sick, I gotta get one of these set up down at the ranch," he says, referring to the golf simulator.

"Yeah it's nice having it, helps keep the scores down. When was the last time you played?"

"It's been a while, not since I moved out to the ranch."

Carl had tried to keep his golf game going when he quit playing hockey but the mental connection between the two caused him to never have the urge. Instead, he got into hunting and long-distance shooting. Other than that, his work on the ranch kept him plenty busy.

Jason continues the tour of the house and into the other room. G's deep into one of his conspiracy videos. He and Carl have a brief and awkward interaction that lets the oldest Wagner brother know that Grant is the exact same as when he was in high school, which was the last time Carl had seen him.

They wrap up the tour in the newly air-conditioned garage slash gym which is fully set up and operational. There are even mats for mixed martial arts training and a couple of heavy bags mounted to the ceiling.

Carl delivers a jab to the punching bag, "Yep. Just as I figured, this place is unreal. I'm sorry I haven't come down sooner."

Jason takes a second to wonder whether he wants to do this now or later, "Why haven't you?"

"Honestly?"

"Well, yeah. I'd rather you not waste my time by lying to me."

"I haven't had a good answer for it. Anything I've thought of just ends up sounding like bullshit and so I'd rather have not said anything. The only two real reasons I keep coming back to are shame and embarrassment. You and Nick, you guys are living your dreams and I... I have been a self-absorbed and enti-tled prick. I've let my life on the ranch become my new identity, like witness protection, and I used the new identity to cut off all ties to my old life."

"But why did you feel like you needed to?"

"That's what I can't figure out. I just keep coming back to the fact that I've been ashamed and embarrassed. Ashamed for how I acted and embarrassed for not doing what I set out to do."

"Carl, no one ever held it against you that you didn't make it to the NHL."

"I know, I know, but I held it against myself. It was all I ever wanted to do, all I ever wanted to be, then it was just over. It was like I woke up one day and knew in my heart that I'd never make it and that damn near killed me. So much so I had to quit. Took me a long time to realize that quittin' didn't help me at all and only made it all worse."

For the first time Jason understands what his older brother is talking about. This was the exact fear that he'd been facing all summer. That lingering feeling that this could be the end, only for Carl, it was the end.

"Why did you stop?"

"Because I didn't want to play if I wasn't going to make it to the NHL and at the time, I was dating that chick, I don't know if you'd remember, you were in juniors. But she and I wanted to move in together and start settling down, and I wasn't going to be able to support our life playing hockey. She and I broke up about, I don't know, six months after I quit. Right around the time you got drafted, and that was when I went off the rails."

"I never even knew about all that. I always just thought your concussions or maybe from me getting drafted pushed you over the edge."

"Nope. The truth is that it's because I was an entitled prick who thought just because I tried hard and loved the game, it owed me something. That mindset almost cost me everything, including my life. It's taken me a long time to appreciate and acknowledge that hockey gave way more to me than I ever gave to it. Anyways. I'm gonna get outta here so you can rest up. Have a good game tonight."

Jason gives his brother a hug, "Thanks bro. Glad to have you back around. Jesus, you're a tank."

Carl chuckles, "Ranch life, baby."

"No shit. Here, I'll open the garage and you can head out that way."

Jason knows that no further conversation is needed. He's happy to have his older brother back in his life. All he ever wanted was an explanation and the truth. He never hated Carl for anything, regardless of his hurt feelings from being ignored by the older brother. He hoped that there would come a time just like this, where Carl would come and apologize and explain himself. Now that it has, there's a sense of peace. Everything around him is clicking and working as it should.

36

PRESEASON CAN MEAN a lot of different things depending on which type of player someone is. For example, veterans and superstars usually don't have to play if they don't want to. Some like to get their legs under them, especially if they don't do much skating during the summer. Players who are new to a team, like Jason this season, will have to play more than the returning veterans because it's a new environment. The coaches and staff want to learn as much about their new players as they can. While he isn't new to the league, he is new to Yotes and sometimes new guys work, sometimes they don't. It all depends on the team and the only way to see it without consequence is during the preseason.

Jason's pregame routine has more or less remained the same since he was sixteen. He always arrives a couple hours before the game starts, heads into the dressing room and changes into his gitch. Next, he tapes a few of his sticks.

Hockey players have all sorts of different ways in which they tape their stick. Different schools of thought lead players to choose certain styles over others. Certain colors over others.

Some suggest taping the handle one way while others suggest another. Some prefer to tape the entire blade, while some, just part.

Jason's tape job is simple. The handle is wrapped in the thicker width white stick-tape, down roughly twelve inches from the top, with no fancy knob or lacing effect. The only other thing he does to the bottom front of the taped handle is write his number: *32*.

He flips over his Bauer Vapor Hyperlite stick to the blade and continues with the same roll of white tape. Starting at the middle of the blade, he slowly and methodically wraps the roll around the front and backside with precise overlap. He continues until he's reached the tip of the blade, or the toe (as it's more commonly referred). When he gets to the toe, he folds the tape over itself to back up over the front of the toe. He rips the tape from the roll and tightens his fold. Next, he grabs a pair of scissors and works his way around the toe so that there's no excess tape flopping in the breeze at the end. He repeats this process a few more times with a few more sticks.

After making sure all his equipment is set up exactly how he needs, he embarks on the next phase of his pregame routine: warming up his body. He starts out with some dynamic stretches. He finds a spot with the other guys and does some high knees, high kicks, then some butt-kickers, then alternating side lunges, and finally a quick sprint. The object is to get loose.

Once the dynamic warm-up is complete, a group of the guys form a circle and grab the soccer ball. The name of the game is either two-touch or sewer-ball, depending on where someone's from. But the rules are that one player serves the ball to another player using their feet. That player has two touches to get the ball to another player. The player last to touch the ball before it falls to the ground, is out. No hands are allowed. Wags loses in a showdown against Clayton Keller. The object here is to stay loose and keep it light.

Currently they share a facility with Arizona State University at the Mullett Arena in Tempe, and in a few years the team moves into their brand-new arena in North Phoenix. Jason sits in his stall in the dressing room, partially dressed in his equipment, as Jacques addresses the team in his pregame speech. His basic message is to go out there and set the tone. He wants his team to force turnovers, be hard on pucks, and win battles along the wall, "Constant net-front presence. Das where da goals are gonna come from. Okay? Deeze guys are gonna be coming *hard*. Let's get out der and stick it to 'em. Lez shove it up their azz, ah?"

The team erupts in cheers as they turn the music back up and ready to go. Jacques reads the starting lineup and then exits the room and heads to his office to finish his preparations.

The guys are done getting ready around the same time and one-by-one they start their walk from their dressing room to the ice for their on-ice warmup. Jason uses the on-ice warmup as a chance to do another set of stretches before joining into the shooting and passing drills with the team.

Fans start to fill in as warmups begin. Kids always flood to the front row on the glass, in hopes of getting a puck from one of their favorite players. Jason notices a kid banging on the glass and signals for the little guy to be ready. He flips the puck straight up and over the glass. The kid flinches as it comes down and has to bend over to pick it up but when he does, he raises it up, and starts jumping up and down excitedly.

As the players feel like they're adequately warm, they start to trickle back into the dressing room as the Zamboni gets ready to resurface the ice for the start of the game. The ice gets really chewed up from players skating around, so the Zamboni comes out after warmups and again after each period. They do it for overtime during the playoffs, but outside of that, it also comes out and does a thick strip down the middle for a shootout when one is required to determine a winner.

Jason uses the time to re-tape the stick that he just used during warmup. For most of the guys, this is just another preseason exhibition game that doesn't mean anything for the actual season. A couple guys are playing in their first NHL preseason game and that is special. But for Wagner, his whole career is on the line, or so he feels. The team they're going up against is Las Vegas, the team that just ditched him for his rival. He has to go out there and show everyone that he is the better player.

The game is under way. Wagner is on the second line playing wing on the left-hand side. He jumps over the boards and gets the puck immediately, he sends it in deep to start a forecheck. The first guy to it is a Golden Knights Defenseman. As soon as he touches the puck, Jason lays a crushing hit and takes the puck away. He comes around the net and passes it to the slot in the middle, where his teammate gets all of his shot, beats the goalie, and puts the Coyotes up to an early lead.

Everyone on the bench leaps to their feet and congratulates one another and then waits for the players on the ice to come through the high-five line at the bench. Wagner's line remains out there for the start of the next play. The face-off takes place at center ice and lined up directly on the other side of the line is none other than Nikolas Karlov. Jason gets set.

"I'm ganna keel you," says Karlov.

"Is your Russian accent even real?"

"Yeeh et's reel muther fucker."

"Cause I know some guys who can turn it on and off when they need to."

The ref drops the puck and Jason rushes for the loose puck. Karlov uses his stick to block Wagner's advance and trips him which the head ref deems a penalty. Karlov makes his angry protest with the ref who made the call, but finally quiets down after being threatened with a misconduct.

Jason heads back to the bench so that the number one power-play unit can start their attack in hopes of increasing the lead with a one-man advantage. Toward the end of the power-play, one of the Coyotes players got a soft holding call by the official. They were simply battling for the puck.

The fourteen seconds of four on four are rather uneventful with sloppy passes taking up most of that time, and now it's the Coyotes turn to be a man down and try to kill a penalty. Wagner is back on the ice to see them through the remainder of the penalty. His job is simple, block passes, block shots, and get the puck out of the zone.

The penalty clock ticks down to zero as is signified by the attacking goalie's slapping of his stick against the ice. The puck is still in the Coyotes defensive zone, but they're now back to full strength, five-on-five hockey. Jason is still on the ice from the penalty kill and will remain there until his team can get the puck out of their own zone. The Coyotes defenseman wins the puck battle in the corner and rims it around the boards to Wagner who anticipated the play and was there in time. He quickly pivots to retrieve the puck and get it high and out. Less than a second after the puck banks off the glass and out of his zone, Jason is knocked head-first into the boards via a hit from behind and is very slow to get up.

No penalty was called on the play, save for the fighting majors that ensued as a result of O'Brien taking exception to Karlov's gutless action. When Jacques requested an explanation, the ref said, "Karlov was finishing his hit and it was Wagner's responsibility to keep himself protected when he had got the puck and there wasn't enough for a boarding when he was the one who turned his back to the guy that hit him."

Jason is called to the dressing room and is suspected of having a concussion. The head trainer takes him through all the tests that are required and deems that he is in fact concussed and will need to sit out until he is healed. When he got hit, he also tweaked his back and that is causing a great deal of pain. "Here's a few of these. I'll get you some more for the recovery."

Jason takes the painkillers and swallows them without the aid of water.

37

CONCUSSIONS SUCK. There's no two ways about it. Injuries in general suck but there's something about a concussion that really sucks. The greatest enemy to contact sports may be brain injuries. Hopefully one day people will be able to treat them just like they would another injury, like a broken bone for example.

"The problem with a concussion is it's not like breaking a bone. It's more like getting a bruise. And you may say, 'Well what's the big deal? I get bruises all the time.' That may be the case, but a bruise on the knee is a long way away from the brain, Mr. Wagner," the team's neurologist holds up a model of a human skull with a brain inside, "See how there is this gap in between the brain and the skull? That is basically filled with Jell-o that protects the brain from the skull. When you get hit, the brain travels through the gelatin because of its inertia," he continues his demonstration, using his hand to move the brain through the gap toward the backside of the skull. "If it's a hard enough hit, the brain will collide into the skull and that is how you get the bruise. Over time, it takes less and less to cause one because the protective Jell-o becomes weaker with subsequent hits."

"So, what're you saying?"

"I'm saying this was obviously not your first concussion based on the MRI."

"I've always passed the tests. There was one I had in my second year, but that was when I was still in the minors, and they didn't make it seem like it was that big of a deal."

"That is the problem that I see in many contact sport athletes, they discount symptoms or sometimes go undetected altogether, but one thing is for certain and that is the brain always keeps score."

"So you're saying if I keep going, I'll end up in a coma?"

"Not necessarily, but I would encourage you to start thinking about a future that's a little easier on your brain."

"Is there anything they can do to reverse it or treat it?"

"There have been a lot of efforts albeit not particularly in the field of traditional medicine or academia, but in other ways that are outside the scope of my medical practice."

"I see."

The neurologist tries his best to be sympathetic to his patient, but he can't even begin to wrap his head around what it would be like to be in Jason's shoes.

"And how many concussions would you say I've got left in me?"

"It's impossible to say because we don't know how many you've had. The only way to truly study a brain and see what's happened is when you are dead."

"Well, we don't want that, do we?"

"No, we definitely don't want that."

"I don't really want to be done right now, you know, I just signed this contract and the season hasn't even started yet."

"I'm not saying you have to be done right now, I'm saying you need to be done *for* right now. If you feel that you are good enough to keep going once your brain is healed, then that is up to you, but I would be remiss if I weren't upfront about the risks."

"No, I appreciate that, how long would you say I'm out for? Eight to ten days?"

"I would say at least until after preseason is done."

Jason winces like he's just been handed a prison sentence.

"I know, it is not what you want to hear, but trust me; if you want to make it through the season and wish to continue playing after, then no playing or hard activity until preseason is done. This will be very problematic if not taken seriously."

"I understand. I'll do what I have to."

"Just rest and try to stay off the screens."

"Can I read books?"

"Yeah, sure. You can read books if you like, but if you start to get a headache or have a tough time focusing, give yourself a break. That is your brain telling you that it is too much activity, thus hindering the recovery."

"Alright. I can do that. Just sucks it happened in the first game of preseason. I just had all summer to rest." He almost says it like he's trying to get out of a speeding ticket. Like the doctor will take pity on him and retract his diagnosis and recommendation for treatment.

"I'm sorry. I know it is a bummer to get hurt like this but it's very important you take care of it properly, so it doesn't worsen."

"I understand, I appreciate it."

"And after ten days you come back in, we'll see how things are coming along and maybe we can make a change. Who knows?"

"Let's hope so," Jason stands up.

The doctor stands up from behind his desk and puts out his hand, "Take care and listen to your brain."

"I will. Thanks again, see you soon."

Jason walks out into the lobby where his brother, Nick is waiting to drive him home. The team didn't want him driving anywhere until after he saw the neurologist.

* * *

ON THE WAY back to the house Jason, doesn't say much, instead he is faced again with the thoughts that his career could be and maybe should be over. He kept thinking to himself, *Why me? Why the fuck is this happening? Huh? Just when I get to come home and play for my hometown team, this fuckin' happens.*

Nick feels his brother's negativity, "You hungry?"

Jason shrugs.

"Let's roll through somewhere and get something to eat."

Nick drives to the nearest fast-food joint and goes through the drive-thru. They eat in the car on the way home so there isn't any evidence of G being left out.

After he gets some food in him, Jason decides his bad attitude isn't going to get him anywhere. He is going to use the time to relax. When it was time for him to relax, he wasn't really been able to on account of the fact he's been uncertain of where he was going to play or even if he was going to play. Now that he's signed a contract, maybe his body and his brain can get the much-needed rest it deserves and come the first game of the season, he'll be ready to go.

"Hey can you swing me by the bookstore on the way home, I've gotta stock up for the recovery."

"Sure. I'm always down to hit up a bookstore."

38

Hannah comes by to visit on a lazy Sunday afternoon. Jeffery is over at her parents' house, and she wanted to check on Jason as well as bring him a care package of sorts. It includes all of his favorite candies as well as a book and a lion stuffy that Jeffery picked out for her to take. Jason's head is pounding as he gets the text that she's already at the house. He quickly reaches into his nightstand drawer and grabs his bottle of painkillers. He takes a few of the pills and downs them along with some water. He slips into his Ugg slippers and walks to the door.

G is on the couch playing his games when he notices his friend groggily walking through the house, "Hey bro, everything good?"

"Yeah, just my head. Hannah's here to bring me some stuff and hang out."

"Oh, okay."

Jason opens the door and sees Hannah with her upper lip tucked under the bottom and the sad look of concern that he thought only a puppy could make, "How are you?"

"I'm okay"

She crosses the threshold and gently hugs him. They kiss and stay in each other's arms just swaying side to side for a few seconds. She kisses him again on the lips and pulls away.

"You poor, poor man," she says.

"I'm okay."

"I brought this for you."

"Thank you, you wanna come in?"

"Sure, what're you up to? What have you been doing?"

Jason looks around and shrugs, "Nothing really. Not really anything I can do except read, take naps, and watch movies or TV. Which I guess now that I'm saying it doesn't sound that terrible."

Hannah chuckles, "Yeah seriously, can I have a concussion?"

"No, you don't want a concussion. They're the worst. But you can hang out and join me for a movie if you're available."

"I am."

Jason leads her to his room where they pass by G who says hello to Hannah.

"I love that your friend from middle school lives with you guys."

Jason laughs in case she's being facetious, "Do you really?"

"I think it's adorable. I also think it's adorable that you live with your brother."

"Really? I feel like a lot of girls think it's lame when guys have roommates."

"I mean I wouldn't say you *need* roommates."

"Right."

"You just like having people around."

"Exactly."

"And who better than your brother and slightly awkward friend from school?"

"See? You get me," He leans in to kiss her again, this time longer, "I don't know if I'm gonna be able to you know... I've got a pretty bad headache."

"That's okay. I still want to hang out even so."

Jason softly laughs, "Okay good. I didn't know if you just liked me for that."

"Like you're just some piece of meat huh? Is that what you're used to?"

"You never know, it's a crazy world out there."

"That it is. You know, not to undermine what I was just saying but, I have heard that sex is good for curing headaches."

Jason smirks and says, "Well then in that case, come here."

He pulls her on top of him and continues to kiss her as he begins to take off her Foo Fighters T-shirt. While she takes off her yoga pants, Jason strips down to nothing and eagerly awaits for her naked body to be pressed up tightly against his. Their two bodies become one for the next couple of minutes as they engage in Jason's new favorite form of headache treatment.

"My head feels better already."

Hannah kisses him on the forehead and giggles. "Good."

"Mmm, much better. What should we watch?"

"Whatever you want to put on. I can rub your head, too."

"You are a goddess."

Jason takes hold of his Apple TV remote and clicks over to his movies. Despite it being the age of streaming, Jason has spent too much time and money digitally collecting movies for his library and will always try to start there when trying to figure out what to watch. Whenever he watches a movie for the first time, he likes to do it alone for some reason. When he watches movies with others, the more times he's seen it, the better. Hannah admitted on their first date that she wasn't much of a movie buff, and in fact, most movies that Jason frequently quotes or references, she's never seen.

He combs over the list of films going by each category. When he gets to the comedies, it doesn't take him long to make his pick, "Have you seen Dodgeball?"

She grimaces like she's about to misspell a word in a spelling bee, "No."

"That's what we're doing then," he clicks play and they begin to watch one of his all-time favorites while she continues to rub his head with the same effect that she had when she first shampooed him.

He gets into the candy she brought, starting with the peanut M&M's. As the movie plays, he finds himself paying more attention to her during all his favorite parts, wanting to know if she enjoyed them as much as he did, and to his satisfaction she did. By the end of the movie, Hannah had to get to her parents so she could pick up Jeffery and Jason was feeling like he was ready for a nap. And that's what they did. She went to retrieve her son and Jason went to sleep.

He slept for about two and half hours and was brutally awakened by the sound of the smoke alarm ringing throughout the house. He reaches for his pills and takes another few as the throb in his skull has somehow synced up with the ring of the alarm.

He comes out of his room to find G cooking on the stovetop without the fan on. He storms over to the fan switch in the living room and then to the sliding door to open it and let out the smoke. Then, he stomps up to G who seems unbothered by the sound and by the smoke. He's cooking and nodding his head to the music that blares into his ear canals.

Jason yells over the alarm, "G!"

Nothing. He yells again, even louder, "G!"

Finally he senses a presence and jumps when he turns to see his very angry friend. Pulling out one of his earbuds he says, "What's up bro? Oh shit."

"Oh shit is right. I was coming out here to ask you the same thing. I was just asleep."

"My bad bro, I had my headphones in and couldn't hear the alarm."

"Did you not see the smoke?"

"I did but I figured the alarm would go off if there was too much."

"Well. It fuckin' did."

"My bad."

"Just fucking think man. Why didn't you have the fan on top of the stovetop on?"

"There's a fan on top of the stovetop?"

"G, I can't handle this right now. There's a fucking button right here, with a little picture of a fan on it. When you start to see smoke from now on, you press it. Got it?"

"Yeah, sorry again, bro."

"And turn the fucking alarm off!"

"I don't know how."

"FIGURE IT OUT! FUCK!" Jason stomps back into his room slamming the door behind. He walks over to his bed and sits on the edge and puts his head in his hands.

A couple minutes later, Nick walks in from training and is able to help G turn off the ringing noise that is currently the bane of Jason's existence.

39

THE END of preseason is upon the NHL and teams are finalizing their rosters. Bubble players are making their way to either the big leagues or back down to the minors. The team didn't feel it was necessary to risk further injuring Jason's head, and so he had remained in concussion protocol through preseason as per the doctor's recommendation. Jason didn't perform nearly as well as he would have liked to over the preseason, but then again, he only had a few shifts, and what he did in those few shifts was good.

Tonight is their home opener against none other than Vegas. Jason is at the rink for morning skate. He feels focused and ready to return. The fact that he gets to have his first game back against the guy that just put him out for preseason is all the fuel that he needs. In order to get to sleep last night, Jason had to take a sleeping pill along with a glass of tequila.

He woke up and grabbed a cup of coffee on his way into the rink. It's his first time back on the ice since his injury. The first thing he notices is how bright the lights feel. The second is there is a dull stabbing sensation midway through his back with every stride he takes. He takes it light and uses the time to ease himself around out there and see if the pain in his back is just from his being laid up for the last month, or if there was really something wrong.

By the end of the skate, Jason's back is killing him. Once he's out of his gear, he heads into the trainer's room to be worked on and see if a massage will do the trick. After that, he alternates between the hot and cold tubs to help with inflammation and recovery. If he hadn't been inactive for the last month, these would be unnecessary steps, but for a guy at his age and with his body damage, they are imperative.

After his body rehab session, it's time for his pregame meal. He's been eating chicken Alfredo before games since he was twelve years old, that won't ever change. The difference between then and now is that the team supplies the meals at the rink after morning skate. Jason doesn't have to go sit at an Olive Garden in his suit on the way to a game with people looking at him and his teammates, wondering why there are kids in suits at an Olive Garden.

He takes his lunch with some of the guys who are also getting their meal in before they head home for their naps. They keep it loose and talk about the other sports that are in season. They know they have a game later that day, there's no sense in them putting their energy toward that at this time. It would dampen the impact for when the time actually comes to handle business. Instead, they gawk over NBA and Formula One highlights.

* * *

NICK'S in the middle of his training session when he gets the call, or rather his gym does. The front desk girl comes running across the mats to where Nick and his coach are working on striking combinations.

"Slow down, Mama. Shit. You're gonna knock yourself out," says Nick's striking coach.

Nick starts laughing and breaks his concentration.

"Oh psh, shut up, you know you like it," she says.

"I do but not when we're at work baby. Slick Nick's gotta stay ready."

"I know, that's why I'm over here. Dana wants to talk to you."

"Me?" he asks.

She nods her head yes. Nick and his Coach look at each other before Nick says, "Go, see what he wants."

Nick's coach and his girlfriend head back to the front desk while Nick starts shadow boxing. G is on the other side of the mats cooling down with a stretch after spending some time working on his jiu-jitsu. G's been going in a couple of days a week with Nick and taking the lunchtime BJJ class while Nick works with his striking coach.

G is drenched in sweat as he comes hobbling up to Nick.

"Sup bro? How goes your sesh?"

Nick executes a combination through the air in front of him, "Good bro, how'd it go with you? Are you guys done?"

"Yeah it was just the three of us and they gotta go back to work."

"Damn. Are you good to chill 'til I'm done? I don't know how much longer I got."

"Yeah sure, I'll sit in the sauna for a little or something."

"Okay, cool."

G continues to stand there like there's more for him to say. "What's up?"

"Have you noticed anything about Jason lately?"

"Not really, what do you mean?"

"He just seems a little quick to snap these days. I feel like I'm walking on eggshells."

"Nah, he gets like that when he's hurt or stressed and can't play. You just gotta give him some space."

Nick's trainer hangs up the phone and starts back over to the boys, "Dana wants you in two weeks."

"What?"

"Lowry pulled out or got hurt or something. He needs a heavyweight."

"What about my fight in a couple months?"

"He said you could keep it if you want it."

"What do you think?"

"Do it. Fuck him up, then fuck up Lemko."

"Chill, G," says Nick.

Nick's trainer interjects, "I think your boy's right. I mean it's not good to turn down a fight when you're in a good place to win. It's kinda quick turnaround time, but we'll just do a shorter camp and finish 'em quick. That'll force a new contract and a shot at the belt. Honestly perfect when you think about it. How do you feel?"

"See?" taunts G.

Nick takes a second to think things over. Now isn't the time for him to be insecure or worried about what will happen if he loses one of the fights. Now is the time to go all in on himself. Put all the chips to the center of the table and hope that he's the winning horse, "Let's do it. Fuck it right?"

"Hell yeah, baby, let's go! You got this. I'm gonna call him back right now and let him know you're on. In the meantime, you go home and get some rest, we'll start our little minicamp tomorrow."

"Alright, sounds good."

They all give each other fist bumps before Nick and G head to the locker room to get changed back into their street clothes.

40

Carl's sitting on his old leather couch watching the pregame show on his TV at his cabin on the ranch. It's a western wooden box that has a roof over head. His furniture is an old and worn leather set that's been in the family almost a hundred years. There is an old, wood burning stove that gets used every now and then but they had gas hooked up back in the seventies so the gas stove is what gets used in the day to day. He's got electricity, cable, water, pretty much everything he could need. He doesn't know why more people don't up and leave their cities for a simpler life.

"Aquí tienes amor," says Maria as she saunters over to him carrying a freshly cracked, ice-cold can of Modelo.

"Thank you, baby," Carl says as he kisses his fiancé on the lips, "You gonna sit down and watch the game with me?"

"Ay, are you finally going to watch a game?" She sits down and cuddles up next to him.

"I was gonna try. Unless you got something else in mind," he says as he eclipses her body with his and kisses her more.

"Later, amor. I want to watch the game with you."

Carl has only watched a couple of sporting events in all the time since he's moved out to the ranch. He watched one of Nick's fights but it was the fight where Nick lost his title early in his career and so he thought it was bad luck for him to watch. He'd tried to watch a couple of hockey games here and there over the years but could never bring himself to watch more than a few minutes.

Maria always thought it was a little strange, being as all the other guys on the ranch couldn't stop talking about sports. Mostly everyone was into football. The main house was a football watch party every Sunday. Everyone that worked on the ranch would come over to the main house and it was like the Super Bowl every single week. Carl would go from time to time but for the most part, he'd just stay at his house by himself and do something to keep busy. No one really knew what ever he was up to. At first Maria liked that he didn't care about sports and never watched them but the more that she got to know him, she realized he couldn't. So, for him to be watching a game by choice now was a big step to her to show that he's done some much needed healing. They sit cuddled up watching the pregame broadcast.

"This is Jason Wagner's first game back since his concussion that he suffered at the beginning of preseason."

"Yeah and you know it was a pretty scary play, not one you'd normally see in preseason but you know, game moves quick and it just ended up being one of those things."

"Yeah a scary play and a scary situation. We're happy to have him back in the lineup tonight as the Coyotes get ready to face off against the Vegas Golden Knights here in their home opener."

"I know he's happy that's who they're up against."

"Oh yeah, well there's nothing better than when a team injures ya or gets away with a cheap shot so to speak and then you get to go up against 'em for your first game back."

"Little extra juice is what you're saying?"

"Little extra juice, that's exactly right. I'd be looking for Wagner to have a big game tonight."

"Well I had a chance to speak with him a little before the game today and he told me that he is focused, he's excited, and he's ready."

"Well that's good to hear, we know the boys definitely will be happy to have him back in the lineup, and we are, too."

Carl chuckles as he takes a sip of his beer. It's a surreal feeling for him to hear the announcers talking about his brother. He briefly thinks back to when he and his younger brothers were young kids watching these games with their dad while mom cooked dinner. The bitterness he once felt when he'd hear the names of guys he'd played with and against being announced for NHL games was gone. He used to turn on a game and see an old line-mate of his out there playing in front of twenty thousand people for millions of dollars while he himself was down and out, working on his family's ranch with nothing to show for it. That made him want to blow his brains out with the pistol he started carrying once he became a cowboy. He knew he couldn't go anywhere near one of Jason's games or that might do him in right then and there.

He ended up just sitting in the car with Maria for a while when they were in town to see the pre-season game. They talked for a while and ended up taking a walk and getting a slice of pizza at one of the pizza spots on Mill Ave. He'd had every intention of going in to watch the game but couldn't bring himself to get out of the car. It wasn't payback for Jason skipping the funeral, he just started getting anxiety about running into people from his childhood, it being his hometown team as well. Maria was cool about it and knew that he was working through his trauma in his own way, as long as it wasn't self-destructive.

When he found out that his brother was injured by a gutless play, it infuriated him that he was unable to do anything. Since then, Carl has kept a distance between himself and his brother. He knew that Jason was in no state of mind or spirit to continue the mending of their broken fences. All he was worried about was getting back out there on the ice. Carl understands that and would've been the same way. They'll be fine and Carl knows that now, too.

"Woah, woah, there he is," Carl says excitedly pointing at the screen.

"I see him."

Wagner is lined up for a face off in the offensive zone on the right-hand side. The puck is dropped and the Golden Knights win the draw back into the corner. Wagner gets the jump on the defenseman to the puck, but instead of continuing his attack, he pulls off the gas just a little. That gives the Knights defenseman time to get around him and win the battle.

"What the fuck is that, Jace?"

He watches Jason then stick his stick out in order to poke the puck free and in doing so accidentally trips the guy and the ref's hand goes up.

"Then you take a fuckin' penalty?"

"Baby cálmate, tranquilo."

"Baby he can't be doing that kind of stuff out there. He needs to have grabbed the puck like he could of if he didn't let off."

"I didn't see him *let off*."

"That's because you didn't ever play, you can't tell. And then, instead of burying that guy, he just reaches his stick out, like *meh*."

"Maybe he's just a little nervous from his head."

"He better not be," he says.

"Yeah, just a tough penalty to take, I mean ya see here on the replay, Wags had the initial race almost won and then at the last second, he pulls back ever so slightly, which allows this Vegas defender to get back and win the race. Then after that, instead of using his stick to try to reach for the puck, he's gotta be looking to lay the body there. Just crush 'em."

"Yeah and as we said at the top of the broadcast, he's been out with a concussion so hopefully it's just knocking some of that preseason rust off that he didn't have a chance to do during the actual preseason."

"Yeah, we're not worried about it, he's always been known for his physical brand of hockey as well as his ability to score goals from the front of the net."

"That's right. Alright well, we're gonna get to see our first Coyotes penalty kill of the season right here after the break."

"How are you doing?" Maria asks.

"I'm fine."

She gives him a look that says she doesn't believe him.

"Baby I'm fine. He's fine. You heard the announcers."

She nods her head and pretends to believe him, and they sit there as the commercials roll. They're close in proximity being together on the couch, but their minds are a million miles apart. The reason Maria knows that is because that's what she's thinking about. If he were also thinking that they would be together physically and mentally. For all she knew, he was imagining himself floating on an inner tube in the middle of the ocean. The ability to read his mind was a skill she had not mastered at this point in their relationship, though there were glimmers of it at various points. Like when she was able to read his mind to figure out where he'd left his long underwear when it got cold. Times like this, however, it was as if he had a force-field up that blocked her ability to even have the slightest hint.

Jason's next shift comes with twelve minutes left in the first period. He's jumped out for the winger that's just come off and is on the attack right away. The Knights D-men go D to D and break the puck out of their zone on the opposite side from where Jason is. He now begins his back-check, cutting through to the middle of the ice, on his way back to his defensive zone. The Vegas forward cuts back toward the center where he easily gets around Wagner who stands there flat-footed, like an immovable object.

"He is playing so scared. He's gonna get sat the rest of the game."

The whistle is blown due to the shot going out of play and into the netting above the glass. The Coyotes change lines and Jason heads to the bench, knowing that he's playing like shit. He's playing scared.

Carl watches and squints as he tries to make out what Jacques says to Jason once he was back on the bench. The cameras cut away before he was able to decipher any words.

41

JASON'S PARENTS sit at home and watch the game from the comfort of their living room. The surgery that Jason's mom had to rid her of the cancer all throughout her abdomen was said to have been a success. Upon completion of the surgery, the doctors had said that it was gone, all the way down to a microscopic level. Shortly before the preseason game the family all attended, she had a follow up visit to do a CT scan. The results came back a week later that the cancer, which initially had started in her ovaries, was now on her liver and lymph nodes and that chemotherapy would be necessary to have any chance at keeping this from going terminal.

She had always been adamant about never wanting to do chemo. When she was first diagnosed, the majority of her friends that had beat cancer using chemo said that if they were re-diagnosed, they wouldn't undergo the harsh treatments again. And besides, she was told that the cancer was gone down to a microscopic level and so she felt like the homeopathic stack of supplements would be sufficient in transforming her body to an environment for which cancer can't live, grow, or thrive.

To everyone's shock and frustration the results of the most recent CT scan prove that the supplements have not been as effective as the cancer cells in the time since the surgery. With so much life to live, she decides that the anti-chemotherapy hill is not the one on which to die. So, she scheduled an appointment with a place in Scottsdale that combines low doses of chemotherapy along with other homeopathic treatments, and their objective is to find the individual's cure. It seemed better to them than the brutish method of blasting away at her whole internal system as a way to simply "kill" the cancer for it to only come back a few years later and then rinse and repeat the whole process.

She's recovering from her first day of treatment and has mustered up enough strength to watch her son's first regular season game as a Coyote on TV. It just about killed her to not be there in the arena where she could yell her infamous cheer, "WEOOOW!" Anytime one of Jason's teams was in town his mom and dad would be at the game and Jason could always hear his mom in the crowd no matter how loud it was. Anytime they were in California for business, they'd drive up and catch a game when Jason was with the Kings. Any game that they weren't there to see in person, was usually there, volume up on the big screen TV in their living room.

"How are you feeling?"

"I'm okay. I'm just glad we're able to watch it all, you know?"

"Yup. Hopefully Jason has a better period here in the second."

She scoffs and shoves her husband.

"What? It's not like he can hear me, I'm just saying. He needs to have a better period, that's all."

She shakes her head and turns her attention back to the screen as the puck is dropped to start the second period. The Coyotes are starting the period down two goals to none. The first two lines set a good tone physically and with puck possession. Jason's first shift of the period comes a little under three minutes in. He gets the puck in the corner and fires a pass to his teammate along the half wall then heads to the front of the net where he's greeted by a hearty crosscheck to his back in between his padding. His teammate passes it to their D-Man at the blue line and he winds up for a clapper. The shot is about at knee level and within a stick's reach for Jason. He uses his hand-eye coordination and redirects the puck passed the blocker of the Vegas goalie and into the net.

The red light signifying a goal goes on and the horns blare. Jason raises his hands in a humble celebration as he and his teammates on the ice come together for a group hug before going through their line of high-fives at the bench. The coach changes lines and Jason watches the replay from the bench and is congratulated again by his teammates as they watch back the clip. Something that Jason hopes he never takes for granted is hearing his name announced after he's just scored a goal.

"Coy-OTES GOAL, his first of the year, scored by number thirty-two, JASON WAGNER. Assisted by number three, JOSH BROWN, and number ninety-two, LOGAN COOLEY."

"OWOW OWOOOOOO."

Jason's mom sheds a tear that rolls down the side of her face as the camera cuts back to the play which is now resumed. Jason's dad gets red in the eyes, but no tears fall as they continue to watch the game.

The Coyotes tied the game up with five minutes left in the

second on a goal that was assisted by Jason from a very nifty cross-ice saucer pass that landed right on the stick of Logan Cooley, who handled the puck and sniped one passed the Vegas goalie. The score is tied at two at the end of the second period.

42

Jason sits in his stall trying to focus before it's time to go out and finish the game's final period. "I'm ganna keel you," is all he can hear in his mind. So far, the coaches have managed to keep Wagner and Karlov on the ice at separate times thus keeping their forces from colliding. That luck has run out as both of their lines were called to start the third period. Wagner gets set on his side when he sees his rival skate over to take his spot at the face-off. The only thing separating them is the thick red center line painted beneath the ice.

"How waz yur extinded vaycaychion?"

Jason looks over, "You finally ready to go?"

The official standing at the center gestures to each goalie and the timekeeper that the time had come to drop the puck.

"Yew ganna die."

The puck drops and so do Wagner's and Karlov's gloves. They square up to each other and engage in a slow dance with their fists raised. The tension can be felt all over the arena. Everyone knows about the bad blood going into the game and is invested in the outcome of this fight. Some even more so than the result of the game itself.

Jason grabs Karlov's jersey with both hands at the shoulders, a trick he used to immobilize his opponent's arms and keep them from flailing. Then he lets go of the jersey with his right and cocks back. He delivers a hard right that connects on the jaw of the sturdy Russian. Karlov fires back with some body shots that land then he transitions to blows to the head and face after ripping off Jason's helmet. Wagner returns with two quick straights that knocks off the helmet of Karlov and then gives a strong shot to the body. Karlov gets the wind taken out of him and tries to grab on, but Wagner blocks his grab and uses his left hand, which is still tightly grasped to his opponent's jersey, to jab him in the face repeatedly before issuing a big overhand right. The Russian begins to buckle as Jason continues to rain down punches. The linesmen intervene to end the fight and escort the gladiators to their penalty boxes.

"Guud fight man. Sorry about da het."

"Good fight, you're good man, thanks for answering the bell."

And just like that, their beef was squashed. For now, at least. Their rivalry first began when Wags chirped Karlov, asking if he had Oreos at the bench. The Russian didn't understand the reference until he asked a couple of his teammates. In the 1998 classic poker movie, *Rounders* the character portrayed by John Malkovich has an affinity for the sandwich cookies while he's at the poker table. Karlov watched the movie with his teammates and was enraged, mostly because even his teammates thought it was funny. Since then, he's wanted to take Wags' head off.

There's something strange that happens when two rivals come together in a battle of fisticuffs in front of a packed arena.

The outcome of the fight and the fight itself can completely change the dynamic of a game and of a rivalry. Respect can be earned. Debts can be paid. Momentum can shift. Beefs can be squashed. Sometimes that's not the case and one fight is just that: one fight among many that two rivals may share over the years. This was the first time these two have had a real donnybrook. The other scraps and interactions on the ice had been just pushing, shoving, and some face-washing after whistles and a lot of chirping before face-offs (Karlov's mostly being death threats). For them, this settled it.

The two men are skated alongside one of the linesmen to their penalty boxes and there they watched their teams play without them. At the first whistle after their five-minute time-out, the doors open, and the crowd erupts in cheers and applause for the release of their imprisoned warrior as he steps back on to the ice and skates over to the bench.

Jason's thoughts in the penalty box are clouded by the painkillers he'd taken in between the first and second period for his back. The only thing he knows is that he feels good and is playing well. As for Marty, *Fuck 'em. Everything's worked out fine without him and I don't need him. Thank God for Sosa.*

He sits there and looks around, taking in the intimate atmosphere of the Mullett Arena in a way that he'd never experienced it before. It was an out-of-body experience to say the least. Was that because of the drugs? Who could say? He knew one thing though: without them he was scared and in pain. The team didn't bring him home to play scared and hurt and he knows that... which is why he kept the pills to himself. The team and the doctors were so preoccupied with the concussion it was almost as if the back tweak never happened. Plus, Jason had done a good job of pretending like it didn't bother him.

The truth was his back was still bugging him a lot and his headaches weren't exactly gone. Earlier that day, he'd woken up from his nap with a mind-splitting headache and a sour disposition. To him though, if there's no proof of something wrong, like a picture that shows a problem, then he better play through it. His MRI and X-rays all clear him to play so he keeps the rest to himself.

As far as the pills go, Jason has to outsource in order to fly under the radar from the team. But being that this is Jason's hometown, it isn't very hard to do. He knows plenty of kids from school that have grown up to be drug dealers. He's so secretive about his continued, occasional use, that not even Nick or G know about it. He doesn't want to freak anyone out given what's happened with Carl. Then he's thinking about Hannah and what she's had to deal with so, he decides to keep it to himself and keep it to a minimum.

The fight helped set the tone for the rest of the game, and the Coyotes get a handful of goals in the third period that hands them a six to two victory. Jason was announced as the game's first star and was asked to give a post-game interview, which he obliged.

"Here we are post-game with Jason Wagner. Wagner finished this game with a goal, an assist, and a fight, which completed the Gordie Howe hat-trick for the hometown kid. How'd it feel for your first regular season game in a Coyotes uniform?"

"Yeah, you know it's pretty cool. It's something you dream of your whole life, to be able to make it to this league and then to be able to do it here at home is just unbelievable. Really, a dream come true."

"You battled through some adversity this preseason, what can you tell us about the recovery?"

"Oh, I'd say it went pretty well, you know. Obviously, I wanted to be back for more games during preseason, but I had to listen to the doctors and just give it the time."

"Well you looked great out there tonight and certainly were a big part in helping bring home the W. How are you gelling with the new team?"

"Thanks, yeah, it's been great. Got off to a little bit of a slow start in the first there, but, ah, we battled back pretty good and got to put it to 'em a little bit which, uh, you know, feels pretty good, not gonna lie."

"Alright, well Jason, thanks for taking the time and we look forward to seeing more games like this."

"Oh yeah, definitely, thanks for having me."

Jason heads down the tunnel and into the dressing room where the team erupts and cheers. They all acknowledge him as the game's most valuable player and pass him the Australian football that they use as a memento for the player who's awarded the unofficial title. The ball came from a team trip to Australia during preseason a couple years back. Now, it's just a part of the team culture. All teams have a token for the player that they agree had the best game. Some teams use a hardhat, some teams use a custom championship wrestling belt with the team's logo on it, everyone's got something.

"Great to get the first one out of the way, hey. Let's stay on it and keep 'er goin boys. We've got a few coming up at home, and then we take this show on the road."

The team cheers and turns the music up loud while they celebrate their first win of the season.

43

Jason stumbles into Hannah's sleepy little apartment. All the lights are off and there is no sound other than the ruckus Jason is causing.

"Jason?" Hannah loudly whispers.

Jason whispers, "Yeah."

"Jason?" now a little louder.

"Yes, it's me," he says as he opens her bedroom door.

She halfway sits up and squints, "What time is it?"

"Late. I'm sorry babe, I was with the team after the game."

She grunts and tells him to join her in bed and sleep over. Jason wasn't exactly tired and was still wound up from the game and their time in Old Town. He got undressed down to his boxers then slides into bed against her so that she became the little spoon. Once he realized she was going to be asleep for a while and there would be no action, he decided to close his eyes and at least try and drift off. Flashing memories come up of various clips from when he was young. He watches his past in third person, like a stranger in the foreground. Each memory comes from a different hockey trip where he's either arriving at a rink or leaving a rink. Nothing happening other than idle transit. Soon he falls asleep.

Midway through his rest, Jason has a terrible dream about a turtle sitting peacefully on a log. After watching the creature in his dream for what felt like an eternity, a crocodile suddenly sprung out of the water, knocked off the turtle, and *SNAP*, ate it in one chomp. He wakes up and feels like he just got another concussion. His head is pounding, and his thoughts are hazy. He quickly gets out of bed and beelines it to the toilet where he throws up so loud it wakes Hannah who comes over to check on him.

"I'm fine," he groans after spitting into the toilet.

"Do you need anything?"

"No, I'm fine, I'll be right there, I'm sorry."

"Don't be sorry. Is it your head?"

"I don't know, I'll be okay, I just drank a little too much after the game."

"Okay."

That was a lie. Jason had only had two drinks while he was out celebrating, and he wasn't even buzzed anymore. Hannah goes back to bed and is quick to fall back asleep. By the time he gets back to the bed she's got a very cute and subtle snore. Jason figures the coast is clear and reaches over into the pocket in his backpack and pulls out his pill container without making a sound. He carefully opens the container and takes a few of the pills with the shot of water that was still in the bottle he brought over.

Jason fully intended to put the lid back on the container and put it back in his bag, but first he needed to stop his head from pounding and spinning. He leans back and lightly closes his eyes a couple seconds, that's all. He tries to focus on a single point of darkness and breathe slow. He observes the explosion of colors that bursts through the black of his set of closed eyelids. He tracks them as they burst slowly, floating across the depth of eternity like waves crashing on the beach. Only these are like waves crashing on the ocean toward the vastness of the sea and they go on and on forever. The memories return and he is soon asleep again.

Groggy doesn't even begin to describe how Jason feels as his eyes begin to peel open to the waking sound of his phone alarm. He grunts and reaches for his phone and in doing so, accidentally knocks over his bottle of pills. It's in that moment he realizes he's not alone in the room. Hannah and Jeffery both startle awake as soon as the pills hit the floor and spill out everywhere.

Jason stumbles out of the bed to try and get the pills in the container before it becomes a big thing.

"What happened?"

"I just knocked over some ibuprofen. I got it."

Jeffery begins to stir and look over the edge of the bed to see his buddy, Jason.

"G'morning, Jason," he whispers.

"Mornin' buddy, sorry about all the noise."

"It's okay."

Hannah gets out of the bed and walks around to Jason's side where the pills are scattered on the floor. She sees that the container in his hand is a prescription container.

"Is it prescription ibuprofen?" she asks.

"No just Advil, why?"

She looks at him and tilts her head to the side like, *Do you think I'm stupid?*

"What?"

"The bottle in your hand is not Advil and the fact that you're lying about what it is tells me those aren't supposed to be your pills."

"You're right, they're from the team, I'm sorry I lied, I just didn't want you freaking out with... you know, everything."

She doesn't know whether or not she can trust him. Jeffery is still on the bed. She glances over at her son who resembles her so much as they're almost identical when compared side by side at the same age. "Come on buddy, let's go make some breakfast."

Jeffery gets down off the elevated, queen-sized bed feet first, walks around the front to his mom, and they open up the door to the day. Jason picks his pills up and refills his container thinking that the coast is clear enough for now.

After Hannah gets Jeffery set up with his scrambled eggs, mini blueberry muffin, and banana, she saunters back over to her room. She stands in the doorway looking onward with a vibration that would suggest a great deal of concern, "Why did you lie if they're, 'from the team.'"

"Because of all of this," he gestures around the room, "this whole room is like a fucking shrine to your dead ex-fiancé. And his heroin addiction started out with prescription painkillers, right?"

She remains silent with an expression of mounting horror on her face at the words that she's hearing.

"Right?"

The horror subsides and turns to pity. To what or for whom wasn't clear, maybe not even to her, but that was the expression nevertheless. "Yep."

"K, well I'm not your dead ex-fiancé. I don't wear bandanas,

I don't play guitar, and I'm not gonna fuckin' start doing heroin. Alright?"

"Okay, Jason."

Tears well in her eyes but not a single one drops as she watches him violently pack his things and leave without saying goodbye to either her or Jeffery. She's torn on what she should do. Up to this point, the two of them were perfect together and he and Jeffery have been getting along so well, it was like they were a little family already.

Something she never did was give benefit of the doubt in her last relationship. She would always jump to conclusions and most of the time she was right. Since his death, Hannah has been through all kinds of different counseling and therapy sessions and throughout her healing journey, she's realized that maybe she's manifested some of these outcomes through her own jumping to conclusions. Who knew what could have been if she'd been more content to give the benefit of the doubt? Probably would have come out the same, but it's up to her to accept that, which isn't as easy as it seems.

Instead of jumping to the same conclusions she would have in the past, she decides to clear out the museum of Jeff's artifacts and return them to his parents or donate them. The only thing she keeps hold of is the scrapbook that was put together with all the photos she and her two Jeffs have as a family for the short time they were one. Jeffery is too young to know or understand everything now, but someday he'll be old enough and by then, he may want to know more. The other bit of stuff that she saved was his collection of vinyl records. Jason told her from the start of their relationship, "Feel free to get rid of whatever of his shit you want, whenever you want, but do not get rid of his records. There's some good stuff in there."

Jason came back over after practice later in the day and apologized. Jeffery was staying the night at his grandparents' house. Jason saw what Hannah had done for him by clearing out all Jeff's old stuff and they made up all over her bed all night.

44

———

Through October, Jason was able to keep his stories straight. To Hannah, his pills were from the team. To the team and his roommates, the pills didn't exist. None of his teammates were aware that he was getting painkillers off the street, and if they were, they'd probably try to help him out or try to get him into the Player Assistance Program, but he wants no part of any program and doesn't need any help. Not when he's playing how he is. He is having one of his best seasons ever, he's off to a great start in scoring and is proving to be a great playmaker as well, assisting on more goals than he has in any other first month of a new season.

Nick on the other hand is trying to shake off his devastating decision loss that he was handed after going all three rounds in the fight he took on short notice. Everyone agreed that he was robbed and that the judges gave the fight to the wrong guy. Even Dana said he felt that Nick won the fight. He also said what he always says though: "That's the risk you run when you leave it in the judges hands, it's the fight business."

Still, it doesn't change the mark on the record. One fight

down, one to go. Nick's next fight is not only a must win but it's a must win in decisive fashion if he wants another contract and a shot to reclaim his title as world champion. He cracks off a quick combination on the heavy bag in their garage.

G opens the door and says, "Hey bro, I'm gonna go meet up with Dallas for some coffee."

"Alright bro, have fun."

Nick doesn't ask but wondered how G is going to get there being as he doesn't have a car and hardly ever drives. He got his license at sixteen like everyone else, but when he wrecked his old hand-me-down Honda Accord a few years later, he spent his total check from the insurance company on everything but a new car. Since then, he just bums rides or takes an Uber or Lyft.

G strolls into the little coffee shop and is greeted by a viciously loud corgi in a tactical harness barking like a hell hound.

The shop owner is a young woman in her early thirties, "He's just saying hello, are you okay with him?"

"Of course. I love dogs. I had an Australian Shepard growing up," G says leaning down to pet his new friend, "Hey buddy, how are you?"

Dallas stands up and makes his way over to G with a smirk and his hand out, "G. How are you buddy?"

G nods his head and puts out his arm after giving his hand a quick wipe on his pants from petting the guard dog, "What's up bro? How's it been?"

"It's been good, is it just you or did Jason come with you?"

"Just me. I think Jason's at practice."

"That makes sense. Well cool, you want to grab a coffee and meet me at the table?"

"Sure."

G orders whatever the barista recommends since he's never been here and isn't much of a coffee drinker to begin with. It's not that he doesn't like it, it's more so that he thinks the whole ordeal is a hassle. Dallas is at the table wondering what this interaction could be about. He was halfway under the impression that Jason would come along with G, but seeing as that's not the case, he'll have to improvise.

G makes his way over to the table, coffee in hand, and takes a seat in the chair opposite Dallas, "Ahhh. This place is pretty sweet."

"Yeah it's a really cool spot. The owner is married to one of my buddies."

"Oh, no way."

"Yeah. Yeah. So, how's everything man?"

"Things are good."

"That's good, how are the brothers?"

"I think Jason's good. I don't see him that much 'cause he's got his girlfriend now."

"Oh yeah, I've noticed. Makes it tough, I've been there. Plus, he's got the season going on."

"Yeah but he's been playing well, so that's good."

"How's Nick doing after his fight? That was such BS judging."

"I know. You saw that? Yeah, he's not happy about it. Like, I've honestly seen him at the gym more than I've seen him at home since he lost."

"No shit?"

G nods his head.

"Damn. He's serious."

"Yeah he is. I'm pumped to see him come back even stronger."

Dallas takes a sip of his coffee, "So what'd you guys think of the stuff we sent over?"

G takes his sip and wasn't ready for it to be so hot. He nods for a second, stalling to regains his wits, "It was eye-opening."

"Right?"

"Yeah, I mean, I've always kind of suspected a lot of stuff like that going on but I didn't know there were legit businesses trying to fight it."

Dallas smirks and nods his head.

"I've watched all the stuff and then even got into a bunch more."

"Are you working at all right now?" Dallas is starting to get the picture for what G is after with this meeting. If he'd been asked a couple months ago if he'd consider G for a job, he'd of laughed and asked "As what?" But now, he is admittedly impressed at G's transformation. The man is dressed normally, he's talking normally, and seems to have acquired a sense of ambition, so much so, Dallas may be forced to reconsider his former perception. He also knows that it was always a long shot that Jason would have the time to be any kind of spokesperson during the season. He'd likely need to wait until the end of the season to be able to iron out more details.

"Not per se," says G, but I've done a bunch of different things in the past. Ever since moving in with the Wagner brothers, I haven't really needed to have a job, so I've just been working on trying to improve myself."

"For sure. I bet that's been nice."

"It's been cool and all but I gotta say, seeing what you guys are up to has triggered something in me, I feel like."

"Oh yeah?"

G nods, "Yeah, I just never knew a business like yours existed." There was a slight pause, but Dallas has been around long enough to know what's coming. "What would I have to do to come and work with you guys?"

There it is. Dallas smiles coolly, "I gotta say, I wasn't expecting this coming here today."

A regular person would start to panic at this stage of the conversation. They've just professed what they want. They're now waiting on pins and needles to hear if they'll get it. But G is no regular person, and if Dallas tells him, "No way, go pack a bowl," that's exactly what he'd do. With no hate in his heart, he would understand.

Instead, he says, "But I'm impressed, and I don't see why not. We can bring you on as like a junior analyst or something."

"Bro, that would be so awesome. Thank you so much."

"Yeah, man. You wanna start on Monday?"

"This coming Monday?"

"Yeah."

"Yeah, that should work."

"Cool, here's another card in case you can't find the last one or whatever, but this is our address."

"Sounds good."

They both stand up and shake hands again before they return their cups to the counter and head out the door. G's ride back to the house is quiet as his driver is an older man from another country that's hard of hearing and can't speak great English. That's fine by G. Inside, his heart is pounding with purpose and excitement. He wonders if this is how Jason or Nick feel before a big game or fight: pure exhilaration.

45

After his last time buying prescription painkillers from a drug dealer, Jason felt he needed help. But he decided it would be on his terms. He scheduled an appointment with Dr. Sutton where his plan of attack is to avoid the topic of drugs and focus solely on the problems in his career. Right now, he's sitting on the comfy chair talking about his injury and his recovery process. Dr. Sutton has endured countless stories of athletes getting injured and recovering, or not recovering in some cases. People may all well be different, but that doesn't keep their stories from coming out similar; if not the same.

Dr. Sutton recognizes Jason as being a lion with at least one thorn in his paw, no matter how well the athlete pretends he's fine. There's something in his eyes that gives him away. The doctor's hunch doesn't color the conversation, instead like usual, he lets his client do the talking. Every now and then he'll insert a question or two in order to pry a little deeper, hoping to get to a root, but for the most part, Jason will say what he wants. Dr. Sutton takes note of that, but also of how he says what he says and sometimes more importantly, what he doesn't say.

"How's everything now?" says Dr. Sutton.

"I'm all good. Head looks good on the scans and same with the back."

"Is there still any residual pain or anything?"

"Not really. I've felt pretty good all month since coming back."

"Looks like it. I've been seeing the highlights on social media. You've been on fire."

Jason chuckles, "Thanks. Yeah, it's been a good month for the most part. Team's playing well. Got a girlfriend. Seems like everything with me is going good right now."

Dr. Sutton wonders why Jason said, "Right now." Was it because he expects it to turn bad sometime soon? "Nice, congratulations on the girlfriend, what's her name?"

"Hannah."

"She the one?"

Jason laughs, "She might be, who knows. She's got a kid so we're taking it slow."

"Oh, how cool. A little boy or girl?"

"A little boy, his name's Jeffery, he's super cool."

"Wow, that's awesome, so you've met Jeffery. Is the dad still in the picture?"

"Yeah, little man and I are tight. And the dad was a heroin addict who hanged himself when Jeffery was eight months old."

"Oh, jeeze."

"Yeah, so, pretty heavy origin story. But they're awesome."

"I'll say. Have you met her family?"

"Yeah, a couple times. Her dad's alright, he's pretty quiet

and doesn't talk much. The mom is a real tornado of anxiety though."

Dr. Sutton laughs, "Oh no."

"Oh yeah. And she keeps calling me Jeff before obnoxiously trying to correct herself."

"Is that the name of the ex?"

Jason nods and forces a smile.

They both laugh and Dr. Sutton tells a story about his mother-in-law from his wedding day. He tells him it's all part of ending up with a good woman. He asks Jason about his family and is pleased to learn that the brothers had put aside their differences and gotten back in contact with each other. He was very empathetic to learn about Jason's mom's condition. He was around the same age as Jason when he lost his own mom to cancer. He's still plagued with memories of the mental warfare that the entire family endured, and the lingering suspicion that the medical system is predominantly driven by greed.

Jason is doing a good job at keeping negative thoughts about his mom at bay, partly because of the drugs he's been taking and partly because every time he goes to visit her while she's in treatment, she acts as if she's got cucumbers on her eyes and her feet in a tub. Of course, that's not the case for her and as soon as he leaves, she goes back to feeling like shit because of what the chemotherapy does to the whole body. But it does make her feel good that she's able to present herself with such strength and dignity to her family and anyone else who comes to visit.

"She'll be good. She's young, she's tough, she's got this."

"Well good."

"Yep," Jason continues to nod his head as he wonders privately what he's going to say or where he's going to go with this meeting. On his prior visits, he had problems that could be talked about. Now, he's got to figure out a way to open up about his problems without triggering any red flags for Dr. Sutton who continues to wait for more from Jason.

"So," says Jason.

"So, indeed."

"I don't really know what to say, usually when I come in here I have more problems, that's why I haven't been in for a while."

"How come you didn't come when you were injured and had more problems to talk about?"

Jason laughs, "I was too worried about getting better so I could play again."

It would take a while for Jason to appreciate the irony of what he just said, and for now, Sutton lets it slide, "How was your mind throughout it?"

"It was good for the most part. Doctors said irritability would be normal for the first little bit but other than that I was pretty much just focused on resting and not stressing my brain while it healed."

"Did they prescribe you any painkillers or give you anything for inflammation on your back?"

"The team gave me a few after it first happened but the league has really cracked down on all that nowadays, and those ran out pretty quick so I just take an ibuprofen if it gets bad."

"Gotcha," says Dr. Sutton, not missing the verb tense Jason used: "take" and not "took". He lets it linger to see what Jason will do with it. *Did he notice it? If so, how will he react?*

Jason caught it as he said it but by then, it had already been said. Now, trying to back pedal he says, "But I've felt good since the first game back."

Dr. Sutton plays it cool, and decides to stick to the hypothetical, "Well that's good. Yeah, the painkillers can be a scary thing. People get hurt, so they go on them, trouble is they're just so tough to stop."

For a moment Jason forgets that he himself is a current closet user, "Yeah, there have been a ton of guys from the league who have had issues."

"Oh, I'm sure. You guys play a rough sport. But it can happen to anyone."

"Yeah, that was how Hannah's ex's problem started."

"With painkillers?"

"Yep."

"Yeah, it usually is. People get hooked on the pills and when insurance stops paying for it, people have to find an alternate drug, and unfortunately that drug is heroin. Now there's fentanyl, too."

"Sad deal."

"It really is. Then the thing with athletes is that money isn't usually a problem, so they're able to continue buying it so long as they continue to play and once they start using them while they play, it's very difficult to play without them.

"How do they get over it?"

"By facing it and getting help, which usually revolves around addressing whatever is causing the person to feel like they need a crutch."

Jason nods casually so as not to give away that he wasn't asking for a friend.

"You know, like when someone sprains an ankle, they walk around on a set of crutches. Once the ankle heals, they shed the crutches and move on with their life. But what people do with painkillers is like, metaphorically, they walk around on their crutches and then when their ankle is healed, they stay on their crutches, or they drop to one crutch, or switch to a cane. Those people need to find out whether or not there's still a reason for them to be crutching around, because if not, drop those crutches and enjoy walking around again, right? Get back to living life. If there is a reason, then fix it. Our bodies are our machines."

"What about the people who can't be fixed?"

"What do you mean?"

"There's been plenty of career ending injuries."

"All careers have to end some way. Especially those in sports. Some are bound to do so because of an injury that can't be healed. Maybe they won't able to play at the top level again, but at least they won't have to go through life with pain."

"That's always been my worst nightmare."

"What's that?"

"Injury ending my career. Not having it be my choice, you know?"

"Would you ever choose to be done?"

"Playing?"

"Yeah."

"You know, I don't know. When I was younger, I would have said never, I wanted to die playing hockey. As I've gotten older, I've realized I'm not at all like Gordie Howe and won't get to play in the NHL 'til I'm fifty. Hell. I might be done before thirty if I don't have a good season."

"Sounds like either way it goes, it's not going to be your choice then."

"No. I guess not."

"Stories of people that don't know when to be done are just as sad a story as the people who get hurt before they're able to 'fulfill their potential'. You're lucky enough to be one of the guys that, should you get a career ending injury next game—"

"What are you nuts?"

Dr. Sutton chuckles, "I'm just saying."

"I know, I've had a good career and there's plenty to show for it. But you can't be talking like that, next game hasn't been played yet."

"What if it has been?"

"What do you mean? You some kind of fortuneteller or something?"

He laughs again, "No, but just think about it for a second. What if the outcome to your next game has already been decided, not by mobsters, not by the league, but the game is decided and so are the fates of every single player involved. Does it make a difference to you?"

"No, I guess not since I don't know what the decided outcome is."

"Exactly. That's exactly right."

"Still man. Can't be talking like that."

"I've always been amused at how superstitious you hockey people are."

"Other sports aren't like that?"

"They are but you guys are in your own world with it."

Jason laughs, "I guess so."

After a little while longer, they wrap up the session and Jason leaves feeling a little better, a little worse, a little guilty, and with his back in a fair amount of pain. As soon as he gets into his Tahoe, he opens his center console and retrieves his bottle of pills.

46

Thanksgiving can be tough on athletes who live far from their families. There are only a couple days off between games, so long distance travel is typically out of the question. Luckily for Jason, he's already in his hometown and all his loved ones are nearby. This Thanksgiving is a little different being as Jason's mom is wrapping up her cancer treatment. She tries her best to make it seem like she's better than ever, but everyone knows how tired she is and how weak the chemo has made her, even in the low doses.

She's sitting on the couch in somewhat of a daze with Jason's dad next to her. They watch Nick play with Jeffery on the floor on front of them, bringing some much-needed joy into her life. Ari snores in his usual spot on the couch, which also incites the occasional giggle. There was talk that Carl and Maria were going to come down, but that depended on the weather and a big storm had made it impossible for them to make the drive.

The other difference is the addition of Hannah's parents. Her brother is not there on account of he's moved back to California so he could be closer to the hoodlums that originally accepted him when no one else would. Hannah's mom has difficulty in social settings, and as a result she has to consume hearty sums of alcohol. She's developed a technique for herself where she pre-games a good amount before they even leave their house. That is so she doesn't have to go straight for a bottle upon arrival. If she shows up already halfway sauced, she looks like she has less of a problem in front of everyone. Everyone except for Hannah, who has a keen sense for when her mother has been on the wine. She and her dad, though he is powerless when it comes to his wife and has all but succumbed to the death sentence that is his marriage.

When it comes to Jason, it should be said that today, he is no better than Hannah's mom. He's been drinking straight tequila since noon in order to prepare for their arrival. Now that Jason's into cooking, he wanted to be the one to prepare the Thanksgiving dinner. Usually, his mom and dad are the ones to make most of the sides and fry the turkey but this year, all they brought was the green bean casserole, and that was because she'd insisted. Jason spent the day preparing all the various sides like the corn crème brûlée, the mashed potatoes, and the mac and cheese. His grandma had a couple of sides she wanted to bring like sweet potatoes and some kind of grape, yogurt, and marshmallow concoction.

By the time Hannah's parents arrive, Jason is already tuned up from the turkey fryer quitting on him an hour earlier when the bird was almost three quarters of the way cooked. In a fit of rage, Jason hatched a brilliant idea to put the oversized chicken on a baking sheet and stick it in the oven to get it the rest of the way. It was a little after that when Jason's parents showed up. They were early to have a little extra time with just them before

Hannah's parents came over. Jason's dad complimented the house and the smells that were coming from the kitchen.

Hannah and Jeffery had come over early in the morning with a whole basket full of toys. Jeffery spent a lot of the time in the game room which required his mom's nonstop surveillance, rendering her useless in the kitchen as a sous-chef. Tequila had to stand in for her and help him get the job done. Ari was on floor cleanup duty, and doing a very good job.

Hannah's dad comes through the door first, and says, "Hey Jason."

"Howdy, happy Thanksgiving," Jason puts out his hand.

"Happy Thanksgiving."

"Happy Thanksgiving," says Hannah's mom in an already exhausted and defeated tone, avoiding eye contact. She immediately scans for either her daughter or Jeffery.

They are down the hall in Jason's room doing a quick diaper change. Jason makes the introductions, and everyone exchanges their greetings and their happy Thanksgivings. Jason swiftly goes back into the kitchen where he can best avoid dealing with her. He checks the turkey by removing the foil that he set over top and sticks his thermometer deep into the seemingly bigger breast. *One-five-six.* Like with chicken, the number he wants to see is 165, not one degree more. Any more than that, it starts to dry out. Any less than that, there's a risk of getting sick. Better safe than sorry, but precision is paramount when cooking a big bird that has a tendency to get dry.

"Just a little longer on the turkey. Almost there," he announces to the group.

"Oh good, I'm starved. I haven't eaten all day," says Hannah's mom.

Neither statements are true but she felt it sounded good, so she said it. Jason ignores her and continues to try and tune out the interview that she was conducting on his mom about her cancer treatment. Hannah comes down the hall and breaks up the conversation with her and Jeffery's greeting. Hannah's mom abandons her interview and is taken by Jeffery's little hand as he wants to give her a tour of the common areas. Hannah makes her way over to Jason and grabs hold of her wine glass, then takes a big swig.

"Same," says Jason.

"I'm so sorry."

Jason takes a big sip of his tequila, smiles and shakes his head, "It'll be alright."

The sides are done and look spectacular. Jason used his chef's torch to melt the turbinado sugar into a hard thin layer of sweet sugary glass that tops the creamed corn in the large cast iron skillet. Hannah has recently gotten into sourdough making and so she made herself responsible for the rolls, which look divine.

Jason takes another big sip of his drink before opening the oven and checking the temp. *One-six-oh, that's good enough for me.* The reality is the turkey will continue to cook for a little bit even after it's taken out of the oven. By the time the bird is done resting, it will be the proper internal temperature, and ready to carve.

Jason uses the carving set his parents brought over. It's the set they've used since their first Thanksgiving as a family. He had watched a couple of videos online for the best way to carve a turkey, so by the time he is done, all the pieces are intact and there is nothing left on the cutting board but the carcass. He has a serving platter for the wings, the drums, and the thighs. And another where he put the neatly sliced breast meat. He put both platters onto the island with all the sides and if there were a dinner bell to ring, he'd ring it.

"Alright everyone, food is ready," he announces to the group.

Everyone starts to fill into the kitchen and begins serving up their food. Everyone likes different aspects of the dinner, and everyone has a different measure for portion control. Nick, for example, requires a minimum of two plates and will sometimes need three. Hannah's mom was the first to fill her plate, the first to the dining table, and was already halfway through eating before everyone was able to join her.

"Should we say a blessing?" Jason's dad asks.

"Yeah, I'll fire one up."

Hannah's mom is incapable of being mortified at her faux pas but does at least put down her fork and fold her hands to participate in the blessing. At the conclusion, she even gives the loudest, "Amen!" Then she puts her eyes back to her plate and doesn't look up until she finishes eating. Jeffery finishes around the same time and she is more than relieved when he ropes her into playing somewhere far from adult conversation.

Everyone who remains at the table pays complements to chef Jason as they devour their food. Jason's mom ate what she could, but for the most part, had to stick to the turkey breast and the sweet potatoes. Although she could eat the sourdough rolls and said those were by far her highlight. Everyone else ate it all, they almost didn't have any leftovers for G, which would have really bummed him out.

He's over with his family where they use the day as an opportunity to pretend they're a happy family. In reality, they all just rag on G. He always says, "That's the last holiday I spend with that group of assholes." Then a month later, he's back for

Christmas. He's always delighted to come home to the Wagner's leftovers. They always tasted better than the leftovers he gets from his own family, and that's only if he sticks around long enough to get any.

Jason finishes his plate and eyes his half drank glass of tequila. He downs it like a shot and heads into the kitchen to clear his plate and pour another one. While he walks, he feels his head begin to pound. He takes a detour to his room and goes to the nightstand where he keeps his pills while he's at home. He quickly takes one, knowing that too many in combination with alcohol could mean death, and leaves the bottle on top of the nightstand.

He hasn't taken any since his last game and is trying to only use them for games. After popping the pills in the parking lot after his last visit with Dr. Sutton, he tried going off them all together. But the result was an immediate, negative impact on his play. He was so noticeably bad in a string of consecutive games that his coach had to cover for him in the media. He'd been good about not giving Jason too hard of a time, but Jacques had no idea there was a drug or alcohol problem. He just thought Jason hit a little bit of a skid and he would be back to normal soon. All players go through slumps, and he felt that Jason was just in a slump.

For the week that Jason was off the pills altogether, he drank more than usual and it was all throughout the day. This might not be uncommon if he were still twenty and it were July, but this is November. Peak season. It doesn't take long to realize that this isn't going to work, and so he decided that he would just use the pills on game days and or if he *really, really needed it.*

Right now, he feels like he really, really needs it. It feels like there's a kid with a bike pump, the hose attached to his head. Every pump sends a throb that makes it feel like his skull is soon to burst. *Maybe this was what Humpty Dumpty was about,* Jason thinks before the next mind-numbing pulse of pain. He closes his eyes and takes some deep breaths and in less than a minute, is up and back in the kitchen feeling somewhat better. Hannah has already started the dishes and is being helped by Jason's grandma. Jason kisses Hannah on the neck and thanks his grandmother after her continued praise of his cooking.

Jason heads over to the couch to join his parents and brother who are watching the football game on TV. Hannah's dad stands awkwardly with his beer in hand, off to the side of the couch where he too watches the game. Not because he's interested but because he dreads social interaction. A couple minutes later, his wife comes into the living room from the game room with Jeffery. She says something quietly to her husband. Presumably that she is ready to leave and to start packing up, because next thing she does is grab her handbag and say in the same defeated and exhausted tone that she used upon entry, "Alright. Well. Thank you all for having us."

It takes Hannah by surprise, not the abrupt exit, but the timing of it. There is never a consistency for this to happen, only that it would happen eventually. She cuts off the water and dries her hands before walking over to say goodbye. Jason takes the cue that he's supposed to get up and formally say goodbye, too, while the rest of his family just waves and says goodbye from where they sit.

"Thanks for everything Jef- eh-uh-uh-"

Hannah's heart skips a beat and sinks into her stomach.

"Jason. My name is Jason. Not Jeff."

"I know that," she says dismissively, "I know what your name is."

"K, well you seem to keep wanting to call me Jeff."

"It's because I was just with Jeffery."

"Oh yeah, I'm sure. What about every other time?" This was not like Jason to be so snippy with someone. Especially when he was dating that person's daughter, but he was drunk, and she had put him over the edge.

"I don't do it all the time. That's so ridiculous."

"You do do it Mom."

"Oh whatever, there you go again. Just rag on me why don't you," she says dramatically.

"Come on, let's just go. Sorry Jason, thanks for having us," says Hannah's dad.

Jason closes the door and he and Hannah head back into the living room to join his family.

"What was all that about?" Nick asks.

Jason looks over at Jeffery, who is watching a video on his iPad then back to his brother, "Her fuckin' mom keeps trying to call me Jeff."

"Who?" Jason's dad asks.

Jason's mom nudges him and subtly makes him aware.

"Oh ohh. Really?" He asks.

Jason nods his head. Hannah just stands there with a horrified look on her face. Not because of what they're saying but because she knows the torment her mom causes other people.

"What's so weird is she *hated* him before he, you know. Like they would get in these loud fights and she and I fought over me being with him and it was all bad. So I really don't know why she does it," Hannah looks over at Jeffery who still is fixated on his screen and couldn't care less for what the adults are talking about.

Jeffery doesn't really know who his dad is, he can't remember him, but now Jason is here and he doesn't call him dad, not yet anyway. How old should a kid be before he's told his dad was a heroin addict who died by hanging himself in the guest bathroom of their family house? It certainly is no question for Jason to be tackling at this stage of his life. He just wants to let things happen naturally and whatever is supposed to be will be. If Jeffery grows to want to call Jason Dad, it would be a tremendous honor that he'd graciously accept.

Jason's parents decide now is as good a time as any to say goodbye and head home. They thank their boys for hosting and thank Hannah for cleaning up, then give Jeffery a big hug. Hannah decides it's time for her and Jeffery to hit the road and get him to bed, so she takes Jeffery into Jason's room to do one final diaper change before they leave. Jason had plans to go over to her place once Jeffery was asleep, but she says she's tired and that he could come over another time.

47

It's been almost a whole week since Jason and Hannah have seen each other for Thanksgiving. They haven't spent that much time apart since their first date, and Jason could tell something was amiss, but he didn't know what. To his knowledge nothing had changed and he hadn't done anything wrong, so he wonders why she's been so cold over the last week. Maybe he's reading too much into it and it's just been because they were on the road, but something in his gut says there's a problem.

They're at a casual wine bar that serves overpriced appetizers and no real food. They've both been sitting awkwardly since Jason finished filling her in on his team's road trip where they won all their games but one. Even as they were together and he sat there recapping his week, it was as if she had lost the interest she once had in him. Again, he feels like something is wrong.

"I have to tell you something."

"Okay," Jason says inquisitively, wondering if she was about to tell him she had fallen in love with someone else or maybe decided that this was all too soon and she did still have feelings for her dead ex-fiancé that prevented her from moving forward.

"When I was changing Jeffery's diaper in your room on Thanksgiving—"

Jason's heart sinks and he begins to rack his brain to try to figure out what she found, "Yeah?"

"I wasn't snooping or looking around or anything, but on your nightstand, there was a bottle of pills and Jeffery grabbed the bottle and so I had to take it from him. Then when I saw the name on the bottle it said 'Mildred Hightower' or something..."

"I can explain."

She puts her arm up and shakes her head no, "You totally don't have to. I'm not going to make you stop doing what you're doing, I've already tried that in a past relationship and it didn't work. I know you're not getting them from the team or even a doctor, and I can't put Jeffery and myself through it again." It was clear she had given the conversation a great amount of thought and rehearsal. Her jaw is strong as she speaks. There is sense of sadness but also of strength in her eyes.

He knew that eventually this would happen, "What can I do?" he asks meekly.

Hannah sits for a moment in deep thought, "I'm not sure there is anything you can do. How can I trust you?" her eyes are now glossed over.

He knows the answer would be simple. He could submit to having her drug test him and she could watch him pee in the cup so she could ensure it was his pee and he could give her complete access to his phone, track his location, and on and on and on. The question he had to answer for himself was did he want to do all that? He had nothing to hide in terms of talking to other women, but when it comes to his use of painkillers that he buys off the street, there's plenty to hide. His eyes begin to water up and he knows that this will be the end if he doesn't show her he can be trusted.

* * *

JASON CRIES the whole way home. He can't stop thinking about Jeffery and how he loves him like his own son. Sure, it had only been only a few months, but the bond they'd formed in that time made it seem like it would go on forever. By the time he gets to his house, the skin around his eyes is red and puffy, his eyes are bloodshot and glassy. He feels dead inside, and when he gets out of his car, he goes inside without saying hello to Ari, to Nick, or to G. He grabs his bottle of tequila from the counter, brings it into his room, and locks the door.

The thought crosses his mind that he could finish both bottles and be done with it all but that isn't the prevailing thought. He turns on the TV in his room and catches the last half of *Goodfellas.* He tries to keep his attention on the film, but the thought keeps coming back to him that the family he had essentially been gifted is now broken up and it is all his fault. Right before he passes out drunk from his tequila, he comes to the realization that he has to get clean, and that means drinking, too.

He wakes up a couple hours later, the TV now showing an infomercial of some new cutting-edge technology for pots and pans. He groans and grabs the remote, "Fuck off," he says aloud as he mashes the power button. The inside of his mouth feels like it's made of cotton and is dryer than the Sonoran Desert. He peels himself out of bed to fetch a drink.

He stumbles over to the kitchen where he grabs a glass and fills it with water from the fridge. He chugs the water then sticks his glass under the nozzle to refill. He looks at Ari who's snoring loudly on the couch, then he glances at the clock. There are only a few hours before he has to be at the rink for morning skate.

When he finally wakes up, it is well beyond the time he had internally set to be up and at his day. Luckily for him, the team's morning skate was optional, and no one was going to be too worried about him missing it. Jason hasn't always been a big fan of the morning skates, but over the last three years, he's really started to implement them so his body can be as ready as possible to play. The fact that he missed morning skate because he was hungover makes him feel like he's back in his early twenties and playing in the minors again. The only difference is, the hangover usually came after something fun when he was playing in the American League. Then he remembers the reason he got buckled to begin with. He remembers his drunken promise to himself and decides he's going to do it. No drugs and no booze. Cold turkey. When he shows himself that he can play and live without them, he will do anything he can to get Hannah back.

48

Sosa finally catches a break in his demanding schedule and he is able to visit his favorite client and catch one of his games. He thought the plan was for Jason to swing by the airport after his morning skate and pick him up, but he's nowhere to be seen. Rather than calling him a bunch of times like a crazy girlfriend, he orders himself an Uber and it takes him to Jason's house. It isn't lost on Sos that Jason seemed to have forgotten all about his coming out to visit when he answered the door.

"Jesus," is all he can say when he sees Jason, "Coach bag you guys at morning skate or what?"

Jason gives a little laugh and leans in to hug his friend and let him in, "No, I uh, missed it. Optional though, ended up getting after the tequila a little too much last night."

Sosa enters the house, "I can smell that." They walk into the kitchen and living room area, "Where are Nick and G?"

"Nick's training for his next fight and G got a job."

"No he didn't."

"Yep."

"Good for him. What's he doing?"

"One of my buddies hired him on with his financial startup as an analyst."

"Get the fuck out of here, no way."

Jason takes a sip of his coffee.

"I swear to God. You want some coffee?"

"No thanks, I've already had like three cups today."

"Alright, but yeah he's really turned it around recently. We had a meeting with my buddy and his partner a couple months ago and G's just been on a mission ever since."

"That's unreal."

"Yeah," Jason nods his head. "It's kinda weird not having him around all the time though, you know? He's got like, business hours where he's gone most of the day and then I'm gone at nights for games, so I hardly see him nowadays."

"Fuck. That's kinda sad."

Jason chuckles at the thought, "Yeah, I guess it is."

"How's Slick?"

Jason shrugs, "Slick's going into his last fight on his contract."

"I know."

"He got the wool pulled over him by the judges in his last one, so he's got a lot of pressure."

"He's got it though, I'm sure he's training hard."

"Yeah he is, it just makes the vibe around here a lot different, you know?"

"I can imagine."

"Did I tell you Carl came out and we patched things up?"

"No, that's awesome. Congratulations."

Jason nods and takes another sip of coffee. Sosa can sense there is still pain and there is more to say though he doesn't pry.

He knows that when Jason wants to talk about it, he'll talk about it.

"So, you ready for tonight?"

"Yeah, yeah, of course, I'm a professional. Who do we play again?"

"Are you joking?"

"Of course I'm joking and of course I'm ready. How are you? How was the flight?"

"Flight was quick, we got in a little early."

"That's always lucky. Sorry I wasn't there by the way."

"No don't worry about it, I just thought you were still at the rink since we were early. If I'd a known you were hungover, I would have been calling you non-stop."

"Sorry."

"I'm just fucking with you buddy." He laughs, "It happens."

Sosa was very understanding on the outside, but on the inside, he was very concerned. It was unlike Jason to behave this way and the fact that he wouldn't talk about what his problems were only made Sosa more concerned. With the start to the season that Jason's had, it doesn't add up.

"Thanks. Everything good with you though?" Jason asks.

"Ever since signing you as my client."

"Come on."

"No, it's been good. During the season I travel around and meet kids that I think have what it takes."

"How young do you guys go these days?"

"It all depends. With social media how it is, you'd be surprised at how many kids under ten are talked to by high level scouts and coaches."

"Wow. You don't represent any kids under ten, do you?"

Sosa laughs, "No, my youngest client is a kid who's fourteen and he's projected to go early in the WHL bantam draft, but other than that, it's mostly kids at least sixteen and up."

"Nice. Well go drop your stuff off and we'll go grab something to eat."

"Sounds good."

While they are at lunch they talk mainly about hockey and the season. Jason eats his chicken Alfredo and stays away from discussing his usage of drugs and instead focuses on his assessment of the season so far as well his outlook for the rest of the year. They've kept in regular contact at least a twice a week but they usually talk about just those games. Jason thinks that the team is definitely good enough for a playoff position but says that it'll ultimately come down to whether or not they get the bounces.

The conversation helps renew a sense of hope for Sosa regarding Jason because throughout their time at lunch, he gets the gleam in his eye again. Sosa was hoping that his earlier condition was purely due to Jason being hungover and that there was not the additive of being depressed as he suspected.

Jason and Sosa head back to the house where Jason goes into his room to take his nap. Before doing so, he implores Sosa to wake him if he's not up and about by three-thirty. Sosa agrees and takes his laptop out onto the coach and begins to work away at whatever he was able to bring with him on the road. He turns on the TV for background and sets his own alarm to be safe.

49

THE GAME DIDN'T GO ALL the way as planned for Jason and his team. They lost three to six and Jason didn't play well. He was timid near the puck. He panicked once it hit his stick. When he didn't have the puck, it was like he didn't know where to be. All in all, it was a poor showing for his first game back being completely sober, although he felt his earlier hangover could have been a factor, so he wasn't ready to give up yet.

Sosa sticks around to catch his client play for ASU the next night and then the night after that is another Coyotes game. Jason hasn't conveyed his reason for staying off the booze for the duration of Sosa's trip, but by the second game, Sosa has taken note of Jason's sobriety. Neither of them drank anything other than water the night before.

Now he's at the arena getting himself ready for another game without the aid of some kind of substance. His nerves cause his tape jobs to be less perfect than normal, but he takes it as a good sign. For the last few months, he's felt nothing. Like a robot that was programmed to play hockey. He's been on autopilot because of the drugs and now he feels it all, the fear, the anxiety, the sadness, and the excitement.

He pulls out his phone to change the song that plays in his ear buds and notices a text from his brother Carl that reads: Hey bro, thinkin about ya. Have a good game!

He smiles and tucks his phone back in the pocket of his workout shorts. Seeing that text message from his brother helps him put aside all his fears and anxieties and soon enough, the nerves are gone. Jason knows his brother isn't the key to his solution but to him in that moment, he represents it.

He goes through the rest of his pregame ritual as if it were just another game and everything is back to the way it was. Before the concussion, before his back problems, before the painkillers took hold, and before he knew Hannah. Just another game.

In the time between then and the start of the game, it was like he was sixteen years old. Like a kid who just got their license and gets to their game extra early because they can. He remembers when he was that age and how much freedom he felt in the hours before a game. It was like nothing in the world mattered outside of getting ready to go play a game of hockey with his buddies. It didn't matter what was going on in school with grades, it didn't matter what was going on at home with the parents, and it didn't matter what was going on with girls. All he had in the world to care about was the contest he was about to partake in alongside each of his twenty other brothers that were in there thinking the same thing.

Jason is going into this game high on life, feeling exactly as he did all those years ago. He almost sheds a tear during the national anthem because he realizes that this whole season he's forgotten to appreciate it. All of it, all the stuff he had dreamed of, from the time he was six years old. Even the sound of his name being announced after he scores a goal. He looks toward the ceiling, closes his eyes, and soaks it all in like he had before but with more appreciation now than ever.

He started the game off strong with three good shifts then had a so-so shift where he ended up getting a garbage goal in front of the net. He put his arms up and feels like he's just scored his first. The boys come in for a group hug and go down the line of high-fives at the bench. He plays well the rest of the period.

Mid-way through the second, Jason finds himself skating hard along the right-hand side. He had come across the ice from his usual left side on a breakout play where the puck was chipped off high and out of their zone. He picks up the puck in stride and continues along the right-side wall, pushing the defensemen back.

As he gains momentum toward the offensive zone through the neutral zone, he knows that it is a one-on-two and he has to create time for his teammate to join him on the offensive rush. He veers to the outside to make it seem like he's going to try to beat the D-man wide, but then buttonhooks at the top of the hash marks. When he executes his stop-turn, he feels his knee snap, and then he drops.

He lets out a load grunt which was heard by the ref who knew to blow his whistle the next time his teammate touched the puck. Jason tries to stand but cannot. The defenseman immediately starts pleading his innocence, claiming that he didn't touch him, and he in fact did not. The whistle blows as Jason's line-mate touches the puck and medical trainers are standing by to quickly take the ice.

"You okay? Is it your knee?" The trainer asks as he shuffles up to Jason.

Jason nods as he tries again to stand.

"Woah, woah. Easy, Wags."

Two of his teammates get on either side of him and he puts his arms across their backs. They slowly skate while Jason glides on his good leg back to the bench where he is then helped by more trainers who walk him down the tunnel toward the dressing room.

* * *

IN THE BROADCAST BOOTH, the announcers are trying to speculate about what they think happened. Jason's summer strength and conditioning coach Ryan Banning sits on the couch in his in-law's house, watching the screen with his hand covering his mouth, fully agape.

"Absolutely crushing to see a guy get hurt like that. It looked like when he went to perform the button hook, he may have caught an edge or something."

"Yeah, for those watching at home, you all saw that he was unable to put any pressure on that leg whatsoever. For these guys to be in *that* much pain, it must be really bad."

"And Wagner is as tough as they come folks. He already battled through an injury earlier in preseason and we'll hope he gets well soon."

Banning reaches for his laptop and goes to work.

EPILOGUE

Four weeks later.

Jason uses his crutch to hold the door as he maneuvers his way into Dr. Sutton's office. Jessica peers over her computer and notices a familiar face.

"Hey stranger. Long time no see."

Jason crutches his way up to the desk, "Hey. I know, good to be here."

"Dr. Sutton will be right out."

"Cool, thanks."

Jessica always wondered whether or not Jason was single. He seemed to check all the boxes of someone that would try and hit on her, but he's never made any advances. He just radiates a casual friendliness.

"There he is. Come on back," says Dr. Sutton from down the hall.

Jason takes off toward the doctor, the sound of his crutches clicking with each step, "What's up, Doc?"

Dr. Sutton closes the door behind them and they each head to take their seats.

"You need any help getting in the chair there?"

"No, I'll be alright. Thank you though."

"Alright."

They each get situated and settled in.

"So..." Jason says.

"So." Dr. Sutton volleys.

"So, I guess I'm done."

"Torn?"

"Oh yeah. Both ACL and MCL. Wiped out whatever was left of my cartilage. Surgery went well but I'm out for the season."

"Man. I'm sorry to hear that. What's going to happen?"

"I have no idea. I was only signed to play here one year, and I was more than lucky to get that. My guess is that I'm done playing and I'll be helping out my skills coach Jake with his clinics. My summer strength and conditioning coach is the one who put my rehab plan together and he says I could be back on the ice by June or July if I stick to his plan. Who knows if it'll be good enough for me to play again or if anyone will take the chance."

Dr. Sutton is surprised at the casual manner in which Jason is able to say these words.

"We'll see what happens in the summer and I'll be paid through the end of the year. But once the season's over, I'll be right back to where I was. A free agent with no teams banging on my door. Including the Coyotes, who I'm sure you've heard by now are moving to Utah for the start of the next season."

"How do you feel about it?"

Jason laughs anytime Dr. Sutton asks him how he feels about something, no matter what it is, "Hah. I feel fine. There's a lot of change going on in my life all of the sudden. Some good, some not so good, but I'm excited for what's to come no matter what, you know? I'm more sad about the Coyotes leaving than my probable retirement."

Dr. Sutton smiles and nods his head.

"When I was in the hospital, Hannah was one of the first ones to visit. And throughout her being there for me, it's made me realize that life would be okay. Even if I never played another hockey game, she and Jeffery would be there with me through it all."

"That's sweet. Sounds like she's a keeper."

"Oh, believe me she is. You know, to be honest, we were actually broken up for a bit there."

"I didn't know that."

"Yeah. I could never tell if you knew or not, but I had developed a little bit of a painkiller addiction from my injury earlier this season. And with her past, she was like, 'Nope, not again', so we were broken up. But she said Jeffery still made her watch the games, so she saw the play where I got hurt." A real smile starts to form on Jason's mouth.

"Oh so she felt bad for you and took you back huh? Once she saw you there all hurt on the ice. She wanted to come take care of you."

"Probably so," Jason laughs, "but she made me promise that I'd clean it up and get whatever help I need so I can be off the pills for good. Now that's what I'm doing."

"I had my suspicions but I didn't want to jump to conclusions. That's never helpful to anyone and I'm glad to hear you're dealing with it. Are you going to go through the program with the league?"

"It's possible, we'll see how things go once I'm off the crutches."

"Literal ones, that is."

"Yes, the literal ones," Jason laughs. "But honestly, I'd rather work it out here if you're able to help me through it."

"Sure. I mean, they're a whole program that's dedicated to helping guys with substance issues, right? But if you'd rather work with me and do something more holistic, we can figure out what the roots are and how to fix them."

"Cool."

"And remind me to get you my buddy's contact info at the end. He played in the NHL and battled through some injuries which led to a drug battle of his own."

"Okay, for sure, that'd be awesome."

"Yeah, his name is Dan Carcillo."

"You know Dan Carcillo? I was a huge fan of his growing up. That'd be awesome to get in touch with him."

"Oh yeah, he and I go way back."

"That's unreal."

"Yeah, small world. He's great. Anyways, how did your parents take it?"

"The painkillers?"

"No, no, sorry, the injury."

"Oh, they're okay. We're all just pretty excited about my mom right now. She wrapped up her cancer treatments and then last week, she got her clean bill of health."

"That's amazing!"

"I know, it's incredible. So we're all just too busy being happy about that to be worried about my career. Plus, my brother Nick won his fight last week and got his new contract, so we're happy about that too."

"Oh wow."

"Yeah, just too much to celebrate and be happy about. I don't even have time to think about my problems or worries."

"That's how it should be. How's your other roommate?"

"G's good, he actually got his own place and moved out once Hannah and I got back together."

"You guys are still cool though?"

"Oh yeah, we'll always be cool. I think he just wanted to be on his own for a change. He's in a really good place and we're all proud of him and happy for him."

"That's so cool."

"Yeah. Nick's gone too."

"What?" Dr. Sutton is shocked, "No way! I thought you guys owned the house together?"

"We did but once he got his new deal, he was invited to move out to California and train with one of the top gyms in the country. He asked me to buy him out so he could go into his new adventure without worrying about money."

"Man."

"Yep. He heads west next week."

"Wow."

"He'll be back for Carl's wedding and I'll get out to visit him once my knee's better. Hannah's from there so we'll go over a bunch, I imagine."

"So you'll be there for Carl's wedding too, then?"

"Yep, bringing Hannah and Jeffery as my plus two. They're doing it at the ranch. I'm gonna be his best man."

ACKNOWLEDGMENTS

Thank you to all of my teammates, my coaches, my billet parents, and my family who has supported me through everything. You mean more to me than I can ever show. I love you all.